Take Me Home

Country Roads Series: Book Three

Grea Warner

Take Me Home
Copyright © 2018 Grea Warner
All rights reserved.

ISBN: (ebook): 978-1-945910-87-6
(print): 978-1-945910-88-3

Inkspell Publishing
5764 Woodbine Ave.
Pinckney, MI 48169

Edited By Jessica Martinez
Cover art By Najla Qamber

OTHER BOOKS BY GREA WARNER

All My Memories in Can't Buy Me Love
Boxset

Country Roads

Almost Heaven

Teardrop in My Eye (coming soon!)

GREA WARNER

DEDICATION

*This book is dedicated to my friends from college. I think
we knew even back then how special those years were.
That small campus nestled in West Virginia was truly a
unique and treasured place – it will always feel like home.*

And, with much love to my family.

CHAPTER ONE

Her voice …it was haunting. She seemed so far away and, worse yet, in pain. But, it was more than pain. She was sad. It was sadness in her voice. And, I knew that voice. I knew that voice well, and I wanted to be there to comfort her. But that wasn't possible, was it?

Her voice became clearer then, and I concentrated on her words, wanting to know what was causing her such distress. "You have to," she pleaded. "You have to take your meds. Everyone loves you. We need you. Please, Finn."

I love you. I need you. Yes, the same applies.

Even though I wanted to say those words, I couldn't. I started to, but something was stopping me. Was it my heart? No. It was emotional, but it was something more. I put up my hands.

"Lara!"

Pressure. There was pressure all around. Next to me. Around me. In my head. In my brain. I needed to escape it. I wanted it to go away. I wanted to be free. I wanted to be me again. But how?

1

It felt like there was pressure on my chest, too. God, near my heart. My eyes were heavy. Regardless, I managed to open them. There was a reason for that pressure. A guardian angel lay haphazardly across my body protecting and watching over me. I was tired. I was so tired. But I wanted to stay awake and just watch. I wanted to soak in the peacefulness before it all came crashing back in. Because, I feared it inevitably would.

"Finn," I heard the voice choke out. But this time, it was mine. I couldn't muster up much more. I was too exhausted. So, I was glad when he lifted his head from my chest and peered his gorgeous, yet bloodshot, eyes into mine.

"Lar? Lara?" I felt his hand on my cheek, but I couldn't quite reply back. "Baby, stay awake, okay? Please. Please. Please. Please stay awake this time."

"O…K…," I managed to squeak out.

But maybe he didn't hear me because he started to get off the bed and turn away. "Hey—"

"Don't go." My voice gained strength as I begged him not to leave — the one thing we had always promised not to do.

"Oh, oh, Beauty." He grasped my hand while using one of his terms of endearment for me. "I'm not leaving. They've tried to make me, but I won't go." Then he clarified with, "I've got to get a doctor in here, though."

"Hospital?" Neither my memory nor my words were altogether sharp. But what I was able to interpret was starting to connect, especially with my now less groggy vision of the sterile, white environment full of monitors.

"Yeah. Yeah. You're in the hospital. Let me get a doctor. You're gonna be all right. You'll be okay. Just …here." Turning his head away from me, he started to scream into the hallway. "We need someone in here! We need someone. Please." Taking a deep, yet staggered, breath, he brought his attention back to me. "You all right? You need to stay awake, okay?"

"Yeah. I awake." God, I sounded like a toddler.

"You're doing so much better than last time."

"Last time?"

"You were awake a few days ago for a little bit. You were trying to talk."

"Oh. Uh…"

A few days ago? When was that? What the hell happened? The voice. Oh. It had been Nola's. What had she been saying to Finn?

My unclear, but racing thoughts were interrupted by the man himself. "You've been kinda in and out the past few days. They wanted to see if you could stay awake. This is good. I love you, Lara. I love you. Thank you for coming back. You can't leave me, okay?"

"Finn…" I breathed out. "What…?" I started, not knowing which question I wanted answered first and not having the clarity in my foggy brain to make a decision.

"So, she's awake again." I looked up to connect the voice with a man in blue scrubs who had approached me. "Really awake."

"Yeah, she just …just now," Finn replied.

Checking monitors while picking up my wrist for a pulse, the hospital staff member spoke. "Well, hello."

"Hi."

"It's nice to actually see those eyes. Blue, huh?"

I felt Finn's hand squeeze mine as he spoke. "I say they're turquoise. But I don't care if they are purple right now, just so they're open."

I couldn't remember what led me to be in that bed, or anything recent for that matter. But, I knew how deeply I loved that man holding my hand. And I also knew I still had a sarcastic side on the other side of my lips. "At least they are natural." I smiled, acknowledging my ongoing teasing with Finn regarding the fake green contacts he wore on stage.

His extreme exhale was full of relief, and he joshed me right back as he wiped his now natural gray eyes. "And to think, all I wanted for over a week was to hear that voice again."

I replayed in my head what he had just said. "More than a week? What?" What does that mean?

I had to think. Why was I in the hospital? Let me stop for a minute and think.

But I didn't have that chance because the bald, bearded man in scrubs said, "My name is Alonzo. Do you know where you're at?"

"The Ritz." I knew I shouldn't have, but my sarcasm had a mind of its own.

When Alonzo looked at Finn bewildered, Finn chastised me. "Lara."

"I'm in the hospital," my hoarse voice said robotically, like a good little kid.

"And do you know your name?"

With my same humor, I nodded my head toward Finn. "*He* just said, 'Lara.'" But then I answered seriously. "Lara Ann Murphy."

The man I now knew as Alonzo applauded my effort. "Good. One more. Do you know who 'he' is?"

"I think I've seen him on some music videos. Yeah, he sings that country crap," I teased, getting just the slightest bit of strength and energy back.

Alonzo smiled. "Yeah. That's a definite identification." With a few arm tattoos peeking out from the scrubs, Alonzo looked like he could be a heavy metal dude.

"He also happens to be my husband." I smiled warmly at my man, who kissed me quickly.

"You're doing great. Let's just do a couple more things, and then I can page the doctor."

"You're not the doctor?"

"Nope. Daylight nurse."

After Alonzo had me raise my limbs, he checked my eyes and adjusted a few things. I was following his instructions, but my mind had started to drift. I was trying hard to recall what had led me to the scenario I was in. I remembered being in the hospital. I had passed out at work, but not for long, and I was taken to the hospital, just as a precautionary measure. But, I was released. Yeah. I was released. I distinctly remembered that. Right?

Immediately after Alonzo exited the room, I reiterated my concern privately to my husband. "Finn? I've been out for days? I'm so confused."

"You've been out for ...well, over a week. A week and a half."

"What?"

That's not right. Fog. Fog.

"You've been in a coma because of the trauma to your head."

"What? No. I remember I felt faint, but I didn't hit my head that hard. And I was released. We already left the hospital. Everything was fine."

"No. What are you tal—" Finn stopped himself. "Oh, that was the first time. Yeah. You don't remember what happened?"

"Yeah, I told you. You came home from ...from ..." Where was it? "From Memphis." See, I knew. I remembered. "And you took me home from the hospital. Everything was all right. The ba—"

My hand flew to my hospital gown-covered abdomen. With that touch, a sudden sinking, acidy feeling materialized in my chest. I pulled the bed sheet down to get a visual perspective of my fear. My stomach was definitely different. There were things I was confused about, but being pregnant was not one of them. I knew I was pregnant. There was a baby. I was pregnant. She wasn't born yet. We still had months to go. Where was she? Because it was obvious that there was no longer the beginnings of a bump. Something was so wrong. I knew it. And looking wide-eyed at Finn, I knew he knew I did, too.

"It's okay," he tried.

"Finn," I said slowly, in fear of the answer to my upcoming question. "Where's the baby? Where's Chloe?"

Just saying our unborn daughter's name made my voice break.

"Lara, you're okay. That's what matters right now." That was enough of an answer – the wrong one – but enough.

Any tiredness I felt instantly dissipated. "Where's the baby, Finn? Where's the baby?" My voice revved up from speaking to screeching. "I need the baby. I need my baby." As I started to sit up, a stabbing pain gripped my mid-section, and I felt instantly dizzy. But the trauma to my body didn't matter. I was going to find my little girl.

Finn was up in a flash. "She's gone, Lara." There had only been one other time I had seen my husband so utterly distraught, and I didn't want to accept that the present situation was painfully similar. Finn's hands went to my shoulders urging me back down.

"No. No. Don't tell me that, Finn. No! What happened? Where is she? What—"

"Beauty, please. You're dealing with a lot right now. Just try to—"

"She's gone?" I didn't let him answer again, though. "You told me you wouldn't let that happen! You promised me you would make sure that everything would be all right! You promised me! You promised me! Why did you let …Oh, my God!" I was screaming and pounding, both at him and on him.

He didn't flinch, though. He just took it. The pain was visible via his red-rimmed eyes, and mine were starting to flood.

Finn backed slightly away when a man entered the room examining the scene. "She knows," my husband said plainly.

"Mrs. Murphy?" The tall, lanky stranger was suddenly by my bedside.

I didn't respond, except to put my hands up to my face. And then I began to rock back and forth, imagining that sweet, little girl still with me …still inside me. As I did, the deluge of tears intensified.

"Lara? Lara, I am Dr. DeHaven. I need you to try to calm down. Let's talk about what we know."

Let's talk? What! What could we talk about? Was what Finn said not true? Then let's talk. Otherwise…

"I want my baby," I managed to spill out between tears, looking at both men in the room.

"We're going to need to talk about that. But, right now, I need you to calm down. You've been through a trauma—a pretty significant one—and we don't want to jeopardize anything or have a setback." The doctor paused. "I don't want to have to give you something to relax you."

"No! You can't do that," Finn pleaded to the doctor and then to me. "Lara, please, please, just—" He went to touch me.

But, he had broken his promise. He had let our baby …God, I couldn't even think it.

I swatted both him and my tears away. "Don't touch me." My words were seething and direct. "What did you do?"

Finn had hit his limit. He stepped back and unleashed his own anger …his own pain. "What did *I* do? I watched you die! God, I was watching you die, Lara! Damn it! Do you know what that was like? Christ! One minute you were fine. And the next, you were falling. And then you were gone. Don't talk to me about decisions!" He stopped and started pacing while raking his hands repeatedly through his uncomely brown hair.

Taking in the scene, Dr. DeHaven directed his comment to Finn. "Maybe it would be best if you—"

Anticipating the doctor's request, Finn interrupted with a solid statement. "I'm not leaving."

The awkwardness was overpowering, but it was broken immediately by two new additions to the room. One was the voice from what I now knew was days ago—Finn's older sister and only sibling, Nola. The other was my mother.

7

"Oh, baby girl, you're awake."

I flinched hearing my mom use those words for me. I was her baby girl. But where was mine? She rushed past Finn and grabbed my hand in hers, smoothing my already limp hair as only a mother could. Her clothes and pixie-style blonde-to-gray hair looked pretty put together. But, the bags and dark circles under her eyes told another story altogether.

I turned my attention to Nola, who glanced from me to her brother. I knew she heard at least the last part of Finn's rant before entering the room. I'd be pretty surprised if the entire hospital wing had not heard it.

"Lara, I'm so glad you're awake." My sister-in-law stood close to her brother, as if urging him not to react any more than he had.

No sarcasm this time. "Yeah," I answered solemnly.

With her eyes wide, yet blinking, my mother questioned the doctor. "Is she all right?"

"Well, we were just getting to that." It was finally his turn to talk again, which I am sure made him happy in the midst of the drama unfolding around him. He adjusted his diminutive circle glasses back to their proper place and spoke. "We need to run some tests and go over some things. But this is what we were hoping and looking for."

Good for you, I thought. This was not at all what I was hoping or looking for. They were talking about keeping me awake, and all I wanted to do was go back to sleep, wake up, and try for a better, happier result.

"So, it might be best if I just have some time alone with Mrs. Murphy," the doctor continued, while looking in Finn's direction.

"Can my mom stay?" I asked, a little more calmly. Even though I was in my early thirties and had been independent for years, I suddenly needed my mommy.

I met Finn's eyes then. There was such hurt. It was as if I betrayed him. But all I could think was that it was the other way around. He had let it happen. He did.

"Finn, let's take a walk. Let the doctor talk with Lara. She'll be all right. She'll be here." Nola rubbed Finn's shoulder. "I think you need a break."

"I don't," he insisted, keeping his gaze on me.

"I do." I scrunched my face and drew my hands up to it, trying in desperation to stop the last few straggling tears. "Just…" Remembering Nola's words from a few days before about Finn needing his meds, I tried to put his needs in front of my angst. "Just go take care of yourself for a little bit."

Doubt stretching across his face, he started to take a step toward me, but I put my hand up to stop him. He breathed out his frustration, turned, and walked straight out the door. Nola nodded her head reassuringly at me and followed in his direction. I knew she would take care of her brother. I couldn't do it. I was angry. I was hurt. I was confused. But, that didn't mean I didn't want to make sure that he was all right.

The room got quieter when the siblings exited. It was almost like an eerie numbness settled in. I wasn't sure if that was the room itself or just my brain …or my very being. I held onto my mother's hand, needing her reassurance—her love. I was used to leaning on Finn, and, if I admitted it, I was sad that it wasn't him next to me. But, it simply couldn't be—not until I found out exactly what happened; how he let them take our baby away.

Dr. DeHaven spoke softly as he explained everything clinically, yet kindly. He first went over the easy stuff. I had cracked ribs and a bruised pelvis. That was the pain that scorched through me every time I moved. Knowing that was nothing compared to the pain in my heart, he cautiously segued to the tougher topics. He wanted to know how much I remembered—what I could tell him about my circumstances. But after much effort and frustration trying to recall with no results, the doctor filled in some of the blanks. He said I was suffering from some short-term memory loss, which wasn't all that uncommon.

He wasn't sure if it was going to come back or not, but it was something that they would be monitoring and encouraging to happen on its own rather than with prompting.

What he did tell me was, my head trauma was caused by a fall. But it wasn't like the lightheaded, momentary passing out at work that had landed me a hospital visit weeks before. No. This one had been more serious.

I had fallen at home, right before Christmas. When I prompted the doctor and my mother for details, I was not given any. Not only because neither of them were present when the accident occurred, but because the doctor wanted to see if I could recover some of the missing blanks on my own.

Instead, what I was told was that the fall had been traumatic enough to have caused swelling around my brain, and it left me in a coma. Once I got to the hospital, they determined that the baby had no heartbeat. The placenta was torn, and it appeared that her skull had been crushed. A D&C was performed.

I closed my eyes, and my stomach lurched when he said those words. What pain could be deeper? I felt my mother hold me tighter and tighter as the information the doctor was giving me became more and more devastating. I didn't remember any of it and, quite frankly, I wasn't sure that I ever wanted to.

"You couldn't do anything to save her?" I choked out as a tear rolled down my face.

"There wasn't anything anyone could do. It all happened instantaneously. You're lucky that your husband was there and called 9-1-1 and that the first responders arrived as quickly as they did. That helped us save your life."

"I fell," I reiterated just to confirm things in my own murky brain.

"It was an accident," my mother chimed in. "Only God knows the greater reason why."

Not sharing my mother's faith, I repeated the doctor's word. "Instantaneously. How quickly life can change."

"Yes, it can," my mother agreed with a distant look in her eyes.

I wondered if she was thinking of my father, who passed away years before in a similar "instantaneous" moment. Although, his death wasn't an accident. He chose to drink and get on an ATV without a helmet.

The doctor broke into my thoughts, telling me that he was going to give me time with my family, but cautioning me not to overdo it. He warned me that I needed to keep stress to a minimum. I didn't think stress was going to be the problem, though. Sadness was. Dr. DeHaven was going to order some tests, and I was going to be closely monitored for the next few days or so, with the hope that I would be released in a couple of weeks.

"A couple of weeks?" I didn't expect it to be that long.

"Mrs. Murphy, you have a lot of recuperation to do. It might be hard for you to understand what happened and to what extent it happened. The recovery process is going to take a little bit of time all the way around. There is the head trauma, of course. You were out for an extended time. And you are not going to have an easy time walking. We'll get the physical therapist in here and get you started on mobility. And, if you'd like, we'll bring in a psychiatrist."

I had been in a coma for over a week. More than a week of my life was simply gone. And more than that, my unborn child…my baby was also gone. It was just so overwhelming and so much to absorb. I knew I wasn't fully comprehending the enormity of it all, and I was so afraid of what was going to happen when I eventually did.

"Lara, you have no idea. You were critical. When Finn's family called, my heart dropped." My mom who had been pretty stoic—especially for Elisabeth Faulkner—broke a little. Reclaiming herself, she stood and turned to the doctor. "Thank you so much, Dr. DeHaven. Thank you. Thank you so much for everything. Whatever Lara needs, you make sure she gets it."

"We will. I'm sure Mr. Murphy wouldn't have it any other way."

He smiled at me and then my mom gave him a hug that I could swear was a little flirtatious. On any other day, it would have made me happy to see my mom start dating again after a string of disastrous men a while back. But I couldn't focus on much more than my grief. As soon as Dr. DeHaven crossed the threshold out of the room, my eyes flooded with the tears that I had managed to keep in check while he did his examination and explanation.

"Mom," was all I managed to get out.

She held and rocked me the best she could from the side of the bed. "Baby girl, it's okay. I'm here."

"I wanted her so much, Mom. We both did. She was so loved."

After giving me my moment, she sat back down and held my hand. "Honey, why were you treating Finn like that?"

"I don't know." I sighed. "I'm just so upset, and I'm so confused. I thought he made the decision...the decision about the baby. But I guess there wasn't a decision," I relented. "And he always told me— always, always, Mom— that he would protect both of us no matter what."

"Oh, Lara, he's not Superman. He's human, and he loves you more than I have ever seen anyone love someone else." Her words made my temporarily halted tears reemerge, for I knew what she was saying was true. "I've seen so many people and so many cases as a nurse, and I will tell you, that young man of yours is rare. He has done everything he could to bring you back to us. He found specialists. He fought with doctors and nurses so he could stay here around the clock. He had his family pick me up from the airport and has me settled in your home. And, on top of that, he was dealing with people and press hounding him. You would think there would be some kind of sensitivity during a time like this."

"No," I managed to squeak out, thinking that privacy and sensitivity goes out the window when you're America's reigning country music entertainer of the year.

"He's been beating himself up every day with worry and grief," she continued. "He's making himself sick."

My mom didn't know that Finn lived with a form of PTSD due to abandonment. Being blindsided by Audrey's broken engagement years ago had triggered repressed memories of his ill grandmother leaving him in a deserted park as a toddler. It was something that only his immediate family and I knew. But, as someone in the medical field, I wondered if my mother could tell that something else was not quite right, especially if what I heard Nola say was true— that he wasn't taking his meds. Without them, he would anger easily and unexpectedly, and feel limited self-worth. He was always good about taking them, but I could only imagine what had been going on in his mind since a triggering event had happened—two people had essentially left him … me and our child.

"But, Lara, he could not have prevented this …this tragedy." She chose her words carefully. "You need to know that. And you need to make sure that he knows that, too." My mother spoke with uncharacteristic strength and candor— a little bit of motherly tough love.

Finn's magnetism and energy weren't just something that happened on stage or in front of the cameras. You knew when you were in his presence. Or maybe that was just me and the depth of our connection. I looked up to see him propped in the doorway watching his wife and mother-in-law. He still looked beat, but, yet, I could tell that he was more subdued. The time with his sister had done him good. His family, even more than I, always seemed to calm and balance Finn.

"Is it all right if I—" My husband started to ask.

Standing and twirling around to face him, my mother answered, "I think I am going to go back to your house now, if that is okay? I might actually get a decent sleep for a change." She touched my face and kissed me on my forehead. "I love you." Those rare, face-to-face words from my mom made me acknowledge the seriousness of the situation even more.

"Me, too," I echoed her sentiment.

"You got the house code?" Finn gingerly took a few more steps into the room.

"Yes, sweetie, unless you've remotely changed it from here." Her attempt at lightheartedness made me realize that it really was true—Finn had not left the hospital.

"No." Finn shook his head with the slightest of grins, while accepting a warm hug from my mother.

"She's okay," I heard her tell him. "You're both going to be okay."

I hadn't seen Nola enter the room, but she was there now, too, and she spoke to my mother. "Here, Elise, I'll walk out with you. I want to call our folks and check on Kelsea."

"Yes. I need to call Lara's brother, too," I partially heard my mom say. Partially because both ladies were exiting the room, but mostly because my focus was on Finn.

"I'm sorry, Lara. I'm so sorry. You gotta know, I would have done anything—" He stopped his own words, did a quick wipe of his eyes, and then locked his hands into his jeans pockets. He looked suddenly like an insecure little boy. More than anyone else in this world, the accident—or tragedy—or whatever anyone was calling it, had taken its toll the most on that man in front of me.

I needed him more than I ever had in my life. And if I knew him, and I did, he needed that reciprocation from me. "Finn," I cried out, as I reached my wire-monitored arm in his direction.

He instantly closed the physical and emotional gap between us by taking long, quick strides over to my bed. He put his long, familiar hand in mine, intertwining our fingers. I silently scooted over to make room for him on my single bed. Obliging, he stretched his body alongside mine and enveloped his arms securely around me. Our heartache sank into each other's souls.

CHAPTER TWO

The next day was comprised of a whirlwind of testing, scans, and people constantly coming in and out of my private room. Medical personnel refilled meds, checked monitors, and took meal orders. And, of course, there were phone calls—my brother, Finn's uncle, co-workers, and friends—as well as visitors. My mother, who claimed the hug with Dr. DeHaven was just out of pure exhilaration over my recovery, brought a home-cooked lunch for her, Finn, and I.

Living in one of our neighboring New York suburbs, Finn's sister stopped by just as my mother was leaving. Nola gave me a homemade get-well card from her preschool daughter, Kelsea. She had drawn a picture of herself—bouncy blonde curls and all—putting a big bandage on a strawberry-blonde woman, who was obviously meant to be me. It was sweet, but it reminded me of my own little girl, who would never grow up to make a drawing like that.

Immediately recognizing my non-verbal reaction, and unfortunately knowing better than most, Nola empathized and apologized. "I'm sorry. I thought it might upset you."

"No. No. I'm glad you brought it." But I immediately

handed it off to Finn, who secured it out of sight.

"She wanted to come see you. But I told her she needs to wait until you get out of the hospital."

"Yeah. That will be bet—" A fact bolted through my brain as if it were a flash of lightening. "We have her play to go to, right?" When Nola and Finn exchanged strange, awkward glances, I questioned, "What?"

"Baby," Finn said tentatively. "That was all a couple weeks ago."

Oh, right! It was now the beginning of January. My brain was so garbled. I was still missing the time I was out and a little before that. "We went to the play then? I don't remember it. I'm sorry." Again, the looks from the siblings made me question what I was missing. "What?" When Finn hesitated with a response, I pleaded. "Please."

"Your accident?" he said. "That was the day of the play."

None of it. None of it was coming back. Nothing was there.

"I don't remember," I said, frustrated. "Why can't I remember?" I knew the psychiatrist and the neurologist would have differing opinions on the answer to that question. "Were we there? I thought I fell at home."

"You did. We never made it." When I didn't offer a response, Finn questioned. "Lara? What? Talk to me."

"I don't know how to do this. It's too much. It's all too much." My voice wavered.

It was. It really was. The baby ...the memory loss ...everything was overwhelming. I looked at Nola. I didn't like crying in front of people, even my sister-in-law, who was more friend than in-law. But there were no emotional restraints left anymore, and I started to sob.

"I know." Finn's voice was calm and serene. He was obviously trying to put my pain in front of his own.

He peppered kisses on my face and then leaned in so that he could hold my head just under his. I saw Nola silently leave the room. Finn used his index finger to softly and rhythmically stroke the length of my nose, causing my breathing to become more natural and my eyes to rest.

***

Unfortunately, the next thing I remembered was waking up screaming, "They took my baby!" I had been dreaming, but, just like everything else, I had no recollection of it. And, really, did it matter? The nightmare was real whether I was asleep or awake.

Finn was near the window. "Reese? I gotta go." He mumbled a goodbye via telephone to his publicist before walking to my bedside.

Without a word, Finn rested his lips on the spot of my forehead where I knew the bruise from the fall beamed like a caution light. It was a temporary, physical reminder of all that was lost. He probably chose to kiss me there on purpose, as it would be just like him to think that the gentleness and love from his body could erase the cruelness from mine. If only.

"You all right?" he asked, pulling away after an extended moment and meeting my eyes.

No. "Yeah." How could I be?

He knew the truth but, nonetheless, questioned. "Sure?"

"My side hurts a little." I admitted to the physical pain rather than the emotional one.

"You want something? You want me to get a nurse?" he asked, ready to jump.

But I was never one for taking much medication. And I became even more selective once I started dating Finn and knew of his past drug addiction. It was something he got into post-college and pre-full-blown fame. It was the time when his body was going haywire and no one knew why. Once he got the PTSD and clinical depression diagnosis, and the right medication and therapy, he made much better choices, and had never ventured down that road again.

"No. I'm ...no."

Finn sat down in the chair next to my bed and looked to the television monitor hanging in front of us. "Do you want to see if there is anything on TV?"

"Neh." I didn't feel like I had the energy to invest in watching something, especially because any storyline most likely would be too sad or, even worse, too happy. What I wanted was answers. "I know you're following the doctor's orders and not telling me what happened. But, Finn, what about the baby? I can't remember no matter how hard I try. But, I need to know."

Surely not wanting to relive that tragic day, Finn looked distressed, but he still let me speak my peace. "What about her, Lar?"

"I know she died, Finn. I know. I understand. But, I didn't have a chance to say good-bye. Why?"

"I don't know, Beauty. There was so much going on. I ...I was a mess. I had to trust what everyone was saying. They didn't know how long you were going to be in the coma. Or if—" He stopped himself. "God, I'm so glad you fought. You fought, Lara. It could have been so much longer ...so much worse. But you've done good." He knew he hadn't answered the question. "But, yeah, with ...with the baby there was a risk of infection or something, I guess. And, regardless, the end result was always going to be the same."

"Oh." I guess I understood. With my eyes getting misty, I asked, "Did you see her?" I imagined our little girl—the one who had just been fluttering around in my belly...the one who we had started a nursery for...the one who made her daddy's eyes sparkle and his voice sing.

He paused before answering and then looked down as he spoke. "No. But I wouldn't have wanted to."

Just like Wyatt, I thought. Finn couldn't deal with the reality ...the finality of death. He cut himself off emotionally when his seven-year-old nephew died unexpectedly nearly two years before. When that had happened, he didn't want any remembrance. He didn't want mementos or to even talk about it. But, now, to his credit, at least Finn was trying. It was probably just for my sake, but I was glad he was listening and trying to answer my questions.

"Everything was going so fast. I didn't have much time to think or react. I told them her name, though. I made sure she was named Chloe." He stumbled a little on that last word before again recovering. "And then, after that…after the baby…my focus was on you. This past week or so was, God—"

"I know. I feel like I woke up running and went full-speed straight into a cement wall."

"Oh, Beauty, I wish there was something I could do. I hate to see you hurting like this."

"You, too." I ran the back of my hand along his cheek, which wasn't just covered with a shadow, but a full brown beard, like I had never seen on him before. "Finn, there is something. Go home. Get a good night's sleep. Shave." I tried a smile.

"What? You don't like the *Duck Dynasty* look?" He joked, trying to keep the conversation light.

"It's not 'my Finn.'"

"I will always be yours." Even though I had used that saying many times before, this was the first time his reply was so serious. He followed it up with a soft—albeit whiskery—kiss.

Before I could cry, I tried again. "You'll have that whole king-size bed to yourself."

"That's the problem," he sulked.

I knew the real reason wasn't the bed, though. I knew he was scared of leaving. I had been watching him watch me and especially noticed the relief on his face every time I opened my eyes from sleep.

"I'm fine," I generically acknowledged, and then continued with more of a directive. "I need you to take care of yourself."

"I am."

But, I had heard that before. He had said he was taking care of himself when we were first dating, and he had been traveling back and forth all the time from his home in Tennessee to my place in upstate New York. He wore himself into exhaustion and made poor choices, including going off his medication. That had led to a tumultuous time for us …one that nearly ruined our relationship.

"Finn …" I cautioned.

"Lara, I'm taking the meds." I hadn't verbalized that concern and yet he knew; we knew each other so well.

"Good."

I really only had that one time to compare it to, but it did seem like he was stable. Was he emotional? For sure. But he was holding it together.

"I need you to—" I started.

But he instantly rebutted. "I need you. And, yes, I couldn't think of anything but you. But between my sister and my folks, believe me, they made sure I was being taken care of. I'm taking the meds."

"You are so blessed to have your family, Finn."

"And your mom. She's been something else."

"Ha! That's one way to put it. She's a bit much, isn't she?" My eyes couldn't help but roll at the thought of my needing-to-please mom.

"No. Well, maybe a little," he admitted. "But, she's been so good bringing me clothes and food even though I really didn't want to eat."

"I bet the house is immaculate, too." I said. "She needs to keep busy when she's nervous. She had a lot of practice with that when I was growing up."

"Yeah." His quiet tone told me he was internally recalling the stories I had told him of how verbally and physically abusive my father had been.

"And there are things that you must need to take care of—obligations like meetings, recordings, contacts, whatever. I don't want your career to suffer."

"All of that can wait. Besides, that's what I have people for."

"You're going to have to send Reese on a vacation for all she does."

"Sounds like a good idea." He smiled. "Maybe we could double date, if she would ever go out with anyone for any period of time."

"Yeah," I answered in monotone.

I didn't feel like warmth and sunshine. Escape? Yes. Fun, frolicking, and friendship? No.

But I tried to keep things light. "She's probably too busy solving your issues to date anyone long enough."

Finn shook his head and then finally relented to my request. "Once you go to sleep tonight, I'll go home. I'll make sure that everything is set for your brother to come back in tomorrow. And I'll look for that razor." He touched my nose.

"Thanks, Cowboy." I used my nickname for him in an attempt to get some sort of normalcy back into a far-from-normal scenario. I don't think I quite pulled it off, though.

***

"There's the little fighter." Lane entered the room in an excited flurry and came immediately to my bedside.

"Only because you taught me to be." I gave praise where praise was due.

I was so happy to see my brother, who, though only a year older than me, had been my original protector; the one who had taken the core of our father's abuse to spare me. I glanced at my mother who, with Finn, had followed Lane into the room. She flinched at the mention of our past life, but was silent, just as she was back then.

"It's good to see you, Lara," my sole sibling continued.

"I guess it should be the other way around," I said. "I know you were here to see me, but I just couldn't see you."

Lane and his wife, McEllie, flew in immediately from their home in North Carolina after hearing of my accident. But neither of their jobs—Lane was a food service manager and McEllie a general practitioner—would permit a lengthy stay, and my mom had reassured them that there was nothing they could do but sit vigil. And, God knows, Finn had taken claim on that task. So, they had gone back home, keeping in touch with my mother until I finally woke. And, now, my brother had flown back.

"Yeah, you were doing your Sleeping Beauty act," Lane joked, as Finn sat down in "his" chair at my bedside after giving me a hug.

"At least it wasn't Rip Van Winkle," I teased, as I rubbed my hands on my husband's clean-shaven face.

"Better?" was Finn's response.

"It's good to see *you*, too," I said.

"Mmmm-hmmm," Finn replied, kissing me sans his furry face.

***

My in-laws were the next to arrive. I found out they had flown in from their Louisville hometown on Christmas Eve, despite Finn's protests, and had been staying with Nola and her husband, Will, since then. Nola and her folks alternated roles of taking care of Kelsea so that someone could always be with Finn.

Having visitors and an array of doctors helped, for the most part, to keep my mind off of my inner demons during my recovery time in the hospital. But, there were times when I was alone—or sometimes even when I wasn't—when my feelings would go on an emotional roller coaster ride. One minute I would be all right, focusing on positive things and making conversation with others. But then the what-could-have-beens would unexpectedly come crashing back for no particular reason. There was no obvious trigger. I would be working on accepting the situation as it was, when, *bam,* I would flash back to Finn twirling me in the air on CMA night when I first told him I was pregnant, or, *bam*, to us hearing that heartbeat for the first time, or, *bam*, to us giving our families the good news at Thanksgiving. The fact that everything changed in that "instantaneous" moment the doctor spoke of haunted me. One step and my world became so different. Those thoughts had my mood changing so much from moment to moment, I wondered if it was how Finn felt when he wasn't on his meds but on a smaller scale.

***

I was released from the hospital a month after I was initially brought in. I thought I couldn't wait to leave the cold, clinical setting and finally make my way home. Yet, strangely, I became extremely anxious when the "all-clear" moment came for me to actually leave. I thanked the doctors, went over the paperwork, got a prescription, and promised to make my follow-up appointments. You would think I would be practically skipping out the door. But, I was hesitant. Because I was leaving. I was leaving my little girl. It was the last place she was with me. The last place she was a part of me. It was the last place where I could picture her being. And I was leaving her behind.

On top of that, Finn's celebrity status was on level ten as we made our final departure. Everyone on the staff had been extremely considerate and respectful of both my medical situation and Finn's right to privacy during my stay. There had not been a glimmer of any press breaking protocol by being on hospital grounds. But when it was time to leave, suddenly hospital personnel came out of the woodwork to not only wish me well, but also to shake Finn's hand and get that last glimpse of stardom firsthand. Considering all they had done for both my husband and me, I tried to be cordial and patient. But I was also emotional and tired.

"Finn?" I glanced from the nurses station back to the room I had just vacated. "If we're going, I need to just go." And then I added, "Take me home…please."

His eyes bounced from the nursing staff to mine, and I knew he immediately understood. "Sure thing, Beauty."

He adjusted my bag on his shoulder, leaned his forehead onto mine, and kissed me in a sweet, reassuring way. PDA was something he didn't do when we first started dating, and he still kept it to a minimum, because he maintained that his private and public lives were two separate entities. The people he loved didn't need to be subjected to something he chose and signed up for. However, since my arrival, the hospital staff had been witness to nearly every facet that made up the composition of Finn Murphy. And his love for me was at the center of that stage.

Luckily, the rest of our exit went smoothly. The main lobby area wasn't bustling with people, and the elevator that led directly to the adjacent, indoor parking garage was empty. With my mind lost in the abyss of nothingness, I was moving rather robotically when Finn pressed the unlock button on the car fob. It was only then that I noticed which car he drove.

"You brought the Jeep?" I asked as he tossed my bag into the back seat.

The red Jeep Wrangler was "my" car—the one I drove. Finn had bought it for me before we were married, after I had casually mentioned how much I loved his Jeep when we were just friends in college. He had since wanted to buy me a different car or, at least, an additional car—maybe a bigger SUV, like a Cadillac Escalade. I could even get it in red. But I didn't want that. I wouldn't drive it. I was emotionally attached to that Jeep. And I guess Finn was, too.

He opened the passenger door for me. Even if it was my car, Finn always took the macho lead when driving was concerned. I had even jokingly consented to it in our wedding vows.

"Yeah, I brought the Jeep," he echoed my words. "I felt closer to you in it. And it makes me think of simpler times."

Just like my manic mind, we twirled down and down the parking garage ramps until we reached the exit gate. The bright sunshine of the crisp, winter day contrasted fiercely with my solemn mood. Our drive home was, for the most part, in silence, which was not the norm for the two of us. We always had something to talk about and tell one another. But melancholy had set in. The ride reminded me of our drive back from Wyatt's beachside memorial— the silence …the loss …the emptiness.

As if reading my sad, silent thoughts, he glanced over at me before saying, "We're almost home."

I attempted a half smile. It would be good to be home… just the two of us without the commotion of the medical world. I knew all that I wanted and needed was my husband's love and strength.

"Finn, do you think you could sing something?"

"Oh, baby, I don't know. I don't really feel like it."

"Okay," I answered quietly.

I understood. I just thought maybe it would make us both feel better. Writing and singing were like therapy for Finn. And hearing his voice, whether it was lyrical or not, always helped soothe me.

After a minute, he said, "All right. Just for you." I didn't have to wonder long what sentimental song would emerge from his vocal chords, because he immediately began singing lyrics from "The Fox." While beating on the steering wheel, he turned to gauge my reaction and said, "Well, do you know what the fox says?"

After belting out one of the silly lines in response, I burst into laughter. We had both made fun of the song in the past but somehow had replayed it numerous times online and knew all the words. It wasn't what I had expected in that car, but he was right to sing it. It was the perfect release, if only momentary, from our portrait of pain.

***

Courtesy of my mother, there was a container of homemade chocolate chip cookies awaiting our arrival home. She knew how much both Finn and I loved them. So, before she returned to Pittsburgh, she left them for me as the ultimate comfort food.

"Well, she's nothing if she's not predictable."

"The fridge is full of ready to heat up meals, too," Finn added.

"She acts like someone di…" …ed. I stopped myself realizing someone had.

Finn pulled me into the security of his torso, holding me silently for a moment. Rubbing my back before bringing me arm's length away, he said, "Why don't you go sit down? I can bring you something to eat."

"I'm not hungry." When I saw the unnecessary concern in his eyes, I added, "We'll get something later. Let's just …just sit in the great room. Tell me something. Talk to me about some producer that doesn't get it, or some crazy fan message, or even about basketball since the Bengals aren't going to the Superbowl."

"They got cheated." He smiled. "Next year."

"Whatever."

As we made our way into the towering great room, it seemed like years had passed since I had been in that house, instead of merely weeks. I started walking toward the stairs. Taking off my shoes, I intended to place them in the basket on the bottom step to take up the stairs at a later time. Even though our master bedroom was on the first floor, I had a separate closet upstairs just for my shoes. That's when I noticed that Finn had stopped. He was steps behind me and was simply staring—staring at me.

"What?" I simultaneously dropped the flats into the basket.

"You don't remember anything?" he asked slowly and methodically.

It took me a moment, and then I realized where I was standing—at the bottom of the stairs. I still didn't know the details about the accident. No one had told me, and my memory was still void. But I knew I had fallen, and I knew it had been at home. Logic said if the fall was that devastating, it was down a flight of steps …the same place I was standing.

"Is this it?" I asked. "Is this where I fell?"

He didn't need to answer. I knew. I knew by the look of not well-disguised horror on his face. That was it. That was the spot that had changed my life. And I still didn't remember a thing.

"Oh, damn," he said with full-tilt emotion. "I'm …I can't believe how close I was to losing you."

I didn't remember. But he did. He probably had every excruciating second engraved in his mind. And he was trying to be brave for me. But he needed me. We needed each other.

"I'm here." I reassured him by reaching out my hand as physical proof.

"I love you." He locked his eyes with mine and stroked his thumb alongside my index finger. "Let's just keep the shoes downstairs for a while, okay?"

"Sure," I agreed, letting him guide us onto the sofa. Snuggled in his arms, I spoke my fear of going upstairs. "I'm not really looking forward to seeing the room, anyway."

Finn didn't have to ask which room I was referring to. We hadn't done much, but we had started to convert one of the bedrooms into a nursery. Besides the sonogram photo, the room had become a collecting place for things we had picked up—a jogging stroller, decorative diaper basket, diapers, a bouncy seat, and wooden letters in pink and white that spelled out "Chloe."

His lips grazed the top of my head before saying, "Yeah."

I turned to face him. I was too raw not to speak honestly. "This hurts so much."

"I know, Beauty. Believe me, I get it." He bracketed my face with his hands. When tears started to pool in his eyes, I felt them form in mine, too. Knowing our joint vulnerability, Finn silently encouraged me to turn back around into his embrace. When I did, he mumbled into my shoulder, "I love you. I'm glad you're home. Nothing else matters."

CHAPTER THREE

Finn was a combination of restless and overprotective for the next couple of days. He hovered around me 24/7. But, there wasn't any reason for such attentiveness. I was more than capable of doing and getting things on my own. It was just that most of the time I didn't care if I did or didn't.

Between Finn and I, we had an army's worth of friends, family, neighbors, and colleagues who genuinely cared for us. They all meant well with their calls and their cards and their food donations. But every time such an offering was made, it picked at a scab that had barely even started to form. I decided just to ignore the ringing of the phone and let the envelopes stay stacked on the far corner of the kitchen counter.

Finn had to stay a little more "plugged in" due to his career, especially since the Grammys were taking place just two days after my release. My husband, via his staff, had backed out of the awards show before I was out of the coma. His absence would be quite noticeable, since he was up for three awards. But the situation was what it was. And, admittedly, while I may not have needed someone to pour me a bowl of cereal or get the mail, I needed him

…just simply him. Even with—or despite—his hovering, knowing that he was around made me feel safer, stronger, more secure.

We ate a late dinner the night of the Grammys. While I picked, Finn devoured his food in between texts and calls. There had been a constant flow of each for a couple hours. Fellow artists, his band, and his team were all updating him on what he was missing. I could tell that Finn was nervous, although he wouldn't admit it. With his CMA Entertainer of the Year award in November, he was poised to sweep all three categories he was nominated in. In between one of the many preshow calls, Finn managed to pour a second glass of bourbon and asked me if I needed anything. I shook my head, tried a half-hearted smile, and continued to rinse off the dinner plates, losing myself in the soothing, monotonous hum of the water evenly flowing from the faucet.

Finn made a point of showing me that he was switching the phone to vibrate as he sank onto the great room's sofa. I grabbed the throw blanket and curled with it into my husband's tight torso, adorned by a simple dark blue T-shirt. It was such a contrast to the dapper suit he would have been wearing if he were at the awards show. And *I* certainly wasn't ready to hit the runway. I would most definitely be in the "Fashion Miss" column with my ill-matched sweats combo, no make-up, and a hairband haphazardly holding back my strawberry blonde hair.

"Wow. They really brought it." I offered a critique of the opening act.

"Yeah. They're gonna be an 'I knew them when,'" he said while tapping his fingers along with the music.

"Opening on your tour really got them to a new level." I knew he wouldn't say it, so I did.

"Sometimes you just need the chance."

"That one person to give you a boost."

I rubbed his hand as we both grew quiet. The hosts attempted a funny spiel, more acts were performed, and finally the first award was given out. I started thinking of another time Finn and I had watched an awards show together on television—right after Wyatt had died. Besides the utter anguish Finn had been going through that night, the one thing that stuck in my mind about that show was the fact that the presenters had made a big deal of acknowledging Finn and his nephew's death. I suddenly became downright fearful that history was going to repeat itself with our daughter. I didn't want that. I couldn't bear that. There was no way I could listen to one more condolence, especially on a nationwide broadcast. The press had been pretty respectful up to that point. There had just been brief updates on my condition—I lost the baby, I was in a coma, I was out, I was released. But Finn's cohorts might think they were doing the right, kind thing by acknowledging our tragedy.

I know I was silent and still for a while, paralyzed in my own prediction. By the time I went to say something, it was too late. The first award that Finn was up for was ready to be announced. I felt him stiffen and shift slightly behind me. I grasped onto his hand. I'm not sure if the action was to support him or for him to support me. Regardless, the presentation went off without a hitch. All except, of course, that Finn did not win Best Country Album.

"Well, there's one done." He tried to sound nonchalant, but I'm sure he was a little disappointed. His album, after all, was chart-topping. "Toray deserved it. She has some good pieces on her album." When I let out a huge gust of air, which I didn't know I had been holding in, Finn reacted. "That sounded like relief. You glad I didn't win?" He smirked as I turned to face him.

"No, of course not." But I stumbled the rest of my reply. "It's just …I didn't know …never mind."

His face bunched up slightly, surely perplexed at what I stopped short of saying. "Wha—"

I interrupted. "I'm tired. I think I'm going to bed."

"What? The show's only half—"

"I'm sorry. You know I support you." I tried another of those smiles that just didn't seem to quite make it. "I know you'll get the other two. I just don't think I can."

God, I hated bailing on him. I didn't have it in me, though . . .none of it. The day had been long. I had gotten through. But it was enough. I didn't want any drama to unfold ... not at that point.

It took him a second but then recognition flashed across his face. "They're not going to say anything." He touched the tip of my chin, causing me to look at him. "I made a point of it."

I almost cried knowing that he not only understood what I was thinking but had the foresight to think of it. "Did you send in speeches?"

"Yep. Kept it generic," he said plainly.

"Really?" I asked and then tried to lighten the mood. "No 'I love you, Lara's'?"

"That is my generic." He gently touched my nose.

I managed a slight smile at his pure sincerity. "I really am tired." One wouldn't think I would be as tired as I had been after being asleep in a coma for so long, but I was. I started to leave his embrace. "Forgive me."

"I'll go with you." He reached for my hand starting to get up himself.

"No. Don't be ridiculous. You're not tired. You are completely jazzed. And you should be. Wake me up if it's good news." I bent down and kissed him with finality.

***

I was awakened by the motion of the bed dipping as Finn climbed in on his side. My back turned toward him, I glanced at my bedside clock. It was hours after the show should have ended. Simultaneously, I felt Finn thread his body behind mine and smelled the alcohol on his breath. I wanted to know what the results were. Did he win both awards? He worked so damn hard, and he deserved it. And I wanted it so badly for him. Yet, I didn't have the energy right then to ask. I let my eye lids lower once more and listened as my husband's breathing turned from shallow to that of deep sleep.

***

I was the first one up the next morning. But that really didn't count. My early rising was due to a combination of not doing a lot the previous couple of days —and, really, since I had been in the hospital—and going to bed too early.

Sitting on the sofa in the great room, I probably looked as lost as I felt when Finn wandered in. His brown hair, still in sleep mode, was askew, and he had a bit of a five o'clock shadow. The weeks had done a beating on him, too. But, yet, in a rugged kind of way, he still looked handsome as hell wearing his favorite non-performer attire of sweats and a T.

"Morning. How you doing?" He lifted my legs off the sofa, sat down, and placed them on his lap.

I attempted a smile, knowing it would make him happy. "Watcha get?" I turned the subject back to him and the awards show the night before. Purposefully avoiding any form of media, I wanted to hear the news directly from the man himself.

He laughed slightly. "A good night's sleep, a kink in my neck—"

He knew what I had been referring to, but, not having the energy or desire to play along, I asked more directly, "Finn, what did you win?"

He reached behind him to a folder lying on the elongated sofa table behind us. Then, pulling out a piece of paper, he handed it to me. On the top of the page was written: *ACCEPTANCE SPEECH – BEST COUNTRY SOLO PERFORMANCE*. Beneath it was the speech:

Thank you fans, friends, and family for your support. It means much more than any trophy I could ever get.

It was short, yes, and semi-generic, but loaded with meaning. "I'm so proud of you," I said, and he handed me the second paper; the Best Country Song speech. "Really?" An actual, genuine smile spread across my face as I read the second:

I am deeply honored and humbled to accept this award. I wake up every day knowing how blessed I am to have the best team surrounding me both professionally and personally. Without my band, agents, publicists, writers, label, country radio, and fans, I would not be able to sing my songs, let alone be honored with a Grammy. Without the love of my wife, I simply would not be.

Touched but feeling unworthy, I said, "I don't deserve that."

"More."

"No. Just like the baby. I didn't deserve to have a baby."

"What? Why would you say that?" If Finn had still been sleepy, he wasn't any more. He was definitely now awake, alert, and alarmed.

"Never mind."

"Lara, I want to know why you said that about the baby."

And then it came out—what I had been thinking almost instantly after he told me the devastating, crushing news in the hospital. "I know I don't deserve to have a baby. The universe was just confirming it. I gave up my child after high school. Why should someone like that, who *willingly* gives a child away, be granted another one? Can you believe that? I didn't want that little boy all those years ago. And now ...now that I did want one—"

He let me get most of it off my chest before interrupting, "Beauty, that was different. Those were different circumstances. You did what was right at the time… for you and for that baby. Lara, one has nothing— *nothing*" —he purposefully and gently lifted my chin so that I was meeting his eyes, which were as direct as his affirmative tone— "to do with the other."

"I don't deserve you, either. There are times when I just don't understand why you love me … why you choose me when you could have any one."

"What?!"

"I'm not any one spe—"

"That's exactly what you are. You are my world. Why do I love you? Baby, you ground me. From the very beginning, all those years ago, when we were just bumbling around as college co-eds, as friends, you knew what to say. You believed in me. And that has never changed. God help me, for as much as I have thrown at you, that has never changed. I am so lucky to be 'your Finn.'" He smiled but continued immediately. "I can just be me with you. You have this mixture of innocence and gumption that make me want to protect you and feel so protected myself at the same time. God, you're amazing. What I want is what we have … unyielding love. If anything, I'm the one who is blessed that you chose me."

Before I could rebut, Finn's phone started to vibrate. It had been lying on the coffee table when I first walked in that morning. There had been other messages coming through before Finn awoke, but I hadn't bothered to look. It wasn't that he would mind me looking, I just didn't have the desire. Besides, I knew they were most likely all congratulatory messages from colleagues.

As he shifted his eyes slightly to the phone, I said, "I don't want to take away from your celebration. I don't want to ruin that for you."

"You… God…" Matching my melancholy disposition, Finn took the phone and ceremoniously slid it across the floor so that is was far away from both of us. "Come here." He coaxed me into the security of his muscular arms.

Every imaginable emotion was flooding my brain. I needed him so much… for all that he was to me— my husband, my companion, my partner, my soul, my love, my friend. But I felt so much guilt for not deserving him and all those things he was to me. And, then again, I felt weak for needing him. Being needy wasn't "me," and never had been. Then there was the uncontrollable sadness, loss, and grief. They were rooting themselves deeper and deeper into my being—even more so since coming home. How was I going to survive?

His embrace was so tight and secure around my body, I could not imagine how anything else could invade us. And that unconditional, silent love only made me ache more. When I started sobbing downright uncontrollably, he just held tighter.

"It's okay. It's okay," I heard him start. But, when his melodic voice broke, I knew it truly wasn't okay.

"I'm sorry," I said and tried again. "It's your day. You should be celebrating. I *am* so proud of you."

"Please…" He shook it off. "First of all, it's a trophy… a piece of metal."

"It's all that you work for."

Ignoring my comment, he continued. "And, second, my day was yesterday. Today we celebrate Christmas."

"Hmmm," I mumbled with a sigh. "Don't feel much like it."

"Well, I, personally, am glad you're here to celebrate it." His voice was soft as he mellowed. He kissed me on top of my head before saying, "Baby, I love you."

"I love you, too." *But I still don't deserve you*, I said silently in my head.

We laid there in each other's arms for a good amount of time before I felt his hand rhythmically rub mine. "Lar?" He took that hand and kissed it before getting up to open a drawer in the nearby cabinet. Returning to the sofa, he placed a jewelry sized box in my hand. "I wanted to give this to you before Nola, Will, and Kelsea got here."

I opened the box to discover a circular necklace with my initials written in diamonds in the center. It was truly stunning. His steadfast love meant more than any glistening jewels, though.

"Thanks. It's beautiful."

"I know you don't feel—"

"It's beautiful, Finn."

"Can I put it on you?"

I pulled my just-below-shoulder-length hair to the side, allowing him access to my bare neck.

Resting my hands on the necklace, I said, "It really is gorgeous and personal. When did you do this? Where?"

"I had it done when we ordered Kelsea's necklace. You just didn't notice that the jeweler slipped the second box into the bag when we left."

"He said something about going to the back to put his business card in the bag."

"Yeah." Finn laughed.

"And then you insisted on carrying it. I thought you were just being chivalrous."

"Well, yeah, of course," Finn started. "But…wait. Do you remember that?"

"Yeah, I guess I do."

"I didn't think you remembered anything from that day." His voice dipped on the word "that" in solemn remembrance of the day that I fell—the day that changed our lives.

"Yeah, I remember going to the shop. I guess I forgot that it was that morning. But …" The memory thing bothered me exceedingly. It wasn't that I remembered every detail of every part of my entire life, but that part was so blank, so erased, it was on a different level. It was extremely agitating. "Uhhh." My hand left my necklace and rubbed my eyes.

Finn's hands, slightly calloused from years of playing guitar, caressed my back. "What's the last thing you remember?"

"I think that might be it— leaving the shop. I'm guessing you drove."

"Yeah."

"Why can't I remember that?"

"I don't know. But, y'know, maybe you're the one better off. I can't get it out of my head."

"I'm sorry it had to happen on the day of Kelsea's preschool play."

"You sure you're all right with them coming by tonight?"

Kelsea, Nola, and Will were coming over to celebrate Christmas exactly a month after the day we all should have celebrated together in Murphy family tradition —in Kentucky with family and trees and merriment. But that hadn't happened. They had instead been gathered around my sterile hospital room while I slept on and on. So, we were having a mini-Christmas redo with just the five of us at our house. It would be simple and mostly done for Kelsea—so she could see me, know I was all right, and reclaim some of the joy of the holiday for her memory bank.

"I can call Nol—" Finn started when I neglected to answer right away.

"No, it's okay. I want to make sure Kelsea gets her gifts." Albeit weeks late. "It will do me some good to see someone happy. Where are her gifts? I want to make sure they are ready."

"I'll get them."

"No, I can—"

"They're upstairs," he said slowly and solemnly.

His words deflated my momentary high feeling. "Finn, you're going to have to let me go up those stairs at some point."

"I know," he admitted. "Just not today, okay?"

I had visions of him standing at the bottom of the stairs, like I was a toddler and he was the parent at the bottom of a slide. That was Finn personified— an honest, caring, true man. And he would be the same way as a father. He just didn't have that chance. All because of those stairs ...and me.

"Lara?" He called me out of my deep, depressing thoughts. "Let me just have this, all right?"

I nodded slightly, and he kissed me his thanks.

***

It was obvious, almost painfully so, that Kelsea had been coached by her parents on how to act around me. Not wanting to confuse the preschooler any further, I did not question or rebut anything that was said or—more accurately—not said. Instead, I focused on making the day special for that little blonde bundle of energy, just as she and her parents tried to do the same for me. They brought all the food for dinner, plus a cake.

"C'mon, Kels," I said to my little niece, who, despite the brisk late January air, was decked out in her sparkly purple dress with matching shoes and white tights. "Why don't you help me serve the cake?"

"Really?" Her smile was almost as big as the one she had when she had opened our gift and discovered her look-alike American Girl doll and necklace.

"Sure. Come on. We'll start with the napkins, because you know how messy adults came be."

As I handed her the extra napkins, she giggled and exclaimed, "They have Rudolph on them."

"Yep. I saved them since Uncle Finn and I couldn't make it to Christmas." Upon my words, Finn, who had seemed to be walking on proverbial eggshells just waiting for the delicate balance to crash, put his glass of bourbon down and started toward me.

"You were in the hospital," Kelsea continued. "Pop-Pop and Nana went, too."

"Oh, Kels. I'm sorry. We wanted to have Christmas

with you."

Finn, now at my side, nudged Kelsea. "Hey, squirt, we forgot the ice cream. Do you want to help me get it?"

"Yeah!"

"Well, let's go then." Finn glanced back at me as he and Will followed Kelsea into the adjoining kitchen.

I turned to Nola. "She's been through too much already in her young life."

Knowing that I was referencing Wyatt's death, Nola silently nodded her head and turned the tables. "How are you holding up?"

"I …you know, one day at a time."

"And what about Finn…you and Finn as a couple? Are you there for each other?"

"Yeah, Nola. Why? Did he say something?"

"No. No," she denied immediately. "It's just … it's so important that you are open with one another, no matter what."

And then I understood. Nola and Will almost didn't make it after their son died so suddenly. There had been counseling and denial and destructive choices amongst their grief. Though our situation wasn't the same, I knew Nola could see how something parallel could occur.

"We are," I reassured my sister-in-law. "It's just hard. It's hard for me, and it's hard for Finn. You know that. But he's gotten better at that. You know I love your brother so much."

"I know, and he feels the same—"

"Aunt Lara!" Kelsea interrupted, running back into the room and belting out, "Uncle Finn said there is only enough ice cream for *boys*!" She emphasized the last word like it was the ugliest one in the universe.

"Did he now?" I laughed, looking at Finn with one spoon in the chocolate container and Will with one spoon in the vanilla container. "I guess that means there's only enough cake for girls, then."

"Uh, I'm not sure about that," Will chimed in.

"And" —advancing toward my husband, I curled into his side, met his eyes, and snatched the container easily away —"Uncle Finn is no match for me." I placed the ice cream on the dining room table.

Kelsea ran into my body, causing me to bend down to meet her full-blown hug. "I love you, Aunt Lara! You're the best person in the whole wide world."

Her hug was so genuine and strong. I smoothed the curls on the back of her head as my tears came silently and fluidly. They flowed in grief for all that I had lost but also in happiness for all that still surrounded me. Noticing, Nola got Kelsea to help her cut and serve the cake. I switched embraces, finding myself once again in Finn's arms.

While I dried my tears in the privacy of my husband's plaid shirt, he echoed his niece's thoughts. "My sentiments exactly."

I pulled away to face him, giving him a slight smile. Putting his forehead to mine, he nodded his head slowly up and down, causing me to do the same. It was just enough to get me through the dessert portion of our day.

Almost immediately afterwards, though, despite my best-concentrated efforts, I knew I had reached my threshold for semi-forced happiness. Daring the tears not to reemerge, I kissed Kelsea on the top of her head, brushed my hand with Nola's as a sign of thanks, and continued into our first-floor master suite, shutting the door behind me.

I knew he would follow. I just didn't know how soon. It was almost immediately. But, yet, I had still managed to change out of my pale dress and into a pair of gray sweats. A comfy, white cami was almost over my head when he entered.

"Finn, go out and be with your family."

"They understand, Lar, if anyone does."

"Kelsea doesn't. I don't want her to think this is her fault. I don't want another day ruined for her. Please,

please go out and be with them…with her. Make her understand. Tell her I am just tired. And that I love her. I'm sure they'll be leaving soon, anyway."

"I don't want to leave you."

"You're not. I'm in the next room. I can't break her heart, and I'm going to if I stay or if we both leave. Besides, I should call my mom back." I reached for my phone and curled up in the tan circular chair near Finn's nightstand.

Recognizing that I had taken my stand and my reasons for it, my husband relented with a message for my mom. "Tell her we need more cookies." He always found a way, if only momentarily, to cheer me up.

"Thanks, Cowboy."

"Yep. I'll see you in a little bit."

***

Over a half-hour later, I was off the phone with my mother. I heard him open the door, and I could feel his presence. Yet, I didn't turn to face him. I was stuck…stuck in the chair … stuck staring at a non-descript part of the wall. I couldn't even tell you what I was thinking of or even if I was thinking. I didn't want to be stuck. I wanted to move on. I just didn't know how.

Acknowledging my disposition and my need for continued silence, without a word, Finn slid his arms under and around me, boosting me into his torso. I wrapped my arms around his neck, feeling the strength in his upper body as he cradled me to him like a most precious newborn. He gently laid me on the bed, where I allowed myself to semi-uncurl. I moved the soft, satiny burgundy colored sheets so that our bodies could slip beneath them as Finn stripped to his boxer briefs and changed into a gray V-neck T-shirt. With one hand, he gently touched me, causing me to scoot over and grant him more room on his side of the bed—the side closest to the door. In the same way I always wanted to sit with my back against a wall, I preferred being further away from the open doorway. It was a deep-seated neurosis of mine. But that wasn't the only one. Since leaving the hospital, I had developed a fear of the dark.

When Finn went to turn off the solo light in the room, I started, "No. I need it on."

"I got it," he comforted.

My only explanation for my sudden, irrational fear was that because the coma was such a deep sleep, somewhere in my innermost self I was afraid of that pure darkness again. In the hospital, there had always been some light beaming from some place. But that wasn't the case in our home. So the first night back, Finn set the flashlight on his bedside table to beam upwards. And, since then, he had turned on our sentimental red lava lamp. I had owned it since college, prompting Finn back then to teasingly give me the nickname Roxanne, after The Police song about a red light girl.

With that comfort aid in place, I went to my next one—I turned my back and snuggled close to Finn's front. His fingers pushed hair away from my face, and I felt his wet mouth make contact with my collarbone. I reacted by moving my body so that I was lying on my back. He curved his one leg so that it laid protectively on top of both of mine. Softly, he kissed my lips. When I didn't readily reciprocate, Finn tucked my head into his chest and seemed content to end our day that way.

I lifted my head, though, needing him to know how I felt…how he made me feel…needing the day to have more plusses than minuses. I kissed him in the same way— not seductively but with the purest of love. "Thanks for your love and patience. I don't think I would be functional without you."

"Lara, you are braver than you give yourself credit for. And I thought we settled that 'thank you for loving me' bit years ago." He touched my nose so I knew he was joshing and then followed up with the good night phrase we had used since our friendship in college. "Sleep tight. Don't let the bed bugs bite."

CHAPTER FOUR

I occasionally have those nights where I am in the depths of sleep—full-dream, deep-breathing, snoring sleep. Then, suddenly, I am wide awake. I know it's because my mind has had a chance to completely unwind and catch up to something it needed to think about.

Such was the case a few nights later when my eyes popped open in the middle of the night. I was thinking of Finn's tour. I carefully and quietly elevated myself to a sitting position in our bed, trying not to disturb the sleeping musician himself. But he must have felt or somehow knew I was up and watching him.

"Lar? Whatcha doing? It's the middle of the night. You all right?" He was groggy, yet focused.

"Sorry about the tour," I said simply.

"What?"

"You didn't have to cancel it after all."

Shortly after Finn had found out I was pregnant, he cancelled his annual summer tour. The baby had been due in summer. And Finn had insisted on being there for not only the birth but after. That meant no tour. Now, all of that was null and void.

"Oh, baby, don't even think about that." He was now a

47

little more awake and sitting up to meet me.

"But *you* must." I peered my eyes straight at him as if daring him to lie.

He took a deep, labored breath. The poor guy was probably having pleasant dreams, and he woke to me and my drama. Even a nightmare might have been better.

"No. Really. I'm not. In the realm of things, that is so unimportant." He took my hand, as if to solidify his statement. "I have no regrets about the decision not to tour this summer. None. You hear me when I say that."

"I have regrets," I admitted. While Finn pressed his lips to the top of my head for an extended period of time, I continued. "I regret thinking I could have it all. I regret loving every announcement, every heartbeat—"

Almost forcefully, he made me look at him. "Don't. Don't say that. You understand me? I know you're hurting. God, baby, I know that. I wish I could take it all away for you...for us."

I started to pull away from him. "Finn, just...just let me go. I need to just—"

"No, Lara. You don't." Speaking firmly, he looked me so straight in the eyes, I couldn't help but look down. He touched my chin, easing my line of vision back into his. "You don't. You need me. Just like I need you. And I am not going to let you retreat like I did." He paused. "Like I did with Wyatt. Have pain...feel the pain...feel the loss, the grief, but don't regret having loved. You can't regret having loved someone ... especially 'our' someone. You taught me that."

I started to deny what he was saying. But realizing how much it took for him to actually verbalize the connection of grief with his nephew, I backed off. I eased further into his embrace, rather than trying to deny it.

"I love you, Lara. Hold onto that. Hold onto us."

"I am." I wiped a tear that I had tried to resist from initially falling. "I am. Forever, right?" That word meant so much to us—when Finn had first used it before we were engaged, I knew our relationship was on a whole new, secured, committed level.

"Forever, Beauty," he repeated with love and confidence.

***

Since my accident had caused us to miss our first wedding anniversary, we decided to instead celebrate it on Valentine's Day. Originally, we had planned on going back to our alma mater in West Virginia. But the drive or even flight would have been too physically painful for my healing body. So, instead, we had a mini-escape by driving into Manhattan and staying a couple nights at the penthouse Finn owned in the city.

Finn was a little shocked when I told him I had already made plans for dinner. He was well aware that I still wasn't in any emotional state to try anything elaborate. But in honor of our first anniversary, I wanted to make the effort. I wanted to show him that, no matter what, he meant the world to me. And, it was easy to arrange. We went to dinner at his uncle Eoin's restaurant, located just blocks from the penthouse.

After being seated by the owner himself, Eoin brought us our food that I had ordered ahead of time. "Enjoy, kids," he offered with a smile, and I wondered how a thirty-one-year-old could still be considered a kid, especially when I felt so damn old.

As Eoin walked off, Finn looked inquisitively at the dinner selection. "Pizza?"

"It's our first anniversary." I paused, still grieving over missing the real one, but then tried to motivate myself. "I wanted to celebrate our firsts."

"Okay?" Still perplexed.

"Pizza was the first meal we had alone together," I explained as I picked up a piece.

"Yeah?"

"Yeah…in college. Right after Olivia and Sam's car accident. You helped me take care of her cats and bought me pizza."

"Ha! Yeah, I remember," he acknowledged, and then joked, "I'm glad you're finally paying me back. I don't know how a poor college kid ever bought pizza."

"It was sweet. You didn't have to do that."

"Especially since I thought you were so stuck up. I guess those Southern gentleman ways my folks tried to ingrain in me kicked in."

"They did a good job," I said, as he gallantly brought the top of my hand to his lips.

"I love you."

"I remember the first time you said that to me." I managed a smile.

"Yeah." His smile was partial, seemingly full of regret. "Seven years late."

"It happened the way it was supposed to. I wasn't ready back then."

"Please don't tell me you consider that kiss in college our first kiss."

"No?"

"You didn't kiss me back." He still sounded heartbroken over that drunken kiss he gave me right before he graduated— a kiss that came completely out of the blue to me.

"So, the bookshop, then?"

"For sure. That was our first real kiss. Also seven years late."

"That was a good night."

"It was."

"And Eoins…" I glanced around. "This was where we had our first date, wasn't it?" I took note as he brought his pumpkin beer to his lips. "That's why I chose the beer. It was what we drank that night."

"Yeah, our first date."

"Well, it really wasn't presented that way." As Finn

diverted his eyes by taking another swig, I asked about something I had been curious about since then. "Finn, were your friends ever planning on coming that night?"

"I can't believe you're only asking that now. That was two years ago." A shrewd smile crossed his face as he took yet another gulp of the beer.

"They weren't, were they?" I said, eyes wide, mouth open.

He laughed and then turned serious. "You knew that, though, didn't you?"

"I figured it out. But, no, not then."

"I didn't know if you would come if it was just the two of us."

"I went to Java Mug with you."

"Yeah, but Java Mug was just a coffee and 'let's catch up' kinda thing. Uncle Eoin's was…" He stopped.

"Different," I finished for him. "But I didn't know that."

"No? You didn't feel like something changed? You didn't feel like after Java Mug, and especially after Wyatt's birthday party, that something was different—different good—different special between the two of us?"

"No," I answered honestly. "Because I always kinda felt that way."

"Yeah." He smiled.

"You were probably right to do the date thing that way, though. I'm sure I would have acted a lot weirder than I probably already did."

"Yeah." He chuckled. "That's exactly what I was thinking—how weird you were, not at all how beautiful and captivating you were in that silvery shirt."

"It blinded you from the weirdness," I joked.

"Oh, Lara, whatever." He knew I couldn't take a compliment.

"Finn?"

"Yeah?"

"I do love you, you know." I heard my voice break, just

like the way I felt I was breaking a little inside each day since the accident.

"Lar…" His voice crumbled a bit, too, and he went to get up from his seat across from me.

"I'm…I'm okay." I needed to be. I needed to be for all kinds of reasons. I needed to be because we were in a public place and my husband was a public figure. I needed to be because I was stronger than these emotions that insisted on grabbing at my heart. And I needed to be because, damn it, no matter what, nothing was going to change.

Still half-seated, half-standing, Finn looked at me hesitantly. But when I nodded positively, he sat back down, reached into his side coat pocket, and pulled out a small wrapped package. "I have a little anniversary gift…thing for you." He handed it to me and reclaimed his seat fully.

"Finn!" I admonished. "We made a pact not to do that."

"I know. I swear, though, it's nothing. It cost nothing." He ignored my exasperated, semi-warning expression.

The thin wrapping was easily removed, uncovering a brown, leather-bound diary with my initials embroidered in red on the cover. It was nice, simple, and, indeed, hadn't cost that much. Sadly, though, I wasn't sure what I had to write about.

When I told him as much, Finn said, "No. No, it's already full." Something in his voice let me know something sentimental was just a page away.

I flipped the cover to the left and saw Finn's writing on the first page. On the top right hand corner was the date—our wedding date. Scripted on the bulk of the page was the following:

Watching you sleep and thinking how even in slumber you are so beautiful. You are so beautiful, Lara. I wonder if you know how much I treasure you…how precious you are to me. I love you so much, baby. You made me the happiest man in the world today and...forever.

"Oh." I managed to get out. "Finn, that is unbelievably sweet. When did you...? On the plane? Going to Ireland last year?" As he nodded in agreement, I started leafing through the pages. Every single one had something written on it. Looking at the dates, I said, "Is this every day?"

"Right up to..." He paused and his eyes dipped. "Well, right up to that day." He didn't have to be more specific about the day where every happy memory ended.

"Oh." I stared at him a second, taking in the wonderment of Finn Murphy. "Baby, that's...oh, God." I reached my hand out to his and then started randomly looking through the journal.

"Well, you know I keep a kind of lyrics journal. I just thought—"

"I love it." I let my eyes rest on his before randomly flipping to the day after my birthday:

How can you do that to me so many miles away? I miss you.

I looked up and smiled. He was watching me intently, warming up to the idea of me reading his personal thoughts about me. I flipped to another page somewhere mid-summer:

Damn! That...you...were fucking hot!

I laughed out loud, blushing again as Finn stretched across the table to read the passage. He did a quick chuckle, too, as I went to another random page. I remembered the fall day:

It's simple days like this—just you and me, the comedy club, chasing after you in the park, when I wonder, what did I ever do to deserve such happiness?

I wanted to read it all. Yet, I wanted to savor every moment. Should I read one a day? I didn't think I could wait that long. Everything was so thoughtful and real and beautiful. A journal of our past year made me think, though. So, I started to turn methodically to one specific page.

"What are you looking for?" Finn asked.

But I didn't answer. He would know when I got there, and he would know why. It was the end of May:

I have a lot on my mind, but never think that you and your love are not in the forefront.

The next page/day:

Your patience and understanding are just two of the many reasons why I love you.

And then one more turn to the anniversary of Wyatt's death:

Sorry I've been such an ass, Beauty. I love you. You make me a better person.

Finn's eyes searched mine, and I flipped the book around to show him what I was reading and recalling. I remembered thinking at the time, despite knowing he was upset over Wyatt, that he was still somehow mad at me. And it hurt that he wasn't letting me in. I thought for sure he wouldn't have written anything on those days. But he had. He was always thinking of me.

"I love you, Lara. I don't want you to ever doubt that."

"How could I? God, this is amazing." I hugged the now-closed diary up to my chest. "Can we maybe go find that bookshop? I'd really like to kiss you there."

***

I had never seen Finn so agitated. Grumpy when things weren't going his way? Sure. Stressed when the tour was ready to begin? Yep. Emotional over his family and me? Absolutely. Erratic when he was off his meds? Sad and true. And even mad when we would have a rare argument. But this seemed to be all of those things rolled into one.

My husband was no saint by any means—past or present. But he was raised to be a good, considerate Catholic boy. And his mother would have had a fit if she heard how many times he took the Lord's name in vain.

Finn was so upset that I truly thought he was going to trash his career completely. I thought if he didn't conscientiously make the decision to walk away, he was going to piss someone off so badly that the decision would be made for him—reigning entertainer of the year or not. Ironically, it was because of that status that he was in such demand and could not shrug off any more obligations. But he was trying to, and it was all because of me.

He was worried about me. And who could blame him? I would be worried about me. I just couldn't get out of my funk. I went through the motions of the day, but with none of the true enthusiasm I used to have.

Logically, I understood that our daughter was gone and that there was nothing that could be done, or could have been done, to change that. My emotions had transformed to a different realm. I had the acceptance, but I still felt the sadness. I still felt lost.

Part of that was because everything I knew prior to the coma had suddenly changed. Everything was different. I was no longer pregnant or anticipating a new life. Because of rehab and other monitoring, I had not yet gone back to work. And I still had vast blanks where my memory should have been from the day of my accident.

At least I would get a chance to change two of those three. For one thing, I was cleared to go back to work. As a technology coordinator, I could do a lot of things from home, but there was still plenty of hands-on help needed in the building itself. Besides, I missed talking with the school staff, and I needed to get my mind off of all things that didn't involve website designs or data input.

In addition, if my memory wasn't back by the time Finn returned, the doctors agreed that he could fill in the missing blanks for me. I knew he wasn't looking forward to either of his tasks —leaving me or reliving that fateful day. But I was determined for him to go, because I knew he needed to—not just for his career, but for his personal cathartic release. He had been taking his meds and going to see or talking with his therapist more regularly. But, for my husband, his real healer was his music.

Finn had agreed—pre-Lara drama—to be a guest consultant on a televised singing competition show. He had been pretty stoked when it was first brought up to him months before, because he had never done something like that. His role had been promoted for weeks on end and announced many more before that. But now, in mid-March, he was regretting all of it.

"I want you to go," I tried. "I want this for you. Even more, I want this for those contestants. There is some real talent this season." I knew that to be the truth, since Finn and I had been watching the show both during and after my hospital stay. "You will be such a good mentor."

"Neh, I—"

"Finn, you have no idea how much other musicians look up to you. I see it all the time. Your opening acts, at the award ceremonies …you make a difference."

"I can't leave you." He directed the conversation onto another course.

"You can."

"I don't know why you don't just come with me."

"Well, besides me going back to work…" When he tried to interrupt, I verbally blew right past him. "I'm easing into it. It's only two days this week and then it's the weekend. Besides that," I trudged right on, not wanting to give him a space to insert his rebuttal. "I don't feel like being around all those people. It's too much. I'm not ready to put on my Mrs. Rock Star face." Don't get me wrong, there were times I loved getting dolled up and pampered and being on my man's arm. But being an unknown New York suburbanite seemed so much more my pace at the moment.

"You wouldn't have to."

"I would," I bounced right back.

"It's mostly behind the scenes. Besides, I could show you around Los Angeles. I never get out there for more than a night. I could show you all the—"

"—places you and Audrey went."

On the mention of his ex-fiancée, who still lived in Southern California, Finn's shoulders sagged. "No." He let it drop, recognizing how much Audrey managed to crawl under my skin, despite knowing that he cared absolutely nothing about her.

"I don't want to go, Finn. And you need to."

"I don't."

"You do. Even if it is just to get away from me and all this sadness." It hurt, but it was the truth.

"That is never what I want—to be away from you." He reached for my hand.

"You need to take care of yourself."

"You may not know it, Beauty, but you are holding me together right now. Taking care of you—"

"Let your music do that for you."

We were going round and round on the same pointless merry-go-round. I could see the frustration in the way he clasped his hands behind his head and let his muscles bulge. I could feel the emotion in the way his sigh was partially a groan. He wasn't just hearing it from me, either. He was hearing it from all of the people on his team. And he knew he was going to have to eventually give in. Trying to be sensitive, I gave him a moment.

"Well, I can get my mom to come early and be with you the whole time."

Mrs. Murphy was one of my and Finn's biggest advocates since the moment we reconnected. And, as a housewife, she could fly out and be with me. But that was not the solution.

"I love your mom," I said honestly. "But I don't have the energy to play hostess."

"You won't—"

"No, Finn." My proverbial foot was down.

He wrung his hand through his hair, turned around and then back again to face me. "God, Lara, you know I'm just worried about you."

"I know," I said a little more softly.

"This isn't fair." Let his pacing begin.

"I will be at work. There will be plenty of people to keep watch." I rolled my eyes slightly at his protectiveness. "Vanessa, for one, will be harassing me non-stop."

"She has classes to teach."

"Finn…she's also my best friend. She always stops by my room at work, and you know how often she has called and visited since the accident."

"I know," he admitted.

"And I will see your family over the weekend for Kelsea's birthday party at Nola's. I will be well looked after."

"All right," were his words, but his inflection didn't match the meaning.

When he managed to slow his stride down, I encircled his firm, tense body and, ever so slightly, I felt him relax. Lightening the mood, I added, "You might consider getting a haircut before you go on air." I thumped my hand on his chest. "And, you know, maybe hitting that treadmill downstairs. The camera puts on ten pounds, after all."

He pulled slightly away shaking his head back and forth and allowing a smile to parenthesize his mouth. "I don't know why I even try."

"Because you love me." I smiled back.

"No truer words," he said, before gliding his lips softly on mine. "I miss you."

"You haven't even left yet." I half-chuckled.

"I miss you, Lar." This time it was with more earnest.

"I know. The doctor said to wait until you get back."

"God, yeah, I miss that …being with you. But I miss you— that spunk, that smile, the way you put me in my place. I've missed my sassy girl."

I smiled. The possessive way he claimed me with his words— in a country singer sort of way—reminded me of just one more reason why I loved him. "Because I'm always right?" I tried to oblige him with some of that spunk.

"Don't push it, Rox." He jokingly called me by my sexy nickname.

"I'm sorry I've been so…" What exactly was I? "That I'm making you worry." I decided on. "I'll be okay. I will. I love you."

"I love you, too …even though you get your way ninety some percent of the time."

"And the other ten percent, I just let you think you've won."

"No doubt. Thanks for at least giving me that." He touched my nose before adding more definitively, "You know I am going to be calling you at least a couple times a day."

"I would be shocked and sad if you didn't."

"Lar…" There was still doubt…still fear.

"Get packing, Cowboy." I cut him off with my words and a slight smile. "And I'm serious about that haircut."

***

Despite him living up to his word and calling and texting me numerous times during the week he was away, I still missed Finn terribly. And it kind of surprised me. After all, I was used to him being away. In all honesty, he was away a good part of our life together, and that had been the case since we had first started dating. He either had obligations in Nashville or events around the country where he had to perform or make some type of appearance. And, while I missed him, I had been used to it. Now, though, when he left for California, my world seemed so empty. Of course, I didn't let him know the extent of that when we spoke, but instead focused on all the details of the *Singer Spotlight* show and my venture back to work.

And, somehow, we made it through. I believe, a little bit stronger. But, like I told Nola, it was going to be one day at a time—one slow day at a time.

Finn arrived home from LA late at night. He texted me that his plane landed, and he was just waiting for the car service to pick him up. We always made it a point to let each other know when we landed. It was more because of me and my fear of flying than for him. But, then again, he also was the one who traveled more. I shot a quick smile emoji back, set my snooze button for another ten minutes, and then crawled out of bed and into the foyer, dragging the bedroom quilt with me Linus-style.

I was curled up on the foyer's built-in bench when I heard the security system announce that the front door was open. I let my eyes adjust to the dim light radiating from the hallway lamp. Standing in front of me, Finn closed the door behind him.

He let his bag drop to the floor. "You didn't need to stay awake." But the exhausted, subtle smile on his gorgeous face told me he was happy that I did.

"Well, I don't know if you'd exactly call this awake," I mumbled as I stood to greet him.

Dressed only in lacey panties and a white cami, I wrapped my arms around his body. In contrast, he was wearing soft black fleece because, after all, it was March, and upstate New York seemed to be having every season in a week's span. I stood still, breathing in his unique Finn scent, which I always forgot he had until we spent a few days apart. His arms secured their claim around my back and we let the wonderful sounds of silence fall between us. I could literally feel the tension escaping my body. And if I concentrated on his muscular frame, I knew a similar experience was happening to my one and only love, too.

When a calm sigh escaped my mouth, Finn pulled me away ever so slightly. "I missed you. You all right?"

"Now I am." I stretched slightly to pull off his oversized beanie hat, then bracketed my hands on his slightly bearded cheeks. Our kiss was interrupted, unfortunately, by my exhausted yawn.

"Yeah, me too." He smiled. "On both accounts."

"Let's get some sleep. My alarm goes off pretty early."

"I know," he replied before kissing the top of my head. And, with that, we both slept more soundly than we probably had in weeks.

CHAPTER FIVE

Despite missing him excessively while he was gone, I think it did do both of us some good to be away from one another. We were more into the routine of our individual lives and, therefore, could be more in sync with the reality of everything else. I felt better—not complete—but better. And Finn's disposition seemed to mirror mine, whether it was because of me or his Californian music adventure.

So, even though it had been a long work day, and I had been up the night before waiting for Finn's plane to come in, when I got home, I was feeling good. I exchanged my work attire for the creature comforts of sweats and a T, and got ready for dinner. After enjoying our store-bought sandwiches and chips, we both flopped haphazardly on the great room sofa and treasured the comfort of "us" by sipping wine and having our feet intertwined.

I knew it was time. I wanted to know, and I felt like I could know. I thought it would make me feel more complete.

"Finn?"

"Yeah, baby?"

"What happened that day?"

"What day?" He started. But when he saw the pleading

in my eyes, he answered plainly. "You fell. You know that."

"No. I mean, what was I doing?" There was still nothing …nothing for me to grab onto or to anchor my memory base.

"Oh, Lara, I don't want to talk about it."

I knew he didn't. And, I knew why. It was too painful for him. But, the uncertainty was just as painful for me.

"I need to. I don't remember. You have no idea what it's like to not have a memory of something so instrumental in your life. And you're the only one who can tell me."

"You were upstairs." He finished the contents of his glass.

"Why?"

"You had just gotten out of the shower and started drying your hair. We were running late for Kelsea's play and you were a little…" He paused as if searching for the politically correct word. "You were a little anxious about that."

Anxious? No. I was probably pissed. I hated being late. Finn didn't have that same gene or characteristic at all.

"Where were you?" I asked.

"I got you something to drink from the kitchen. We got caught in traffic picking up Kelsea's gift and didn't get a chance to eat. You don't remember any of this?" As I replied with a "no," Finn dropped his feet from mine. I could tell he was getting more upset as the story developed.

"So, I went upstairs…" I encouraged him to continue on with the next plot point.

"You went upstairs to find your shoes." Finn stood up then. I watched him look in the direction of the staircase, as if he were recreating or—worse yet—reliving the scene in his mind. "I saw you on the landing. You were bending down and adjusting the strap of your shoe. I was thinking how good you looked in that turquoise dress—how it showed off everything just right, especially those gorgeous matching eyes." He smiled slightly at me. At least he had a good memory tied to the drama. "You then kinda went sideways and cried out this God-awful sound. And, before I knew it, you were tumbling down the stairs." Finn started shaking his head.

Things were getting too emotional for him, and I knew he didn't want me to see his vulnerability. It wasn't that he couldn't trust me. He knew explicitly that he could. It was that it was always in his innermost being to protect me. And over the past couple months, that meant putting on a brave front, despite his own feelings.

I allowed him a breather before stating the obvious. "I fell."

For me, it was easy. I had no memory. The only emotion or pain that I felt at the moment was watching my best friend hurting.

"I was calling 9-1-1 and running to you. You weren't moving. It was like…" He verbally stumbled, not being able to say it.

But it didn't matter. We both knew what it was like. It was like Wyatt.

"The cops were the first to respond. It seemed to take forever, but I was told it was only a few minutes." As he began rattling off the events, I could only imagine the commotion it caused in our private, gated community. "Then the fire department got here in another five minutes or so. They did what they could until the ambulance arrived in, I don't know, another five or ten minutes after that? There were just people everywhere. But you were still so still. God, Lara, it was awful."

I should have stood up to comfort him. But I was still digesting all the new information that he had just told me—vital new information. And my brain was on overdrive. I was retracing his words in my mind—picking up Kelsea's gift, running late, shower, hair dryer, not eating…

We were both beyond quiet then. I was quiet because I was slowly coming to realize what had really happened that day and my part in it. Finn was silent because he was now emotionally spent, and because he was looking curiously at me—concern streaked across his already worried face. I'm sure he could tell something was wreaking havoc in my mind.

"I did this." I curved my knees up to my chest on the sofa. "I did. It's my fault. Oh, God."

"No, Lar." Finn was subdued but definitive. "No. It was an accident."

I still might not have remembered anything from that exact day, but I did remember events before that. I remembered what the doctor had said after my prior fainting incident at work. I had vasovagal syncope. His instructions were not that difficult or unreasonable to follow. I was to drink plenty of fluids, stay off my feet as much as possible, not get overheated, and reduce stress. From what Finn just described, I blew all of those in one sitting.

"But everything the doctor said …I should have slowed down. I …that hot shower. I …"

I knew I was starting to ramble, but I couldn't help it. It was one thing to think it was an accident. It was completely another to know that I caused it.

"Lara…"

"Oh, God." I didn't let him speak. My skin was feeling hotter by the millisecond, and I felt almost as if I was back in that foggy cloud upon awakening from the coma. "You were… you were trying to get me to…" Eat, calm down, etc. etc. "You have to hate me. You … oh God, you hate me, don't you?" I had started the conversation by looking at my husband, but now I could no longer meet his eyes, my guilt was so bad. "You have to hate me. What I did to her. What I did to our daughter. I killed her." My spread-out hands were embedded in my face now. I had blamed *him* at the hospital, when in reality it had been all my fault.

As I felt his body sink onto the sofa next to me, Finn's strong hands pried mine away from my face. Somehow, he was remaining semi-calm. "Lara, Beauty, no." He managed to lasso my hands into his strong and determined ones. "I couldn't hate you. There's no reason to. Listen to me. It was an accident. It was a horrible, horrible accident. And I am as much to blame."

I met his naturally gray-colored eyes then. "No, you're not. Don't, Finn. I know you're just trying to take everything on just like you always do. But this is me. This was all me."

My husband continued to plead his case, though, while ever so slightly releasing his firm, protective grip on my hands. "I stressed you out that day. I did that. We shouldn't have been going to the jewelry shop the morning of her play. I should have gotten dressed and been ready, but I wasn't. I should have insisted on you sitting while I got those damn shoes. You know how much that eats at me? You want to talk about guilt?"

I could see the sincerity in his watery eyes. I could even understand how he was rationalizing that the incident was his doing. Although I knew the things he blamed himself for were not the cause of my fall. I made poor decisions that fateful day.

"Don't hate me," I reiterated with a cry.

"Baby, no. I love you so damn much."

He pulled me into his embrace and held me there until both of us stopped shaking. And then we just held on some more. In fact, we stayed that way until the sun rose the next morning.

***

Luckily, the following day was Saturday. Finn spent most of it in his studio on the lower level of our house. He had to catch up on a lot of work and follow through with some things from his time on *Singer Spotlight*. Since our semi-cleansing talk the night before, he seemed more comfortable leaving me to do my things while he did his.

One of those was working in our yard. Despite having professional landscapers, I pulled some weeds and planted some flowers that were not terribly aromatic and, therefore, wouldn't bother my highly sensitive nose. It felt so therapeutic. And, for the first time, I truly got why my mother used gardening as her escape when I was growing up. I could rip out the things that were threatening to strangle life out of others and plant beautiful things in their place.

Our day ended with pizza, salad, and a suspense thriller on TV. Finn enjoyed the movie much more than I did. I had had enough shocking surprises in my life. But with his arms wrapped securely around me, nothing seemed quite so bad.

At the conclusion of the film, Finn had to follow up with some more work. But I was ready for bed. So when he eventually made his way into our bedroom, I was already securely snuggled under the sheet. He removed his shirt and started taking off his jeans before going into the adjoining bathroom to brush his teeth.

"Got everything done already?" I asked, as he crawled into his spot mere inches from mine.

"Decided the rest will have to wait," he answered.

I leaned over and kissed him, thinking how good it felt to have him in our bed again, and how lonely I had been while he was in California. He let his tongue dip into mine momentarily and then turned so that I could spoon into him. We laid there silently for a few minutes before I felt Finn's lips on my bare shoulder right before the spaghetti strap. I tilted my neck allowing him to explore further. I couldn't deny that I loved his touch, whether it was his sensual lips or his manipulative hands, which had now found their way under my cami and to my bare stomach.

I turned so that I was lying flat on my back. Everything but the pads of his thumbs, which were creating slow, circular motions just under my breasts, had stopped moving. He locked eyes with me. I knew he wanted permission to continue.

"I need you, Lara," he spoke with love and honesty.

"Yeah," was my one syllable response.

I needed him, too. And the doctor had given us the green light. I didn't know why, but something was holding me back. Nevertheless, I exiled my cami over my head and started my hands down to the rim of my husband's boxers. He moved his hands so that they were working with mine while he started his kissing parade from my neck down to my breasts. When his mouth met my stomach, I suddenly knew why I was hesitant. The last time we had made love, I was pregnant. Finn had loved kissing my ever-so-slightly ballooning stomach and had done so with extra tenderness. I couldn't help the flashback and, consequently, sucked in two quick breaths.

"Hey...hey," he said reassuringly and kissed me softly on the mouth. "You want me to stop? I'll—"

Just knowing that he would do that, and it wouldn't be easy, made me reaffirm one of the millions of reasons I was so in love with that man. "I want you to know that I'm still a little numb, but I love you, and I want this," I answered as truthfully as I could.

"I love you, too."

It felt good to be with him as close as we could be. But we were off. We weren't in sync. I was distracted by the many emotions still ravaging my head. And I knew Finn could sense it. Even if he didn't say it, I could tell by the way he held me ever so closely afterwards. It was like he was afraid I was going to disappear. And that, after all, was his worse fear—being left behind.

***

I woke up a couple hours later to find the bed empty. Ironically, it was Finn who was gone. I knew that he wasn't far away, but a little bit of irrational fear did sneak in during those wee hours of the morning. I threw my undergarments back on and ventured out of the bedroom. One step into the great room and my momentary apprehension was put to rest. I found Finn sitting pretzel-style on the recliner, watching television.

"Hey, Beauty." He grabbed the nearby remote and turned the volume of the TV down to nearly nil.

"Hey," I echoed back, while he stretched his legs out. Taking it as an invitation, I climbed onto his lap. Once situated with his arm securely holding me in place and our faces nearly touching, I said, "I'm sorry, Finn. I know I wasn't completely … it wasn't you."

"Rox, you have nothing to be sorry about."

"I'll get there. I promise."

"There's nothing wrong with being vulnerable. You forget, I fell in love with you when you were vulnerable."

I didn't know what else to say. The understanding that man had was almost inhuman. I decided to simply accept it and leaned my head onto his chest.

Focusing my eyes on the television, I asked, "Whatcha watching?"

Reaching for the remote, Finn turned the volume back up. "Brings back memories, huh?"

Finn was watching *House Hunters*. It was the program that he had teasingly called his favorite show when we first met up again after seven years post-college. It was the show that was on when we had our first more-than-just-a-quick-peck-on-the-lips kiss, and then shortly after that I had fallen asleep in his arms.

I looked back at him. I had been right. He, too, was troubled by the scene in our bedroom, and he was resorting to simpler times. There was no way that show just happened to be on when hundreds of other cable options were available. And I was never more glad that I had followed him out to that great room. We needed that second closure to our night.

"Want to fall asleep on my shoulder again?" He rubbed my arm.

"Just so I get to start with that kiss first," I said and smiled.

"Vavoom," he teased, reminding me of the word I had said after drinking just a little too much wine on an empty stomach that night in Nashville a few years before.

I lightly hit him in the chest and then went in for a series of light feathery kisses. "Thanks for always remembering the important stuff."

"You make me want to." He gently guided my head back down to his chest.

***

Just a few days later, we celebrated my April fourth birthday quietly by ourselves, which was just perfect. And then Finn had to fly to Vegas for the ACM Awards for a few days, and then to Nashville for about a week for, among other things, a Make-a-Wish appearance and a gig at the Grand Ole Opry. He tried, once again, to convince me to join him. But I couldn't take that much time off work. Besides, I wanted and needed to be there. There was a lot to be done. And, in reality, work stabilized me. Finn conceded to my side quicker than he had the time before, although it took some coaxing. I knew he was still concerned, and I also knew to expect a nearly constant correspondence between he and I while he was away.

I heard such correspondence via my cell phone's "Roxanne" ringtone that Sunday night while I was in the kitchen. I knew Finn was most likely calling to tell me that his flight was in and that he was back in the New York area. Knee deep—or, more accurately, wrist deep— in chopping vegetables, I didn't go to the great room to retrieve my phone, instead letting it go to voice mail. A number of peppers, onions, and tomatoes later, I finally heard my husband's sexy voice, via voice mail, telling me that he missed me and that he had, indeed, just landed. I went into our master bath and got in the shower. I had decided to make an effort and get semi-dressed up for his return. After putting my hair in a loose bun and tying myself into a navy colored wrap dress, I went back into the kitchen to put the tortilla wraps in the oven to warm.

That's when I heard Finn's voice bursting through the front door. "Lara! Lar! Where are you?"

"I'm in—" I had started to say my locale when he entered the kitchen.

"Oh." He exhaled. "Hey. Are you all right?" He finally dropped his suitcase and guitar case right in the middle of the kitchen and reached his arm out to my shoulder to draw me to him.

"Yeah. Yeah. I'm fine. What's up?" I asked, concerned that he was so concerned.

"You didn't return any of my texts. I thought something was wrong."

"What texts? I got your call that you were waiting for the car service."

"I …just now …a little bit ago. Wanted to see if you needed me to pick up something for dinner." His voice was returning to a normal pace as he looked to the stove and the numerous items spread across the center island.

"Sorry, I didn't check. Maybe I was in the shower. Anyway, I decided to make dinner. How about that?" I grinned. I was secretly proud of myself, since bagels, eggs, and sandwiches had been about the extent of my culinary skills since the accident.

"That" —he relaxed and traced his finger around my grinning lips —"is perfect."

"Well, I'm just about done. You have good timing— must be a musician thing."

"Ha!" He laughed and then greeted me properly with a kiss as warm as the sizzling chicken in the pan. "Looks good."

"Fajitas." I declared of my culinary creation.

"Well, I wasn't talking about the food." When a blush actually crept onto my face, Finn followed up with a more direct statement. "*You* look really good."

"Thanks. I'm trying."

"I know you are, Beauty."

"I'm getting there, Finn. I don't want you to worry."

"I do."

"How was your flight?" I asked changing the subject.

"Talk about not worrying." He smiled and then reassured. "It was uneventful."

"The best kind." I tried a smile and returned to the skillet.

"Can I help?"

"Take the wraps out of the oven? And maybe drinks?" I turned off the chicken and transferred it to a serving plate. Then, while I was placing the chips, salsa, and condiments on the dining room table, I heard the blender start churning. I smiled to myself reimagining the first time Finn and I had margaritas—the first weekend we were truly together. Since then, the sour alcoholic drink always had a special place in our hearts. I was taking the dishes from the cabinet when he sidled up behind me, putting a margarita in my hand. "Good choice," I said turning around.

"I thought you might approve." He smiled back and clinked his glass to mine before taking a healthy sip. "God, I love that dress." He let his eyes wonder the entire length of the garment. "It really accentuates everything just the right way."

"You mean my breasts!" I teased.

"Well, yeah," he admitted. "And other curves, too." He took our glasses and placed them on the table before interlocking his hand in mine and gently encouraging me to twirl.

I felt free and happy as the material lifted and danced along my legs. Once I made the complete 360 degree spin, Finn pulled me closer into his embrace and started swaying me into a slow dance. I welcomed the rhythmic rock that only a musician could get perfectly timed without music, and I sank into the warm feeling of comfort and love.

"My girl ... the dancer." He wrinkled his nose in a pleased "told-ya-so" kind of way.

I was never a dancer. I detested the thought of being on display and shied away from the intimacy that slow dancing brought ... until Finn. Until he got me to lower some of my internal walls. Until he loved me.

"Because of you and only with you," I claimed.

His mouth lovingly and playfully found mine. When I started unbuttoning his emerald green, plaid shirt and then dipped my hands down onto his hips, he smiled. "You know what those hands on my hips do to me."

"That was the idea, Cowboy," I confirmed.

"Dinner?" he questioned in a way that I knew he was hoping my answer was...

"Dessert first." I was letting go— no hesitation this time.

He kissed me with more purpose then and didn't stop as we waltzed all the way into the first floor master suite. Finn shrugged his shirt off, removed his shoes, and started going for his belt. But I put my hands on his and finished unlocking the leather band that matched his sleek black pants. At the same time, I felt his hands manipulating the tie of my dress. And then, simultaneously, both of our garments feathered to the carpet. I heard Finn's stifled groan of admiration before he kissed me so strongly that we both tumbled to the floor. He planked himself on top of me smiling softly before going for the front clasp of my lacy, teal bra. Then I felt his hand inside my matching panties; his finger teasing, taunting me. With his mouth on the space right between the sides of my open bra, I stretched my neck back, closed my eyes, and started to squirm in pleasure. I wanted him so much right then, physically and emotionally, I couldn't stand it. But...

"Finn," I panted. "I'm going to get rug burn."

He laughed right along with me and said, "Okay, baby." And switched his hand from my front to my behind, cupping my bottom securely in his ample hands and lifting both of us.

As my husband carried me to the bed, I pulled the elastic out of my hair to release my full length from the bun. Once he laid me down, Finn ran his hands, from top to bottom, along either side of my body. And then he started again from the top with his mouth not missing anything—my forehead, each eye, the bridge of my nose, my cheeks, lips, chin, neck. He was purposefully taking things slow. It was so different from the other night. It was like we hadn't known how to act with one another after a tragedy. And, now, we were rediscovering and learning how to live again.

When his mouth found my panty line, I couldn't take much more, though. My body was naturally lifting up toward his. It was as if there was a magnetic force between us.

"Easy, my sexy Roxanne," Finn teased. "Let me enjoy myself." And at the same time, he snaked my panties down my legs gently using his teeth.

"God, that is so damn hot," I cried out.

"My *wife* is so damn hot."

I felt his expert hands discard my panties and then slowly begin their path up my legs. When they reached my thighs, I sat up to meet him as he was kneeling ready to take off his boxer briefs. "Let me," I partly whispered.

After we detangled his legs from his briefs, he stopped, looked seriously at me, and said, "I was so afraid I was losing you."

We were both now physically and emotionally naked and vulnerable. I cupped his face in my hands. For the first time, I was truly seeing his fear and, at the same account, understanding that we were going to make it through the darkness.

"It would have been impossible without you. I love you

so much."

His reply was to kiss me so sweetly and slowly that I totally lost myself in it. I didn't realize that he was also lowering me back down onto the bed until I felt us completely together. We had had sex countless times before, and somehow that time was completely different. Finn was methodical just like his kisses. He took his time and reached deep into me …into my heart. I knew he felt it, too. We didn't speak, but we both knew we didn't want that magical moment to end. We merged into one another repeatedly, feeling each other's love, lust, and release.

Finally, trembling from all three of those things, we both basically collapsed. We laid on our backs, side-by-side, for a couple minutes. Finn was the first to speak. "Am I still breathing?"

"Need some mouth to mouth?" I teased turning on my side to face him and placing my hand on his bare, hard chest. "I might have a little . . .Oollll…." I yelped as he pulled me swiftly on top of him.

"You amaze me."

"Ditto." I rubbed his chest before sinking my head down onto it. "You make me feel so beautiful."

He gently put his hand to my chin and tilted my head up so that our eyes would meet. He wanted my full attention. "That's because you are. Tonight was beautiful. I love you. I love us together."

CHAPTER SIX

Nothing would ever be the same. That was a given. That was a fact. But life didn't stop. We learned to move on— by remembering and sharing, not regretting and shielding.

And we needed every ounce of strength from each other to do just that. During the next few weeks, emotional dates cruelly reemerged on the calendar. First, there was Mother's Day—something I wasn't. I poured my thoughts and energy into my own mother and mother-in-law, even though both were long-distance. And then I gave the rest of my heart to my husband, who knew to keep things simple and serene.

Next was the second anniversary of Wyatt's death. Unwarranted guilt still clung to Finn like a wet winter coat. He could never get over the fact that he was the one with his nephew that fateful day when a car, driven by a man having a stroke, careened out of control and fatally struck Wyatt.

Unfortunately, in a role reversal, I was the one who was away that extended weekend. I was attending a mini-college reunion that my friend Haylie had orchestrated. She owned a bed-and-breakfast a couple hours north and wanted to assemble a few of us girls.

I initially had hesitated in joining the gathering— first because of the loss of Chloe and not feeling like socializing, and second because I hadn't seen most of those women since college, and I didn't know what to expect when it came to the inquisition of Finn and our life together. Being married to a celebrity put a whole different spin on other personal relationships. But Finn had encouraged me to go. He thought it would do me some good to get away, as I knew it had done him in LA. After all, it was a small group, and he had known them in college. And, I had learned to be discreet when it came to my personal life. Hell, I had learned that even before college.

Taking the day off of work, I left the Friday of Memorial Day weekend. Finn helped put my things in the Jeep and asked me to text him when I got to Haylie's. I pressed my lips to his for an extended moment, wanting him to feel our love. Even though he hadn't mentioned it, I most certainly knew he didn't forget that Sunday was the anniversary of Wyatt's death. But Finn seemed okay. He was in good enough spirits and had a conference call within a half-hour of my departure. The rest of his weekend entailed other work obligations, including deadlines on new lyrics and scheduling details.

In some sense, Haylie, the others, and I were instantly transported back in time, and nothing had changed. We naturally fell into the rhythm of our friendship. But, in other ways, our worlds were all so different— locations and careers and kids and divorces and losses and loves. I didn't want to divulge any more than necessary, but my recent life had been well documented via the tabloids. Although curious, thankfully, the girls were sympathetic and respectful when I didn't offer much.

That was, until the second evening of my visit. That was, until a couple bottles of wine were opened and we were playing Truth or Dare, as if we were still back in school. It was my turn, and I was already dreading it. Having been witness to the dares involving drinking and aerobatic feats, I knew I had to choose "truth." And, depending on the question, I knew I might not be one hundred percent truthful.

"Finn ..." Olivia, my best friend from college, was the questioner. "He's smokin' hot in bed, isn't he?"

Only Liv, I thought, and sighed. I was actually kind of surprised it had taken her that long to go there. She obviously had put on polite restraints the first day. But everyone knows that in Truth or Dare, everything is on the table.

When I didn't respond immediately, still taken in a little by the brashness of the question, Olivia pursued. "Look, she hasn't even had one sip of alcohol and her face is beet red!" If the collective group of women weren't already staring at me, their scrutiny grew upon Olivia's declaration. "Slammin' hot, huh?"

I couldn't help it. Olivia's no-holds-barred, straightforward way made me giggle and bring my hands up to my face. It reminded me of how easy our friendship had been before we had—other than a yearly Christmas card—lost touch shortly after graduation.

"Lara, your choice. Is it truth, or is it dare?" she reminded me.

I uncovered my face and smiled. "Slammin'," I admitted and then partially covered it again.

It felt good to be carefree for a moment—to be a girl with no immediate burdens on her shoulders. And I hadn't given away any deep, dark secrets. In the worst case scenario, if any of the women decided to go to the press, which I knew they wouldn't, what could be printed? That Finn's wife says he's good in bed? That would hardly hurt his reputation.

"Ha! Hot damn! I knew it!" Olivia screeched, taking another drink.

Seri, the most innocent of our bunch, said, "I've seen

some of those award shows. The way he talks about you … it's so sweet."

"And that song he wrote—" Haylie started.

"'Lara's Song,'" Seri interjected.

"I remember that song was just coming out when you were here last time. You weren't even engaged yet."

"You were here? Why? When was that?" Olivia asked, seeming a little hurt that she hadn't been to Haylie's before.

"A couple years ago now. Impromptu," I answered.

I wondered if Haylie ever knew why I had suddenly took refuge at her bed-and-breakfast back then. Finn and I had—unbeknownst to most of the world—split up due to what turned out to be unwarranted accusations by the press of his drug use. I certainly didn't want to bring that up. Casually talking about my sex life was one thing. Two years ago was completely another.

Luckily, when I eye-balled Haylie, she got the hint and changed the subject … sort of. At least her question would deflect Olivia. "Does he sing to you, you know, when you two are—?"

"Haylie!" I bellowed but internally grateful. "I think I answered my one question."

"Okay, I guess you're right." She chuckled. "How about a mini-break? I need to call the kids at my in-laws and say good night." Besides closing the bed-and-breakfast for the weekend, Haylie's husband had taken their two kids to his parents so Haylie could host our get-together. From the way it sounded, Haylie had done very well in the husband department, also. And I wasn't just talking about in bed.

"I should call home, too," Seri announced.

"I need to get a drink. Lara?" Olivia lifted her head in my direction.

"Neh. I'm just gonna go out and get some fresh air. I'll be back in a few."

"All hot and bothered thinking of Mr. Smokin', huh?"

"No!" I said, slightly exasperated. Although, I was thinking of Finn. But it was out of concern. I wanted to call him in private and make sure he was all right … make sure he was dealing with the weekend okay.

When I went out to the barn to call, I considered telling him about the Truth or Dare conversation, because normally he would say something sexy and provocative back to me. But, judging from his quiet demeanor, I decided against it. Instead, I asked how his writing was going and internally hoped that was the cause of his subdued mood. He claimed the lyrics were going well, but slowly. I was just finishing up our conversation when I heard Olivia enter.

"I love you, too," I said into the phone and then smiled to acknowledge my friend.

Olivia, clearly a little tipsy, belted out in the direction of my phone. "Love you, too! Smooch, smooch. Kiss, kiss!"

As I shook my head while rolling my eyes in a joking manner, I heard Finn's voice from across the line. "Who's that?"

"Olivia," I replied.

"Figures." It was hard not to miss his exhale.

"She's leaving! Lara's leaving now." Olivia started yelling purposefully for Finn to hear. "Heck, maybe she'll never come back. Say goodbye. We're gonna go find us some real men."

Any hopes that Finn could dismiss those words were immediately dashed. "Put her on the phone."

I glared at Olivia. She didn't know how the word "leaving" affected Finn, especially when it came to me. I let go of being upset with her and instead tried to pacify my husband.

"She's been drinking," I tried.

"Put her on the phone, Lara," he said with even more directive.

I sighed softly and handed the phone to Olivia. "He wants to talk to you."

Olivia took another swig of her wine. "Hey, Lover," she cooed into the phone.

I couldn't help but cringe ... not only because of the Truth or Dare conversation but because, even though she had never said it out loud, I knew back in school that Olivia sort of had the hots for Finn. She had been madly, crazy in love with Sam. But if Sam hadn't been in the picture, I am pretty sure she would have gone straight after Finn. Nothing would have ever come from it, though. I knew then, and certainly now, that Finn didn't think that highly of Liv. He had been one of Sam's best friends, and didn't like how Olivia had him whipped. I saw a different side of Liv, though—a girl who had no stability in her life. She was estranged from both of her parents and her siblings because of her parents' bitter divorce. She was all alone. I understood that. And, because of all the instability, Olivia craved control. Sam had let her have it. But when they entered the real world, it no longer worked. They ended up divorcing five years into their marriage. Ironically, just like her parents before her, it was not at all civil. But, thankfully, it did not involve any children. I didn't know the true reason behind the split, but Finn, who had lost touch with Sam, was sure that Olivia simply grew tired of her husband and needed a new challenge.

"How's it shakin'?" I focused once again on Liv's voice—the one speaking to *my* husband. "It's been a while. We were just ..." I watched her face slightly twitch in a sure reaction to whatever Finn had said back to her. "Well, that's rude." She grew quiet again, and I wondered what he was saying. Finally, she responded. "When did you get so uptight? I was just joking. Maybe—" She stopped mid-sentence and looked from the phone to me and back again. "He just hung up on me."

Crap! He was pissed—really pissed. I took my phone back from Olivia, visually confirming that the call was, indeed, dead.

"What did he say?" I inquired, trying not to sound too

anxious.

"He said" —she took a sip of her wine— "it hasn't been long enough since we've seen one another, went off about how you are not leaving him, and then started in on how I treated Sam. I didn't deserve—"

"I wouldn't leave him," I said plainly and most truthfully.

"What?" Confusion creased her face. "I was just joking."

"We've been through a lot."

"I know," she said this time with a much more sober, somber inflection. Everyone knew of my recent miscarriage and coma. "But, geez, Lara, what's wrong with him? Is that what becoming a super shit rock god did to him? Turn him into a pompous ass?"

"He's not. Really. He's just protective of me and our love. And this weekend brings up ..." I started and then decided I didn't want to divulge anything more, even though Wyatt's passing had been a matter of public knowledge, too. "Never mind. I need to call him back."

"Sheez. Don't send my regards. We're going to hit the bar. You're coming, right?" Olivia hadn't changed. She was still part bully.

"I don't know."

"Why not?" she asked incredulously. "Come on! It's girls' weekend. Call him, do the whole 'I love you' thing and then let's go. Never would have guessed you two would become the power couple you are, by the way. He never said a word to me back then." I knew Finn would never have entrusted anything personal to Olivia, but I let it go as she continued. "And you ... well, I pegged you dying an old cat lady." Amused with herself, she smiled, but she probably wasn't too far off—if it hadn't been for Finn ...and my allergy to cats ... and, it seemed, standing in that barn, suddenly an allergy to hay.

"Olivia!" I rubbed my itchy nose and chuckled. "Just give me a few. I'll meet you in the house."

"You better." She wagged her finger at me parent-style before trailing out of the barn.

I immediately tried to call Finn back. If I wasn't already concerned, I was even more so when he didn't answer. Stunned at the non-response, I hung up without leaving a message. After all, the caller ID would register my number. Was he mad at me? Did he somehow believe Olivia? Surely, he couldn't. I waited, hoping that he would call back. Then I realized he might think it was Olivia calling, since she was the last one on the phone. So, I redialed and this time left a message.

"Hey, why aren't you picking up? Olivia's gone. Just ignore her." I paused, half-expecting him to pick up mid-message. But phones hadn't worked that way in years. "All right. Call me. Please." I finished.

I went over to the stall and petted Haylie's daughter's neighing tan-colored horse. She was a gentle animal, and the repetitive motion of my hand stroking her body soothed both of us. Ten minutes later, when I was just about to give up and leave, a text came in from Finn.

I love U.

Grateful, but still needing a little reassurance, I texted back: *Forever. Call me.*

He ignored my request, but did text back. *Go have fun w/ your friends.*

It concerned me that we weren't speaking voice to voice, and I wanted him to know that. *Finn?*

Letting it go.

I had to believe him. At the very least, I knew for certain that he was trying to make it all right for me. Plus, he was probably being super conscientious, knowing I had a bunch of women with me.

So, reluctantly, I let it be, but not without telling him that I loved him, too. *xxoo*

I did go to the bar. And I did laugh and relax despite offering to be the designated driver and constantly thinking of Finn. Even though his words via text seemed encouraging, I feared something was off. And by the next day, Sunday, I knew I had to cut the girls getaway short and drive home to be with my love.

***

I didn't tell him. I just said my goodbyes to my college friends and drove home. I anticipated what I would find. Yet, somehow, it still shocked and saddened me.

When I entered our house, I discovered Finn in the great room. He didn't hear me at first, despite the garage door opening, as well as the door from the garage to the house. When the rap of my heels hit the great room floor, though, he quickly scrambled to close his laptop in an attempt for me not to see. But it was too late. I saw the photos of Wyatt. I saw the selfie of the two of us just after I told Finn I was pregnant. And although those images made me sad, it was the sight of my distraught husband that brought on the deepest pain. Looking like he hadn't shaved since I had left, Finn sat on the sofa with a half-empty liquor glass in his hand and a similarly filled bottle at his side.

"Lara?" Drunk. Confused. As I placed my bag down on the floor next to the sofa, he took a final swig of his bourbon. "What are you doing here? You're not supposed to be here. Right?" He tacked on the final question at the end, as if he doubted his sense of time.

"Oh, baby." I started to sit down next to him, but he abruptly stood up.

"Lara," he cautioned. "No."

"Let me help you." I joined him on my feet.

"No. No. You're not supposed to be here." When he glanced down, I followed his eyes to the coffee table and the sonogram resting innocently on it.

The image stabbed me with sadness but also gave me strength. "I need to be. I want to be."

"I don't want you to be. I didn't want you to see this."

"What? To see you? To see that you have feelings, too? Finn, God, baby."

Oh, how my heart broke for him. But, it was my turn to be strong ... my turn to be the one who held us together. With the memories of Wyatt especially poignant that weekend, and me being away, Finn had finally let himself unravel and feel the tragic loss of our little girl.

"Thank you for being strong for me these past few months," I continued. "Thank you. I don't know that I ever told you that. But it shouldn't have been at your expense." I moved toward him, putting my hands up to his whiskery cheeks, wanting to kiss him ... wanting to ease his pain. When he resisted by stepping back, I wasn't deterred. "I know you miss Chloe." I tackled it head-on. "I can't imagine what you went through that week or so— losing her and with me in that coma. And today ... this weekend, it's—"

"I'm..." He started but then looked away.

"I'm sorry I left. I knew I shouldn't have gone to see the girls. Look at me." Then I emphasized, "Tell me."

"I just ... I wanted to feel." His eyes met mine ever so briefly, but then, as if in disgrace, dipped toward the floor.

I think every emotion smacked me in the gut in the matter of a millisecond. I was hoping he was just emotional and drunk—which he was. But I had a deep-down fear that it was more. The humiliation in his eyes, along with his words, confirmed to me that he purposefully went off his meds.

I chose to settle on the emotion of love and forget all the other conflicting thoughts. "Feel me," I said with conviction.

"Did you hear what I said?"

"Yes. Did you hear what *I* said? If you want, you can push everyone else away, but I'm not going anywhere."

I thought that would help. I thought he would feel secure and let me in, knowing that I wasn't leaving. But he didn't. He just looked at me sadly and turned.

Pursuing, I followed him into our bedroom. "Finn?"

He spun around and locked into my eyes. Cupping my face firmly, he lavished an aggressive kiss on and in my mouth. In the second that it took me to react, he just as quickly retracted his stance.

"Oh God, Lara. No. Please go. I'm not right right now. I'm not in control."

Taking a breath and assessing the situation, I said calmly, "You don't need to be in control. It's all right. Let go. If you don't think you can talk right now, that's okay. But you need a release, and it can't be with any more alcohol." I moved toward him again and kissed him. "Let me help you."

"I don't want to hurt you. That would ruin us."

I spoke the truth. "I'm not scared of you, Finn."

"Maybe you should be."

Even though his eerie delivery admittedly shook me, I knew him, and I was confident in his love for me. "Finn, you told me you would never hurt me…and you won't. You won't let that happen."

He hesitated for a second and then swiftly, with determination, had me pinned up against the wall. My eyes closed, I felt his body pressed snugly up against me. He was so close and so needy. I tasted the alcohol as his greedy mouth merged with mine. And even though I despised the flavor, I relished his desire and tried to meet his intensity. He was in emotional distress and needed me to be there for him. And I submitted not only for Finn's sake but, in reality, for mine, too. I needed an escape. Besides the weekend and Finn, there was something I was holding in … something that could change everything. And, God help me, I didn't want to think about it. I knew I would have to … and soon. But having my husband's body collide with mine felt like the perfect diversion.

After tugging my capris down, Finn's assertive hands went to my red, patterned T. Awkwardly, because of the fevered pace, he managed to remove it before clawing at my front clasp bra. I tried to help but lost my balance and started falling toward the floor.

"Fuck!" He belted out, and only for that minor second did I fear that he really could lose control.

But he managed to catch me and at the same time, holding me securely, draw the comforter from the end of the bed to lay beneath us on the floor. I couldn't help but do an internal smile thinking of my rug burn comment a few weeks before. He would take care of me. He couldn't hurt me. It wasn't in him.

The relentless way his body met mine forced me to grasp the comforter on either side of me. He was completely the one in charge. I had my eyes closed, absorbing his aggressive body, when I felt something wet drop on my face. I looked up to see the pain escaping my husband in another way— tears were silently falling down his cheeks and onto mine. Aware that I was witness to his vulnerability, Finn entombed my eyes with his firm hand. But I kissed him. I kissed that hand covering my face until he slowly withdrew it. And then I kissed the tears on his cheeks. I felt Finn ease. His body then slowed as he collapsed onto me.

Immediately after, as he laid next to me on the floor, one of his ultimate fears started to escape from his mouth. "Are you all r—"

I stopped him mid-thought. I wouldn't even let him finish because if I hesitated, it would destroy him. And even though our encounter was more intense than I was used to, it was not in malice, and it was very much consensual.

"I ... love ... you." I separated each word to emphasize the truth and power of what I said and because I was still catching my breath. At the same time, I curled into his chest, which had remained clothed by what was now a slightly sweaty yellow T. Feeling tense under my head, I rubbed his muscular abs and drew even closer waiting, wanting him to speak.

It took a moment, but it was worth it. He rested his chin on my head and finally let go completely. "Lara, I miss them so much. It's hard, you know, to move on … to know that I couldn't do anything to save either of them and, yet, to be so grateful that you are alive … that you are here."

"I am. I'm here. And it's because of you…because of you and your love. Don't bottle things up. Don't sto—" But it was me who stopped. I didn't want to push it. I didn't want to risk the progress that had just been made.

He took my chin in his fingers and tilted my face toward his. "Say it."

I adjusted slightly so I could meet his eyes. "Don't do that again, Finn. Don't risk going off your meds." My bravado started to fail as my voice cracked and my eyes got a tad watery. "Don't. Please."

"I'm sorry. I thought I just wanted a couple of days to feel …" He tried to explain. "I let you down."

"You … no. It's okay to feel. Just don't hurt yourself doing it. And don't shield me from it."

He gently extracted me from him and pulled up his dark gray sweats, which were only somewhere near his knees. I took note then. My capris and panties were similarly dismantled around my ankles. My purple bra still dangled haphazardly off my shoulders. We were a mess. Our physical appearance mirrored the mental state that had provoked our emotional love making.

Finn saw me taking it all in and, without a word, scooped me up and carefully laid me on our bed. After peppering a few kisses on my lips, he went to my feet and removed the capris and then pulled my panties back up my legs. He looked at me, then. It was only for an extended second, but it said a lot. I could see his regret, his love, and his gratefulness. But when I went to speak, he got off the bed and walked into the adjoining bathroom. Just like so much of that evening, I didn't know what to expect.

I pulled the satiny sheet on top of me and laid there

still to listen. From the adjoining master bath, I heard the sure tell rattle of a medicine bottle and a glass of water being filled. I felt my shoulders immediately sag in relief and appreciation.

When Finn reentered our bedroom, looking a bit remorseful, I acknowledged his undertaking with a slow closing and opening of my eyes. Then I reached out my hand to him. He readily took it and climbed back onto our bed. He held me then. Or, was it I that held him?

"Once I sober up," he said. "I want a do over. I want to make love to you … the right way."

"Sleep," I soothed. "If I'm with you, it's always right."

"Lara …"

"I need to sleep, too. I'm wiped. I don't want to think about anything but counting sheep."

But it wasn't sheep I was counting, and I didn't necessarily fall asleep readily. I was counting days. It was the end of May, and over the weekend I realized that I had not had a regular period since losing the baby. I understood that it sometimes took a little bit of time after a pregnancy. So, I wasn't concerned medically. But, so many of those days were a grief-filled blur. I hadn't been thinking right and not caring about anything but my loss. Certainly not about protection and certainly not about getting pregnant. And that was what could be happening. I could be pregnant…again. It was like a maddening flashback of my summer after high school. Fear and hope rolled into one because, this time, I had no idea which result I wanted. And, until I knew for sure, I wasn't going to tell Finn, especially with the emotional roller coaster we had both just gone through.

CHAPTER SEVEN

"You told me I didn't hurt you," were the words that I woke to.

"What?" I adjusted my eyes. I couldn't believe how late I had slept in considering how early we had gone to bed. But I am sure the events of the evening had drained me into a tired stupor.

Finn was sitting near the edge of the bed, simply staring at me and creating a noticeable gap between our bodies. "Lara, you told me I didn't hurt you," he said once more.

"You didn't. Finn—"

The way his eyes ventured down to my exposed breasts made me stop mid-sentence and look myself. There were a few slightly inflamed scratches stretching from my left breast to the center of my chest. I had neither noticed nor felt them. Now, a little more awake, I crossed my arms in front of me.

"I'm fine." I defended my body and, in essence, defended him.

"That is not fine," he countered, very stoic in his delivery.

"It is. I'm fine. Besides, who has the fingernails? It was probably me."

"Let me look at you," he interjected. When I didn't respond directly, he gave a more definitive directive. "Please, Lara, sit up. I need to see."

Silently, I did so. I allowed the rest of the sheet to fall past my lap. I knew he didn't hurt me. But knowing that he was upset, I would let him examine me to put his mind at ease. He lifted my hair and ran his hand along my bare back, then pulled the sheet the rest of the way down gliding his hands along my legs. I might have been turned on if I didn't know what the premise behind his touch was.

"Ahh, fu—"

"What?" I asked alarmed and drawing my legs back from his hands.

"There's bruises. There's f-ing bruises on the back of your legs."

Stunned, I turned and positioned my legs so that I could see what he had. There were. Two sets. My left leg had a defined bruise with a couple smaller ones nearby, and my right leg just had a couple of the smaller ones, although not as pronounced. They weren't painful. Again, I didn't even know they were there. But I did figure out when I must have gotten them.

"God, Finn, that's ... that's just I'm sure when you caught me. Baby, you didn't hurt me. You were making sure I was okay. I'm fine," I reiterated for what felt like the hundredth time.

"I'm so sorry."

My ache was not the bruises or scratches. It was emotional. It was for him.

"Please don't. You needed me. I needed you. I am not sorry at all. Don't make me feel like I should be. I don't feel that way, and I don't *want* to feel that way."

"Lara, I told you before, if I tell you to get away from me, next time please listen."

"Don't even say—"

"I have to."

I dug in with all the determination that I had because I

needed him to understand. I needed him to mourn and feel. I needed him to not treat me with kid gloves. I just needed him. And feeling the queasiness suddenly throughout my body, I really had a feeling I was going to need him even more if what I was suspecting was true. "What you have to do is hold me and love me."

"Lara …"

"Hold me. Love me," I replayed because that was all that needed to be said. It truly was all that either of us needed.

"You know I do." He inched forward and lovingly, securely obliged my request.

***

Finn had to immediately leave again for a few days to film some videos and do some promo work. He seemed a little more at ease leaving this time. And I secretly found it ironic. He had been so scared to leave before — first because of my condition while I was pregnant with Chloe, and then later when I was so emotional after losing her. Little did he know that it might be happening all over again.

When Finn flew back into New York the following Sunday, he was going to stay at his penthouse because he was set to appear live on one of the network morning shows the next day. Originally, since I was now officially on summer break, I was going to meet him in the city and go with him Monday morning. But I cancelled at the last minute, right before he was ready to board the plane in LA. My indecision on whether to join Finn, along with other things up in the air, was making me cranky.

"You told me you were going to meet me at the penthouse. What changed all of a sudden?" he asked across the line.

"I don't know. I—" A sneeze stopped my sentence.

"Bless you."

"Thanks. The lawn service just cut the grass." I said, before producing another sneeze.

"What? Were you helping them with it? Your allergies sound bad."

"Ha! No. Just sensitive because I'm tired. Finn, it doesn't make sense."

"What doesn't?"

"Meeting you in the city. I want you to be with me, but you're going to be preoccupied. You'll be busy the whole time, being pulled every which way. So there's no point, right?" That, admittedly, came out a little snotty.

"Geez, Lar, don't overreact. I was just looking forward to seeing you tonight, that's all. I guess maybe you're right. I'll just have to wait another day." He paused. After hearing the airport loudspeakers calling out passenger names and flight numbers in the background, he continued, "Are we good, Beauty?"

Tears threatened because of his sweet sentiment. "Yeah."

"Yeah?"

"Yeah. Be safe. Text me when you land."

"I will. Lara?" He didn't give me time to respond. "I love you."

"I know. Sorry for changing the plans."

"Baby, are you sure——?"

"I love you, too."

"See you tomorrow at home, then?"

"For sure...tomorrow...home."

***

That next morning, I sat on the sofa with my biscotti and honey sweetened coffee watching my handsome man on television. Dressed simply in black slacks and a gray T-shirt that accentuated his bulging biceps, he was just finishing singing his current single when I decided to text him. I knew his phone would be back in the green room and that he still needed to meet briefly with the hosts, but I wanted him to know I was thinking of him when he did reunite with his cell.

Looking HOT, Cowboy.

Even though he only appeared on screen for a few minutes after that, it was twenty some minutes by the time he responded. *Wish U were here, Roxanne. Rushing me to the car for my next meeting. See U soon.*

I smiled and talked myself into getting off the sofa. I was determined that it was going to be that day. I needed to find out one way or the other. No more procrastinating. No more indecisiveness. I went to the bathroom and peed on that little stick. And then I chickened out again. Instead of just waiting the few minutes for the results, I stripped out of my gray shorts and red cami and went to take a shower.

***

It was that time between afternoon and evening when Finn arrived home. Hearing the door shut, I yelled that I was upstairs and would be down in a minute. I expected some kind of disapproval from my husband, as he was still a little anxious about me going up the stairs. But I got none, which I took as a good sign. My memory had never come back of that infamous day in December. But my shoe collection had. Over Memorial Day weekend, probably at the height of his distress and just before I came back home, Finn had managed to move all of my shoes down the stairs and into our master bedroom's walk-in closet. It was more crowded, for sure, and some of his things were displaced, but it made Finn feel better.

As I made my way down the stairs and into the great room, Finn was also entering, but from the direction of our master. He was mid-shirt change—this one was a dark gray hue with a few buttons on top. He was also blinking his eyes, which told me he had just removed his fake green performer contacts. He greeted me with his usual embrace, followed by a quick kiss. "Hey, baby."

"How was your day?" I asked.

"Well, interesting."

I almost didn't hear him, as my brain seemed to be on delay. "Interesting? Huh…what's that mean?"

"I'll tell you in a minute." He started pouring himself a drink from the liquor cabinet. "How was yours?"

"The same," I admitted.

"Oh, yeah?" He took a swig from his glass but didn't pursue further. "Do you want to maybe go out for dinner?"

"Uh, yeah, I guess. Sorry, I can't seem to decide on what to have."

"You all right? Yesterday—"

"Yeah. I … I just need to tell you something."

"Yeah? Me, too." Finn sat down slowly on the sofa, causing me to do the same.

"You go first," I said, thinking I would quickly hear about another Finn Murphy accolade or a trip scheduled.

But that wasn't it at all. He looked at me and then spoke in the same fast motion as pulling off a bandage. "I saw Audrey today."

And, just as quickly, I was off the sofa. "Ahhh, c'mon."

Give me a break! Had it been raining? Because it sure was pouring.

"Lara," Finn said with exasperation, surely anticipating my reaction.

"What?" I denied my own feelings.

"Let me explain." He left his glass on the coffee table and stood up to join me.

"What did she do, follow you from California?"

"What? I didn't see her in California. I'm not even going to…" Shaking his head and trying not to get more upset, he continued with his original train of thought. "It was a fluke. She's in town for some work retreat thing. Their radio station in California is affiliated with the network. So, a few of them were there. She didn't even know I was going to be a guest."

"How do you know all of that?"

"Well, I talked with her after my segment." After the show …in that time that it took him to text me back.

"Great." It was one word, but boy did it pack the sarcastic punch.

"What? It was like a five-minute conversation, and I'm telling you about it. No omissions."

Well, he got me on that. "No omissions" meant we told each other everything. It started as an informal agreement after he had withheld telling me he suffered from PTSD. That omission nearly drove us apart. Then Finn had even inserted "no omissions" into our wedding vows. The truth was, though…if anyone was keeping something back, it was me.

"Weren't you worried that someone would see that?" I said, with a bit of spite, knowing how press-protective Finn was, especially when it came to his personal life.

"That's exactly it. She approached me. I couldn't just ignore her, Lara."

"Let me work through this." I turned and walked toward the wall of windows. My world was swirling. I just needed a pause button— just for a moment.

"What? You want me to apologize?" His patience was wearing thin. He was surely tired from traveling, a busy day, and now an "irrational" wife. "I didn't know she was—"

I swiveled back around, not wanting to see the contrasting beautiful day just outside those glass French doors. My patience, or more accurately my nerves, were at a limit, too. "Stop it, Finn! Let it be."

"It's you that—"

"God!"

Why did it have to be Audrey? And why now? Finn and I didn't argue often. Get moody, need our personal space, disagree … sometimes. But this was turning into a rare doozy, and it sure was reminiscent of one of our previous ones.

"I can't believe this is happening again," I exhaled more than said.

"What?" He raked his hands through his hair; his trademark sign of frustration. "You're not making sense. I haven't seen her in years. And I certainly didn't want to. You have nothing to worry abou—"

I cut him off. "The same way, too."

"What, Lara?"

"We're arguing … it's about Audrey—"

"We never talk about her," he practically yelled. "I'm damned if I do. I'm damned if I don't."

"And I have to tell you that I'm pregnant." With those words, silence crash-landed in the room.

Slowly lifting his head, his natural gray eyes met mine. Still, it took him a moment to speak. And, then, when he did, it was only one slow word. "What?"

"Yeah. Ironic, huh?" I thought back to my last pregnancy. I had been getting ready to tell Finn he was going to be a dad just as Audrey had shown up asking his staff if she could see him.

"What?" He reiterated, probably completely overwhelmed.

"Audrey … last time I tol—"

"Damn it, Lara!" he partially bellowed. "I don't care about Audrey—didn't last year, don't now."

"I know."

I did. I shouldn't have made the reference. Besides the irony, she had nothing to do with what was happening. I realized when Finn mentioned her that I had made her an instant, infamous Lara wall. I was trying to deflect with her and not deal with the pregnancy straight on.

Hearing my acceptance, Finn mellowed and changed to the subject at hand. "How? I mea—"

"Well, obviously, I wasn't on birth control while I was pregnant. God, I haven't even thought about that for a year now. And I was so out of it, right after … right after the miscarriage. I wasn't thinking about anything …certainly not taking—"

It was starting to register in my husband's psyche. "Are you sure?"

I could have gone up the stairs to the room that we had decorated for our not-meant-to-be daughter and gotten the positive home pregnancy test. It was in that nursery that I had placed the white stick, trying to come to terms with the reality of it all. But I had left it there because this pregnancy didn't feel like the one before. It didn't feel like we did in November when we were both so full of excitement and anticipation. Somehow, everything was different.

"My allergies, tired, moody … I took the test. Yeah. Positive." Then I delved right in. "We haven't talked about this … about trying again … or not. I …I don't know if I can go through what hap…" I couldn't continue. I was so scared of everything this child could mean— love, fear, loss, hope.

"Oh, Beauty." Still surely shell-shocked, Finn remained the stand-up guy he always was and reached out to me.

But I knew I was a time bomb ready to explode. My emotions were running wild. And I knew if I let him hold me, I would break for sure. Those Lara walls were definitely building because I did not want to feel any sort of love at that moment. So, as the first tear pooled in my left eye, I started to back away.

"Lara, please, let me hold you."

When I went to wipe the tear away, I felt the scar. Located directly outside the corner of my eye, it had been there since that fateful summer night right after high school. I thought I could do it by myself back then, but I was wrong. Now I knew I couldn't. But I also didn't have to. I just had to let Finn in.

"Lar?" He tried one more time.

Bringing both of my hands up to my face, I plowed

head-first into his chest. I felt his chin on the top of my head a moment before his arms encircled my back. And I sobbed.

***

Needless to say, we didn't go out for dinner that night. I couldn't even tell you what I ate— some leftover. I vaguely remember a pasta—some kind of noodle, some kind of cheesy sauce. We didn't speak of the pregnancy or, for that matter, Audrey, for a few hours. It was an unspoken silent pact. I think we both needed a chance to absorb. Later, I found my solace in the oversized jet tub in our master bedroom. Finn must have found his in a bottle.

After my body and semi-soul cleansing, I came back out to the great room to find Finn sitting on the sofa. His legs, crossed at the ankles, were propped up on the coffee table, and he was holding a glass of bourbon while seemingly staring into thin air. I sat down next to him and, without a word, placed my cheek on his cloth-covered chest. He set the glass down, allowing his arm to naturally wrap around my shoulders.

After a couple silent minutes, I felt his lips rest on top of my head. And then, a moment or two later, he straightened back up. So I did the same. He used the soft backside of his hand to brush my cheek. Stopping at my lips, he replaced his hand with his own lips, slowly at first and then a little more decisive. I could feel the proposition in his motion.

"Finn, no." I pulled slightly away.

His lips this time found my shoulder near the spaghetti strap. "I—"

"You told me I could always say 'no.'" I dipped my head as he lifted his.

"I meant that." He spoke with the utmost sincerity. "I just ...I want to be near you. Are you mad at me? Do you blame me for this?" An obvious reference to the pregnancy.

What? It took me a moment to process. No. If anything, I blamed myself.

"No," I whispered and then looked up to meet his eyes, which were glazed with emotion. Then, a little more strongly, I reinforced my response. "No."

He looked at me for more feedback. I tried to organize the chaotic thoughts that had been ravaging my brain since mid-morning. Well, really, for a couple of weeks.

"It's just a shock. I know I … we … should be happy about it. Right?"

"I know you're scared." God, how could he look right at me, through me, and nail my feelings flawlessly?

"And you're drinking," I recognized that he was bordering on a little more than his usual intake.

He confirmed it with, "I didn't say I wasn't scared, too."

"But are you happy?" I realized he could be both, but I definitely needed an honest answer.

After a pause, he said, "I'm happy if you are here. But, Lara, it does … it scares me. And, no, we haven't talked about it—trying again. Beauty, listen, you know how much I wanted our little girl and how much any baby would be so loved and happy. But it's the thought of losing you…" He blinked his misty eyes before parenthesizing my face with his hands and kissing me with care. "Look, let's talk with the doctor. One thing at a time. It'll be all right."

I wanted to believe him. I did. I trusted him more than I trusted anyone in my life. But he had told me everything would be okay before, and it wasn't. It wasn't. And way down deep, I knew I was already starting to fall in love with this child, and I couldn't let that happen. Could I?

***

Just over a week later, we were confirming what, in our hearts, we already knew. The doctor had just gotten done explaining that there was no reason I couldn't have a normal pregnancy. Finn and I both heard it. Yet I knew by looking at his face and feeling the odd tingling of what was probably my blood pressure, neither of us quite believed it.

"I'm scared," I admitted to the doctor.

I reached for my husband's hand. I'm not sure who was holding on tighter. If my nails digging into Finn's palms bothered him, he didn't let on.

I continued. "I don't want to go through what I did last time. I … I can't."

"*We* can't," Finn tagged in.

Dr. Weinstein spoke in a purposefully calming voice. "First of all, every pregnancy is different. You told me that in your first pregnancy you hadn't experienced any of the symptoms that you did with this last pregnancy."

"No," I reiterated, thinking the major symptoms I had as a pregnant teen were shame and secrecy.

"Well then, let's see what this one brings. And, let me tell you, if there is even the slightest sign of any issues, we might do the bed rest thing, or admit you for the rest of the pregnancy. Until then, we just closely monitor you and keep you on a healthy lifestyle regimen."

That should have been reassuring. But for my husband, it didn't seem to be. Finn loosened his grip on my hand and started to turn as if he needed to pace the room. But I denied him. I squeezed tight, needing him to hear my words as much as I needed to verbalize them out loud for myself.

"I'm stubborn," I started. "I've learned to be. I've had to be." I looked to Finn who slowly blinked once acknowledging the pain in my past that made me the way I am. "And I want our baby." I glanced to the doctor and back again to Finn, who squeezed my hand. If we had decided anything, it was that if the doctor said it was safe, we definitely wanted the child. "But I don't want to die. It took me years to get the life I want." I softly smiled at Finn to acknowledge his part in my happiness— the main, essential part. "And it's not been long enough. I will do whatever you tell me to do to the T."

"Okay, then. That's what we'll do." The doctor smiled reassuringly. "Let me get your paperwork, unless you have any other questions."

"Yeah. Yeah. I do." Finn let go of my hand and posed his question to the doctor. "When is the baby due?"

"Oh, sorry about that," Dr. Weinstein lamented. "With everything else, I forgot to tell you. Looks like the baby was conceived around the end of April. So that means mid-January. Jan—"

Finn interrupted him. "Oh, thank goodness."

I looked to my husband then. What was that comment about? And then it dawned on me and, admittedly, disappointed me a little. Finn had given up his summer tour because of Chloe's due date. I wondered what conflict this baby's due date could have had. Surely Finn realized it wasn't going to be next summer.

"You're sure. Not later than that?" he asked.

"Nope. Definitely too far along," Dr. Weinstein confirmed. "If that's it, let me get that paperwork. I'll be right back."

"Thanks," I said. When Dr. Weinstein closed the door behind him, I scrunched my eyebrows at Finn.

"What?"

"What's with the due date? You worried the baby will interrupt another tour?"

"Huh?" He sounded genuinely confused. "What are you … ? Oh. No." Realization seemed to smack him in the face. "No, Beauty. I don't care about that. I told you."

"What then, Finn? You seemed so relieved."

"I … I wanted to make sure that it wasn't that day."

"What day?"

"Memorial Day weekend," he said solemnly. "I didn't want our baby conceived like that."

"Oh."

You could have heard the proverbial pin drop. I had no

idea he thought that. He hadn't realized I had already been pregnant then— the day I came home and found him in so much pain and anguish … drunk and off his meds.

"No, I was already pregnant," I said quietly. "I was only piecing it together that weekend. It would have been all right, though," I tried.

"I'm going with fajita dance night," he said with a slight smile on his face.

"Maybe. I'd like that, too." And then, after a pause, "We're having a baby then, huh?" I could see the uncommon tears in his eyes, and I knew the macho side in him needed to subtly wipe them away. I let him do it before saying, "Finn, you know what today is, don't you?" Although he hadn't said anything, I knew how meticulous he was about remembering the important stuff.

As predicted, his answer was soft and swift. "I do."

"It's like we're getting her blessing."

His hand loosely covered his mouth as he nodded his head up and down. It was on what would have been Chloe's due date, that I knew we were one hundred percent on board with having a baby again. And I had to trust that our little guardian angel would make sure everything would be all right this time around.

CHAPTER EIGHT

I managed to get back into bed without waking Finn. It was Sunday morning— just a few days after the doctor's appointment. I curled my body behind his in an effort to force him to face his nightstand, where I had just placed a surprise. On my touch, he murmured a pleasing sound and grasped my hands, which were on his stomach. Then he must have opened his eyes.

"What are those?" He turned to lay flat on his back and look at me.

I smiled. "Do you like?"

"Can't ever lose with roses, Cowgirl." He spilled out a similar answer to the one I had given him when he first bought me roses years before. "But I think I should be giving them to you, not the other way around."

"Happy Father's Day," I pronounced—it would unofficially be his first.

"Huh. Yeah," he said, registering the fact and nodding slightly in my direction.

"I love you."

"You are so damn strong. I admire you so much."

I pulled my body on top of his and kissed him. Then, stretching up, I started to pull at the tie in front of my black nightie. It needed to be loosened in order to get it off. Finn, noticing what I was doing, brought his hands up to help. But when the tie was undone, he let his hands drop.

"You sure?" he asked, knowing quite well that we hadn't made love since I told him no after the pregnancy announcement.

"Well, it's not like you can get me any more pregnant, Stud. And, the doctor said I need stress relief." I was determined to get back to normal because I believed that would be the only way to successfully nurture this child. "I'll try meditating with you if you want to do that instead," I teased, but it was true that Finn did rely on meditation as part of his therapy, and also to write lyrics.

"I think I like your stress relief a little bit better right now." His smile was turning more into a grin.

"Let's have some slammin' hot sex, then."

"Slammin'?" he questioned inquisitively.

"Olivia term."

"Oh, brother." He shook his head. "I was kinda rude to her, huh?" He spoke of their Memorial Day weekend phone conversation.

"Maybe a little. But nothing she couldn't handle," I replied. "She'd probably be majorly turned on right now if she knew we were talking about her at this particular moment."

"Oh, God. There's a thought I need completely erased from my head." And with that, he twirled me over. Planked on top, he started slowly and gently running his hands along my body and kissing me.

I didn't want slow, though. I didn't want to think. I wanted to be in that moment. Yes, I knew I needed to be careful. But that was with certain things— food, water, heat … but not love. With that in mind, I reversed our positions and started to pull his white tank over his head. I left it covering his face, though, while I nipped at his chest.

"Oh, Jesus!" Finn quickly discarded his tank top. "You

got thi——?"

"We got this." I said, kissing him and needing us together. That was the only way we would survive. And then we rocked just as loud and intense as a sold-out concert.

***

Now, with the new pregnancy, neither of us regretted Finn previously cancelling his summer tour. It was the ideal opportunity for us to really listen to the doctor's directives and live a stress-free couple of months together. Finn managed a heavenly mix of being romantic, yet sexy, and concerned, yet not overbearing.

Once the beginning queasiness eased up, my appetite came back in full force. Finn and I cooked together more that summer than we ever had before. And, often, we would find time for a walk around the neighborhood followed by a bowl of ice cream …and always water. "Dr. Finn" was adamant about my hydration habits.

My husband's big gesture, though, was to take me to Bermuda in the beginning of August. I had never been there, although Finn had. He had stopped there on some kind of country music cruise while he was still "up and coming." This would be the first time he would have any kind of extended stay, though. And it would be one of our most treasured memories of that summer. We were both able to disconnect from the rest of the world as we stayed at a luxury golf resort and explored the island's shops, caves, and aquarium. And, of course, there were the famous pink sand beaches, where we managed to do all the typical stuff—building sandcastles, dipping our feet in the cool water, lounging in Adirondack chairs— without the prying eye of press or fans.

Unfortunately, our last day there was marred with troublesome news. Soaking up the summer sun, which thankfully didn't feel so oppressive due to the cool ocean breeze, Finn and I were sitting poolside when he started getting a series of texts and phone calls. I knew our vacation was coming to an end, and he would have to meet some work obligations again, but there was something about the way he kept walking off and around when he was on the phone. And there was really something about the foreboding crease on his forehead.

When he reclaimed his seat on the chaise lounge next to mine, after yet another phone call, I stood up and encouraged him to scoot forward on his seat. Sitting behind him, I rubbed his shoulders which were beautifully exposed, as he was only wearing red swim trunks. "What's going on? What's wrong?"

"Nothing," he claimed, but those tense shoulders told me otherwise.

Moving so that I was now sitting on his outstretched legs, I continued my line of questioning.

"Finn?"

"Baby, it's nothing to worry about. I love this yellow suit by the way."

My bathing suit was a simple two piece with boy shorts and a tank to cover my expanding belly. It was not conversation-worthy, unless you were trying to use it for topic distraction. And, for sure, that was the case with Finn.

I continued. "Last time you were like this, you started rambling on about me signing some damn prenup." I smiled so he knew I was joking.

I needed him to relax. I needed him to tell me what was bothering him so I could help. Because the last thing Finn should ever do is keep things bottled up.

His light laughter was a welcome relief. "Yeah, which you really should have."

"I did." Before he could interject, I continued. "I signed what I would agree to. You know I wasn't going to sign anything that said I was going to get any of your money. Besides, it's a moot point. I got all that I want right here." First removing his aviator sunglasses to reveal his gorgeous gray eyes, I then kissed him. "Well, except for you telling me what's wrong. I want that. No omissions, Murphy."

He smiled, sighed, and relented. "It's Carter."

"What about Carter?" I was certainly concerned about Finn's drummer—he was an important part of my husband's life and career—but was secretly glad there wasn't something wrong with any of our family members.

He grabbed his black tank, which had been draped over the chaise lounge, and put it on over his taut chest. "C'mon. I'll tell you, but I don't want to do it here."

Knowing that he needed privacy, I agreed by nodding my head and gathering up our towels. As I laced my hand in my husband's, I couldn't help but worry about what the reveal might be. He squeezed back tight and led me the short distance back to our hotel room.

***

"What?" I asked when Finn had still not offered any information once we were in the room.

His ominous, squinting eyes told me he was debating something, even before he confirmed it. "I just know how this is going to impact you."

My skin prickled with fear. "Is he all right?"

"Yeah."

I breathed a little easier. I thought of the relaxed drummer, who was also Finn's best friend. He was easy to get along with and was always smiling and jovial during the summer tours when I had traveled with them. What could it be? I tried to mentally put the pieces together—something bad, plus Carter's personality, plus something I personally was not going to like.

"It's not drugs, is it?" I questioned.

Finn knew that was a deal breaker for me. And it was for him, too. Thank goodness.

"No," he instantly denied. "You know I wouldn't tolerate that. You know I run a clean camp."

"Okay…" I still didn't know.

"His mom is in the hospital."

"Oh." While that wasn't great news, I thought the other possibilities that were scrambling around in my manic head were probably worse. "Why? What's wrong?"

Again, he paused. "Lara…" How he slowly said my name—my full name and not one of his nicknames for me—I knew I had to brace myself. "Carter's stepdad beat her."

There it was. There was his reason for the hesitation. There was the reason his eyes even-more-so zeroed in on me as I gasped. He knew. My husband knew my childhood stories. He knew how I would react.

After a second or two, he continued. "It's pretty bad. She had some kind of seizure or stroke because of the whole thing."

"Oh, my God." My shoulders sagged, taking in the sadness. But then they immediately gathered back up in anger. "Where is he—the step dad?" I knew I spit those last words out with venom. I definitely meant them that way. But before Finn could answer, another question popped into my mind. "God, Carter has siblings, right?

"Yeah," he answered my second question. "A brother and sister."

"How old are they?"

I remembered Carter talking about his age difference from them, since it was his mom's second family. He had never known his own father. He had been raised by a single mom for many years until this other guy—an obvious loser—came along.

"They're both in middle school."

"Oh. Are they all right?"

"Yeah."

"Carter?"

Even though Finn had answered that same question in

the beginning of our talk, it had a different connotation for me now. This time I was asking more from an emotional stand point than a physical one. But I'm sure I already knew the answer.

"He's...I don't know. He sounds overwhelmed right now."

"What...God...what about this stepdad? He's not free is he? I hope the guy was arrested and they f-ing throw away the key."

"Calm down, baby." Finn captured my hand with his and bent ever so slightly to meet my eyes. "He was, and there's going to be a hearing."

I released a breath that must have instantly been captured in my lungs. The escaping air was because that guy was being held accountable and couldn't hurt anyone else. But it was also because I had such the opposite of a man in front of me—protecting me and wanting to make sure I wasn't hurt just by the topic of conversation.

"You're going, right? You're going to Nashville?" I asked while trying to do what Finn had asked and calming down a bit.

"Yeah. Yeah. I'd like to. Not to the hearing, though. My team doesn't want me involved in that, and I get it. But, I'd like to check up on him and make sure we're helping as a band family with support or lawyers or whatever."

"I want to help. I want to go with you."

"Lar, are you sure? You don't need to. It might not be good for you."

"I want to be there." When he squinted his eyes, I continued, "Carter needs support, and I'd like to be there for you, too."

"Yeah. Okay. I'd like that." His shoulders relaxed in appreciation. "Let me change our flight reservations, and then I just want to spend the night on that balcony, holding you, watching the sunset, and being thankful for what I have."

***

When Carter showed up at our home in Tennessee, he arrived via taxi cab. He looked worn and gaunt. And he most certainly didn't have the positive demeanor that he usually possessed—one that would keep everyone on tour in good humor and one that flirted and fell briefly for my friend, Vanessa, two summers before.

"Finn's not here," I stated, as I ushered him into the great room. "He went for a run, and then he was going to see you."

"Ah, well, change of venue." He slurred, and I immediately realized that he was not only sad and down, but he was drunk.

"Do you want something to drink? Water? Coffee? Tea?" I quickly offered positive choices.

"No," he replied. "Lara, it's good to see you."

"You, too, Carter," I said honestly. "I'm so sor—" I started to cite my feelings on the reason we had made the trip in the first place.

"How are things?" he interrupted.

Recognizing a deflection when I heard one, and realizing he might just need a moment of not talking about what went down, I answered as if it was any other day or any other visit. "It's good now. We're …" No one knew about the new pregnancy, and we wanted to keep it that way. "Things are getting better."

"That's good."

"Why don't you sit down?"

"Uh…no. I don't think I can. I need to move." The jittery part of being drunk was mixing in with his sullen state. "You know, Mrs. Murphy, I think I'm a little drunk." And then he gave me that playboy smile and wink he was famous for.

I decided to play along with the humor. "Well, duh, yeah. I figured as much, Mr. Obvious."

Carter burst into laughter. But, almost as quickly, his shoulders dropped, and he looked to be near tears. He then completed the trifecta by shaking his head back and forth, as if it was going to clear everything completely.

"Do you want me to call Finn? He's probably close by. He's just running around here somewhere…didn't take a car."

"Neh, he'll be here soon enough."

"Can you talk with me?" I offered, knowing by his sheer presence that Carter came to our home for refuge. "I want to help. And, believe it or not, I pretty much know what you're going through."

His eyes seemed to take on a sudden glint of sobriety when he heard my words and looked up at me. I never told anyone about the child I gave away. But it wasn't necessarily a secret that when my dad had drank too much, his fists found different, non-traditional punching bags.

"Sorry 'bout that, Lara-Li."

"Yeah." I paused in reflection and then asked, "How's your mom?"

"It's gonna be a long road. She'll be in a rehab facility for a little bit because of the stroke thing, but she's going to be all right."

"That's good." Not only was I glad for his mom but that he was opening up.

"Catch this," he started. "I have temporary guardianship of Colby and Genevieve." He literally laughed as if he had said the most absurd thing in the world.

"Your brother and sister?"

"Yeah. How wrong is that? Like I am role model material. I'm not Mr. Rules and Regulations. I'm not Mr. Settled Down. But I'm the only one."

"First of all, it's not wrong at all. I'm glad—super glad—they have you." I paused. "Does that mean your step dad—"

"He's not getting them. I have the lawyers working on

113

it. Already making sure Mom gets that PFA."

"Good. Good."

"I'm a little worried about them, though. The shit they've seen growing up…It's not the first time, but this was the worst. I was out of there—grown—before it started. My sister? She seems spooked. And Colby? I'm just afraid he's gonna think that's how you treat a woman."

I shook the flashbacks of my past life out of my head and said with confidence, "Then you set them straight."

"Like I'm an example when it comes to women." He rolled his eyes.

"You a—"

"I'm pretty sure Vanessa would not agree." He had trouble looking at me straight on that time, and I think it had little to do with the alcohol.

"You didn't hurt her."

"Physically. But—"

"You could have manned up with the breakup a little better, yeah. But she's all right, Carter."

"Is she? How's she doing?"

I decided to answer as generically as I could. "She's … she's good. She's all right."

"Seeing anyone?"

The truth was, Vanessa wasn't. But I didn't want Carter to know that. He had enough on his mind without adding my best friend, too.

"I don't think we should talk about—" I cut my own sentence short when we heard the front door open.

"Saved by the bell, Lara-Li." Carter tried that swooning smile again.

I had to admit, though, I appreciated my husband's sense of timing, even if it was unplanned. "In here," I called out.

Finn was stripping out of his sweat-soaked white T and gulping some water when he joined us in the great room. "Hey, baby." He gave his normal greeting.

"Hi, there, yourself, sweetheart," the drummer teased,

114

and I shook my head with a grin.

"Carter. Hey, man. Didn't know you were here."

"Glad you at least still have your shorts on," Carter jazzed back.

Finn peered his way and then greeted me with a proper kiss. "Everything all right?" he softly spoke into my ear.

"Yeah," I answered.

"Why didn't you call me?"

"We were talking." I nodded positively in Carter's direction.

"You drunk?"

"Appears so." Carter partially laughed. But when Finn sighed, Carter took it negatively. "What? You think I should be sipping lemonade and singing 'Don't Worry Be Happy'?"

"No, of course not. I didn't say that."

"Sorry I can't live up to your standards." He clipped a couple of the words.

"What? Carter, I'm just trying to assess the situation. I want to know what I can do for you, man."

"Ah, fuck it. I just needed a friend, not a judge."

"I *am* your—" Finn started.

"You know… a friend like I was when this one left you." Carter nodded toward me as my eyes widened, and I wondered how things got so tense so quickly.

"Leave her out of it." Finn was instantly more defensive.

That time was the worst in our history as a couple. Plus, it had been directly before the most tragic event in Finn's life—his nephew dying. He did not like having it brought up.

But Carter probed on. "You were trashed … destroyed … not even a semblance of—"

"Carter, stop it." The tension in Finn's body radiated onto mine even though we were about a foot or two apart.

I took the slightest of pauses in conversation to try to pacify the situation. "Boys, we're all on the same team here, okay? Everyone wants the best solution. Everyone understands the stress. Carter, just talk with Finn, all right? Know that we're here to help...no matter what...no matter how. That's it." Because Carter seemed to relax with my words, I decided to let the bandmates have time on their own. "I'll be out back if you need something."

Finn squeezed my hand tightly and seemed to search my eyes. I think he was a bit embarrassed by the vulnerability that Carter had revealed in him. But he needn't have been. I knew the sadness that had surrounded us back then, the same way I could see the sadness in the situation at hand. I pecked him on the lips, released my hand from his, and proceeded out the patio doors to the outdoor living area.

***

When Finn came out a little while later, he was alone. I stood up from the sofa, where I had been listening to calming instrumental tunes via the outdoor stereo. Despite not knowing what had occurred, I knew Finn needed me. I silently wrapped my arms around him and felt the steady beat of his heart through the fresh T-shirt he was wearing.

"Is everything okay?" I asked.

"Yes...no. I'll tell you later, but I gotta get him home. He needs to be with his brother and sister."

I pulled slightly away and looked through the glass doors to see Carter walking in circles and holding a coffee thermos. "Yeah."

"I'm not sure how long I'll be."

"You be there as long as they need you," I encouraged while admiring the gorgeous sunset just beginning over the horizon. "Tell him he has my support."

He rested his lips on my forehead before replying. "I will."

"And, you ..." I said, softly gliding my finger along his five o'clock shadow. "You have my love."

"Thanks, Beauty. I think we're both going to need it."

I watched him walk back through the patio doors and into the great room. He clasped Carter's shoulder firmly from behind, and the two of them walked toward the garage. Letting my body sag in relief, I suddenly felt so alone. It was then that I realized the evening had been an emotional experience for me, too. I wanted to call and talk to someone. And, oddly, Vanessa was the first person I thought of. But, for sure, I couldn't do that. She would probably be pulled right into all things Carter again and that would not be good for either of them...at least not yet. So, instead, I sat in silence and held onto yet one more secret.

CHAPTER NINE

It was some time after I had gone to bed that Finn made it back home. I was in bed, but due to the energy of the day, I definitely wasn't asleep. The adjoining sitting room's nightlight illuminated Finn as he peeled off his dark ball cap, gray hoodie, and coordinating tennis shoes before flopping down on the bed beside me. Not bothering to change out of his T, shorts, and socks, I knew he had to be exhausted. But I also knew he would need to talk.

"Everything all right?" I questioned in the semi-darkness.

"It's late ... even later in Bermuda. You should be asleep."

"Finn?" I asked again.

"I'm all right. What about you?"

"Yeah. Yeah, I'm fine."

"I'm sorry he brought up all that crap from a couple years ago." I should have known that would be the primary thing on my husband's mind, especially when talking with me.

"It's nothing I didn't already know. And he only brought it up because he was drunk and things seemed so unstable to him. He wanted to make sure he could trust your friendship." When I didn't get a response, I asked, "How is he?"

"He quit the band." On that comment, I propped myself up a little higher on my side so that I could really look at my outstretched man. "What? Why?"

"Too much going on...too many responsibilities. He said he wouldn't be able to keep the commitment."

"Oh, God, that has to kill him. He's as passionate about music as you. That's why he was drinking, huh? He knew he was going to have to tell you and lose that. Isn't there something—"

"You know what I told him?" He didn't give me a chance to guess. "I told him my very wise and beautiful wife would not let him quit, and to not make any rash decisions ... to see how things go.".

"I'll give you wise." I smiled.

He pulled me gently toward him so that my cheek rested on his chest and my legs entwined with his. Then he spoke most earnestly. "How are you really? I'm sure talking with him about what's happening with his mom made you think about things you didn't necessarily want to think about."

"But I lived through it, and they will, too." I rubbed my hand on the part of his chest that my head was not covering. "In some ways, I think talking with him actually helped."

"That would be nice." Still in a reflective mood, he kissed me on top of my head. "Thanks for coming to Nashville ... for being here for Carter and me. It means a lot."

I tilted up to meet his eyes. "Finn, you'd do the same for me. You are always there for me."

"And I always will be." He gently moved me so that he could first kiss me on the lips and then on my pregnant stomach. "Get some sleep, Bed Bug."

***

The end of August brought another scheduled doctor's appointment. And, thankfully, everything appeared good with both me and the baby. The baby was definitely taking up more room in my body and demanding more food. But I had no symptoms of vasovagal syncope or any other ailments.

When Dr. Weinstein stepped out for a moment, Finn told me that when I heard the good report, I lit up like the proverbial pregnant woman glowing. And I believed that was true. I felt so good.

"Do you hear that, little one? You're doing good. Hang in there." I looked up to see Finn staring at me. Then I realized why. Neither he nor I had talked to this child directly as we had with Chloe. "Do you want to?"

"Neh," he said and then, just so I wasn't disappointed, added, "Not here." But I think he still had his emotional restraints on.

When the doctor came back in, he had papers in his hand. He asked if we wanted to know the sex of our child. I glanced at Finn. I should have expected the question, but my solitary priority since confirming the pregnancy had been staying healthy for the baby.

"Uh…" Finn started, but I knew the answer even though we hadn't discussed it.

"No," I said and even adverted my eyes from any printouts that may have had me knowing or guessing.

"No? Are you sure?" came the doctor's voice.

Dr. Weinstein was personally taking care of everything involving this pregnancy. And he knew that we had found out the last time. But that was just it. Last time, we found out it was a girl. We gave her a name. We started with the pink stuff. We were more attached than attached could be. No. No, we couldn't know now. "The Baby" would be its name—gender to be revealed. My sturdy emotional walls weren't going to come completely down when it came to the child growing inside of me.

So, despite a great checkup, there was a little cloud over us. It made us think, Finn in particular, of all that could yet happen. We were almost back home when Finn started on me about not going back to work at the beginning of the school year, which, of course, was only days away. He was concerned about all the steps in the building. I confirmed that I would always have someone with me and would take the elevator when I could. And then he wanted to make sure I ate enough. So, I reassured him that I would have a snack drawer and use it daily.

But the real truth of the matter was, I needed to be at work. If I didn't, as the pregnancy grew more real, I would become more obsessive about it. And I couldn't do that. Because along with obsession comes worry, and stress was an absolute no-no. Finn told me to let him obsess about it. But we both knew his schedule was increasing again, and he couldn't be around 24/7. It didn't matter what logical rebuttal I had for my husband, though. He was determined to get his point across.

"Look, Lar, it's simple. I don't want you working …not while you're pregnant," he said once the garage door was going down and we were making the transition into the coolness of the air conditioned house.

"Finn, we've been round and round about this. What happened last time had nothing to do with where I was. Geez, I was at home when I … when it happened."

"The second time," he emphasized. "And why do you have to be so stubborn? Most women would love to just have their feet up."

"Oh, okay, Mr. Chauvinistic Pig," I teased.

He eased up slightly but was still honest. "You know that's not true. I just worry about you."

"And I know how lucky I am that you do." So, so true.

"Then why can't you just pacify me a little?"

Resting his hands on top of his head, I could tell he was ready to start pacing in frustration. But to deter the action, I went up behind him and wrapped my arms securely around his torso. I kissed his back through the red and black striped polo he was wearing. Beneath my lips, I could feel his muscular frame strained from his extensive exercise routine but also surely a little because of stress.

When my arms rubbed his upper chest, he relaxed. "That wasn't what I meant."

"I know. C'mon, you can have your way with me, caveman." I was trying desperately to keep the conversation light.

He turned around to face me. "Don't make fun."

"I'm not. I just need it to be all right. I can't worry about you worrying about me."

"Then how about just promising me that you will leave work at work and come home on time."

"Seems like a deal," I answered and sealed it with a kiss. "Except, I might do some online stuff just at the beginning."

"You drive me insane." I wasn't sure by the way he said it which way his emotions were going. That was, until he kissed me so passionately that I ended up taking a few steps back. "Make-up sex?" he asked, taking a breath.

"Were we arguing?"

"You wouldn't think so." He semi-laughed.

"Do you think you could maybe start with one of those famous Murphy massages? My back could really use it."

"Love to." He stroked my leg, prompting me to climb his body so he could carry me into the bedroom.

***

Even though it was one of the most hectic times of the year—both for those in the education field and, I guess, country music stars—we handled it with ease. We celebrated Kelsea starting kindergarten. Her classroom was actually just a door away from my office. So I often had a chance to see her during the day. She thought she was so special having her aunt in the building. I wondered if Wyatt would have outgrown that feeling, had he lived.

The first time I felt the baby move for sure, I was at work. I had felt some fluttering before, but I didn't want to say anything until I was sure that it wasn't just gas. I kind of laughed to myself right in the middle of editing an article for the district's website. It confirmed to me that I was right to return to work. If I had been at home, I would have thought about nothing else and made comparisons to Chloe and the milestones she didn't have.

The movement was more pronounced nearly a week later. Finn and I were lying in bed. I could feel myself starting to fall asleep when it felt like my body had converted into a popcorn machine.

"Finn!" I screeched.

"What? What's wrong?" When he sat up quickly, I realized he had been a little further into slumber than I had been.

"Sorry," I apologized. "Nothing. Nothing is wrong. It's right." I grabbed his hand and placed it on my stomach.

"Was that—?" he exclaimed.

"Sure was. I'm glad you didn't miss it," I said as he caressed my stomach.

"Lar? I want to tell our family."

I closed my eyes. I knew we should. I knew it was beyond time. It was just another one of those "scared to say it out loud" things. Last time, we had told everyone much, much earlier and look how that turned out.

"Just family and friends, though, right?" As far as I was concerned, the press didn't ever have to know. I was my husband's wife in that matter for sure.

"Yeah," he agreed as I reopened my eyes. "We can call tomorrow. Everyone should be off work because of Labor Day. It's probably best that we do it before I leave, anyway."

He wasn't fooling me. I knew exactly why he wanted to announce our news before his departure. And it wasn't only because of excitement. It was for one specific reason and one specific family member.

"I'm sure Nola will be glad to come over and/or call and check in on me," I smirked.

"I love you, Lara," he replied in that teasing sing-songy voice of his.

"I know you do, Finn," I said in a similar tone, shaking my head. I appeased him, though, because I knew it would make him feel better while he was away.

The congrats that came from our families came whole-heartedly after the initial shock. I think they were all a little concerned, too. If they didn't say so directly, you could hear it in their specific questions. But no one was as concerned as much as my mother. I knew it was because I was her baby, and because she had been in the hospital nearly as much as Finn had been while I was in the coma. But I called upon her medical skills to rationalize that I had experienced none of those complications with the little boy that I gave up. And she should know. She was the only one who knew my secret besides Finn.

***

My husband was only gone a day when the nominations for November's CMA awards were announced. Finn was up for Song of the Year, Male Vocalist of the Year, and Entertainer of the Year. Anticipating his call, when it actually came, I immediately put my phone on speaker and pressed play on the stereo. DJ Khaled's preset song "All I Do is Win" blared out.

I could hear Finn belly-laughing in the background. "Okay, okay. Turn it off."

I lowered the volume of the music and turned off my cell's speaker option before softly speaking into the phone. "Hi."

"I've really turned you into a lyric aficionada."

"Yep, me, Ludacris, and Snoop," I agreed and then

teased, "I'm gonna get a hold of your phone and switch that to your main ring setting."

"Don't you dare!" He laughed. "And I haven't won anything yet. They're just noms."

"Congrats, baby."

"Thanks." That was enough accolades for Finn, though. "I miss you already."

"Me, too. Thanks for waiting to call until I got home. That song wouldn't have been very professional to play at work." I semi-chuckled.

"Thanks for being home on time."

"You got it. Doing anything to celebrate?" I asked.

"Shit, no. They've got me so jam-packed with stuff to do, it's practically illegal for me to make this call."

"We'll celebrate when you get home then—that, and your birthday." It was just a few days away.

"Hmmm…looking forward to that," he said with obvious sexual undertones.

"I bet you are. I'm afraid it's not going to be a full Baltimore this year." I referenced the year I surprised Finn on tour in Maryland and we stayed up most of the night making love.

"You okay?"

"Yeah, Finn," I said in my most reassuring voice, suddenly sorry that I even alluded to anything not being one hundred percent. "Just tired. Regular stuff. Nothing, and I repeat— nothing—to worry about."

"You s—"

"Yep."

Hearing my quick interruption, thankfully, he let it go. "How about a half Baltimore?"

"If an old man like you can keep up," I teased, happy to be back on track.

"Can't answer that the way I want to right now, Rox. The crew are already looking at me wondering what a half-Baltimore is. I've gotta roll. Love you."

"Love you, too."

And then I pressed the speaker's volume up once more. "All I Do Is Win" picked up toward the end of the song. It was right in sync with Finn's laughter.

***

The next few days went by remarkably fast. That's usually the case when you're having fun or keeping busy. I was definitely doing both. While work was the busy part, for fun I saw the latest romantic drama with a couple of women from the neighborhood. When they started gossiping/comparing/complaining about their own men afterwards, I bailed. It was one of those "regular life" things I couldn't indulge in. Even though both Finn and I really liked the people in our exclusive neighborhood, we never let our guard down, not knowing who would take certain things to the press. Besides, I knew what I had and, as long as we could keep the drama ratio down, I sure was happy.

My cell phone rang sometime after the end of work on the day that Finn was set to fly back home. I recognized my romantic leading man's ring tone and smiled. I would be seeing him that night and couldn't wait.

"Hey," I answered.

"Where are you?"

"Where are you?" I turned the question around. "You getting ready to board?"

"No. I'm here ...at home. I got an early flight so I would be back before you even started to worry."

Ah, yes, he knew me well. I had an unknown-origin fear of planes, and the fact that Finn had to fly so often drove me semi-insane. I would have been tracking his flight soon enough.

"Oh," was my response.

"Where are you?" he asked again, this time a little more tentatively.

"I'm—" I started.

"Don't lie, Lara." His interruption came out like a parental dare.

"I wouldn't," I said slowly and glanced at the clock on the wall. Crap, I had no idea it was so late already. I had been so caught up in… "I'm at work," I admitted.

"Jesus!"

"Finn—" I wanted to pacify his immediate anger but was cut off.

"We had a deal, Lara. You made a promise."

"I know. I didn't reali—"

"Get home. Now." It wasn't a request.

"I'm all right. I'm just looking over some papers while waiting for things to copy. I'm sitting." Everything I should be doing … but being home.

"Now, Lara." Frustrated. Adamant.

"Stop." Now I was getting upset because he was upset with me. It was an old reflex of mine after dealing with an alcoholic father growing up. "I need to get these things done so the year doesn't get away from me. Plus, with Open House coming up—"

"There's no one in that building in case—"

It was my turn to interrupt and disagree. "The janitors are here. One is even a volunteer firefighter. I'm taking care of us." I used the plural word, hoping that it would soften his mood. "I've got snacks and plenty to drink."

"Damn it, Lara. I think you care more about that school and those kids than you do your own."

What? What! I had to replay that in my mind to make sure I had heard him right. The harshness in his words and his tone made me so sad. I took a deep breath and tried to see it from his perspective. I tried to think about how worried he was and what an unbelievable caring man he was before I spoke.

"Finn, I know you're upset. I know you didn't mean that."

I heard the regret in his voice even if he didn't acknowledge it through his words. "Just come home."

"I will. Don't worry. I love you." When he didn't say anything in reply, I continued. "I just have a little more to finish up. So, I'm going to hang up now." But, again, I got nothing but empty silence. "Finn? Okay?"

"What do you want me to say?"

A little taken back by his rigid response, I paused and then started to say, "Well, I would like—" —him to tell me that it was okay and that he loved me and missed me. But I knew that life was more drama than romance. What I got instead of those words was the abrupt silence of an ended call. "Finn? Are you still there?" I questioned regardless of already knowing the answer.

If the purpose of his final non-statement was to make me feel bad, he did a great job. It wasn't morning sickness or anything pregnancy related that left the sudden queasy feeling in my stomach. It was Finn and how bad I felt that we were arguing. I felt like I had betrayed him—albeit not on purpose—by not coming home on time. I knew I should have stopped mid-stream and just packed it up and gone home at that point. But I was upset, and I needed to calm down first before driving or facing him. Besides, I did just have a little more work to be done and then, like I told him, I would be home. He could use that time to calm down, too.

I couldn't do it in silence, though. I thought too much that way. So I cranked up the radio and dove back into the paperwork in front of me.

I had just gotten back from making final copies at the copier. All I needed to do then was get things ready for the next day. I was starting to separate Open House papers into different grade levels when the radio unexpectedly went silent. Because my nerves were shot due to our argument, the sudden change of noise level actually caused me to scream.

"Ahhh!" I dropped the papers on the floor and turned around to look at the now soundless radio, which ironically had just been playing one of Finn's songs. "You scared me." I acknowledged the singer himself, who was standing next to the machine.

I had half-expected him to come to the school, because that's the kind of guy he is— abandons everything else to protect the ones he loved. And I half-wanted him to be there to reassure me that he wasn't as angry as he sounded on the phone. But the strained look on his face made me wary.

"What are you doing here? How did you get in?" I asked, thinking of the secured building while reaching out to hug him.

"Your buddy, the firefighter" —he denied my embrace by shrugging me off and taking a step back— "let me in. And, by the way, he agrees with me that you should be home."

"I've gotta finish," I said quietly, while still monitoring Finn's temperament.

"You don't! You don't see anyone else here, do you? I'm taking you home. Let's go."

"You're right. Everybody's left. But, Finn, most of the staff stays a lot of the nights especially in the be—" I don't know why I said that. Probably because I knew it was the truth. But, for the greater cause, I most likely should have just kept quiet.

"I don't care about everybody else!" He interrupted with such magnitude that it caused me to jump a little. "Everybody else is not my pregnant wife. They didn't fall down a flight of steps a few months or so ago. They weren't on the floor ... Christ, Lara!" He stopped himself after becoming too emotional, especially for a public building—even if it was ninety-some percent vacant. His pain made me almost fall apart.

"I'm sorry. It was just a rough day. The copier jammed, I had to present something to the board, I met with Xenia, a teacher was absent so I had to—"

"Have you been doing this every night since I've been gone?" At least he didn't scream the accusation.

"No." I placed my fingers under my eyes willing them not to tear up. "I swear to you.

You can ask anybody. Yes, I decided to stay a wee little bit today because…" I looked at him. I was always honest. I demanded it of him, and he expected it from me. "Well, because I didn't want to go home any earlier just to think about you getting ready to get on the plane. My mind would be occupied here."

He turned around, and we both stood silent for a moment. As I breathed in and out slowly, he finally turned back to face me. "All right. Let me help you so we can leave, okay?"

"Yeah?" I tilted my head unsure if I heard right.

"I'm pissed, Lara," he acknowledged with acute accuracy. "At least let me use up some of this energy."

"I'm sorry. I really didn't mean to stay this late." When he didn't immediately respond, I tried a different approach, only realizing afterward the similarities of how my mother used to try to pacify my father when he was in an alcoholic rage. "I remember Open House a few years ago. That week changed my life." I tried a small smile, thinking of the first time Finn and I had seen one another after seven years out of college— he had walked into that same room on the day of Open House.

"Give me some papers to organize or something." He didn't smile, but I saw the slight change in his gray eyes. "And quit flirting with me."

I closed my eyes for a moment with gratitude. And before picking up the papers, which I had haphazardly thrown upon his arrival, I questioned, "Finn?"

"Yeah?"

My answer was to wrap my arms around his torso. He might not have known it, but the hug that he denied me earlier meant everything to me. There wasn't one time that I could remember when he did not instantly hug me after we had been apart. Maybe because I grew up not receiving hugs, I knew the power of them with Finn.

"I'm mad, Lara." His embrace, as well as his voice from behind my back, were tense, but both were also secure. "But I love you."

"I know." To both.

CHAPTER TEN

Finn purposefully waited until I pulled my car out of the parking lot first. Then it was his headlights and face I saw in my rearview mirror the entire ride home. It was semi-nerve- wracking. I didn't know what his mood was in that car or what it might be once we got back.

As we walked from the garage into the house together I tried a fresh attitude at the new venue. "Any thoughts on dinner? I didn't expect you back until later tonight. So I just planned on making a sandwich and having Sheldon and Koothrappali keep me company. Yep, big plans—a rerun of *The Big Bang Theory.*"

"That's fine." He didn't chuckle at my pop-culture remark. "I'll help you make it. But I'm probably just going to eat in the studio."

"Oh."

"I have some work to do."

I bit my tongue ... hard. He just got done with a tirade about me staying late at work, and he couldn't eat a sandwich with me because of his? Knowing that it wasn't quite the same situation, I did a cleansing breath and let it go.

"How are things with Carter?" I tried, knowing that

Finn had planned on checking in on his friend and bandmate before he left Tennessee.

"His mom's still in the rehab facility, but hoping for outpatient soon," he answered as I got out the plates, vegetables, and condiments. "Stepdad serving his time. I told him we could talk about, you know, the band shit in another month."

Finn started placing the meat and cheese on the bread as I said, "So you think he's going to still—"

But I didn't get any further. His phone rang as he reached for a beer. And, just like that, I lost him and any chance of defusing the still very active grenade in the room to the person on the other line.

"Hey," Finn spoke into his phone. "Yeah, I'm just getting in … I know … Let me pull it up and give a listen…" Somehow managing to hold his beverage and sandwich, he continued to talk on the phone and head toward the lower-level studio.

***

I waited awhile after finishing my meal and straightening up before making the venture to his home office. When I entered, he was at the desk with his headphones on. His foot was tapping as he was jotting something down. But, because he was facing the door, he saw my approach. So, he pressed a button and removed the electronic device from his ears.

"Everything all right?" I asked tentatively, not sure if I was asking about the music business or our personal business.

"Getting there." His answer could have pertained to either.

"I'm gonna go to sleep soon. It's…well, it's been a long day."

"Yeah." He sounded as drained as I felt. "We were right in the middle of working on something when I decided to leave Nashville early. That and Carter's absence doesn't help." His face showed nothing but strain, and I knew my presence and actions were also a contributing factor.

"I'm sorry I messed up and that you're so upset with me. I'll be good about coming home. Get back to your stuff and maybe in the morning you can forgive me."

"Lara…" He started to rise, but as he did, I turned and headed out the door.

I didn't want to argue anymore. I understood that he didn't want me working late considering what happened with my last pregnancy. And even though I was not putting myself or our baby at risk, it was a legit enough reason to make him concerned and, therefore, mad. But it wasn't until he had left me alone that I had time to digest more than just my sandwich. He was also upset that, although accidently, I had broken a promise. Knowing what trust and truth meant to both of us, I am sure that must have felt like an additional dagger in his heart. And just as I was not going to jeopardize my health or the health of our child, I sure didn't want to jeopardize our love, which was fostered on friendship and trust. I deserved at least one night of penance.

***

I didn't realize I had fallen asleep. I knew I had tried for a while, but my mind was still spinning and trying to relax without immediate results. But I must have. Because it was the house security system that woke me up. No, it wasn't an alarm going off. It was simply the computerized voice announcing that the back door had been opened. I adjusted my eyes to read the bedside clock illuminating 1:04 a.m. Why was Finn going out the patio doors? The system announced his arrival back into the house only a minute or so later, followed by a notice that the door from the house into the garage had opened. Now I was a little more awake. I sat up praying that he wasn't thinking of driving anywhere at that time of the night. But, this time, his entrance back into the house was even quicker.

It was only when I heard him bounding up the stairs, in a way that it appeared he was taking them two at a time, that I realized he wasn't on a journey for himself. He was on a mission to find me. It really hadn't dawned on me to let him know that I was going to sleep in the guest room. Although, I'm not sure why not. We had never slept apart when we were in the same abode.

"Lara? God, baby. What are you doing up here?" he questioned, entering the room. The mixture of concern and relief on his face was illuminated just by the nightstand lamp— the one I had adjusted to the lowest dimmer setting before going to sleep.

"You're mad," I answered matter-of-factly while readjusting the pillows behind my back so that I could sit up straighter.

"I'm not—" he started. But if he was being honest…

I interrupted but not in a confrontational way. I wanted him to know that I understood and accepted the situation. "You are. I hurt you. You went to your studio the minute we got home. I know you needed time or space or something. I get it. I thought this was one of those separate room times." His eyebrows furrowed in confusion, so I explained. "Remember, before we were married, you said if we got mad each other, we should—"

"I … yeah." He cut me off as he sat on the bed's edge close to where I was propped. "But, baby, I'm not that upset." He closed his eyes for a second and when he reopened them, spoke again. "I was scared, and it set me off. It's hard for me not to think of what happened before. I'm trying. You've gotta know, though, that the only thing that could really hurt me is you not being around … you leaving. So, no, I don't want this. I don't want you in another room. I want you in our room where we both belong."

"I'm sorry...for staying late, for scaring you..."

"For having a guy find his bed empty on the first few hours of his birthday..."

My heart sank right along with my shoulders. Of course I hadn't forgotten his birthday. I just had misplaced the timing amongst the angst. "I'm sorry."

"You can make it up by giving me a kiss."

Grateful that maybe he wasn't as mad as I had initially diagnosed, I wet my lips and tipped up to meet his. I softly feathered a few kisses that were readily reciprocated. Gently, he brought me into his chest, but I was already naturally drawn there.

"Happy Birthday," I murmured into the pale blue Polo shirt that he had yet to change.

He pulled me slightly away to make sure that I was looking him in the eyes. "It might just be." He kissed me on the forehead and laced his hand through mine. Without another word, he guided me out of the guest room and down the stairs.

***

Finn and I were able to get back to being ourselves with one another almost instantly. It definitely helped that I got home, if not on time, then a few minutes early each night. And then there was the fact that the pregnancy was simply going well. With each passing day, I knew I was making strides and was less likely to experience vasovagal syncope.

Kelsea stayed over our place the first weekend in October. Nola and Will had decided to get away for the weekend. They needed the time as a couple and as a way to reflect on their lost son. It would have been Wyatt's birthday that week.

Finn cleared his schedule and became totally immersed in the three of us having a fun time. I couldn't wait for him to be a dad. I adored the way he played freely with his niece as if he were a child himself, yet acted like an authoritarian when he needed to. He had, thankfully, gotten over his fear of being responsible for her, which he developed immediately following Wyatt's death.

The baby seemed to want to get in on the excitement, too, and was particularly active that Saturday evening. "Here, Kels," I said. "Want to feel the baby? It's doing somersaults or flip-flops or something."

Kelsea got up from the sofa, where she and Finn were making rubber band bracelets, and walked over to my spot on the floor. She cautiously placed her hand on my stomach and removed it quickly when the baby bumped around. "That's weird!" she cried out.

"As weird as you doing flips, buttercup," Finn exclaimed grabbing her from behind and carefully flipping her feet over head.

Kelsea continued to giggle an infectious, innocent giggle, even after Finn put her right side up. I caught the happiness in his eyes as he reached out his hand to me. I let him help me up and off the floor, where I had just finished my prenatal yoga and stretching routine.

We weren't on the sofa a second before Kelsea bounced right in between us. "Is it a boy or a girl?"

"We don't know." I semi-laughed at her enthusiasm. "It's a surprise."

"That's what Mommy said. But I hope it's a girl. I could share all of my things with her."

"That's sweet, Kelsea." I smiled, caressing her blonde bouncy curls with my hand. "You're going to be a great cousin."

"What do you want, Uncle Finn?"

"I just want the baby and its mom to be healthy."

Finn looked over the top of his niece's head at me. When asked that particular question, most people say exactly what he had. But, for my husband, I knew it held a truer meaning.

Before I could reflect too much, Kelsea did it for me.

"The other baby …it died."

"Yeah, it did," I agreed with a touch of sadness.

"Why did it die, Aunt Lara?" She looked up at me, with those light brown eyes, truly wanting to understand.

"I—" was all the further my explanation got before Finn interrupted me.

"Kels, quit bothering Aunt Lara." He shifted his position on the sofa slightly.

"Was it sick?" She was looking up at him now.

"No," I answered.

"Did it have an accident like Wyatt did?" She swiveled her head back to me.

"Sort of."

"Kelsea …" Finn's voice had a bit of warning in it that probably only I detected.

"Why couldn't you save it?"

"Kelsea, da—" Starting to swear, he caught himself and, instead, stood up and yelled, "Geez!"

Kelsea, stunned by her uncle's outburst, looked wide-eyed at him and then at me, wanting some kind of explanation. I glanced over at my husband, who had his hands on the mantle and was facing away from us. I took a calming breath and tried to figure out what was appropriate to say.

"It's all right, sweetie." I squeezed her hand. "We know you don't understand. It's just that sometimes adults don't understand either. Sometimes talking about something that makes you sad is hard. But if you want to or you want to talk about your brother, you know you can."

"Uncle Finn, are you sad?"

As she asked the question, Finn turned around to face us. I looked in his direction, willing him to find the right words. He didn't need to lie, but he did need to put that little girl's mind at ease because obviously she thought about these real-life moments almost as much as we did.

"How could I be sad, sweet stuff?" He started back toward us. "I am in the company of the two most gorgeous girls in the world."

Kelsea puffed up like she was queen of the universe. He lifted her momentarily from the sofa so that he could sit next to me with Kelsea on his lap. We exchanged looks—mine grateful and his making sure I was all right— before Finn encompassed us both into a group hug.

"Ah! The baby just kicked me!" Kelsea cried out, breaking our squeeze.

Knowing and feeling that was, indeed, the truth, I teasingly put blame elsewhere. "I think that was Uncle Finn!"

"Uncle Finn!" Kelsea playfully shouted.

And, soon enough, they were both off the sofa chasing each other around the room. It was so fulfilling and peaceful to watch. It was happiness personified.

I'm not sure who tuckered out first, but Finn had a good excuse when Reese called. Kelsea and I let him be and decided to start making dinner. It was only a few minutes later, though, when Finn joined us and explained what the call was about.

He popped open a beer from the fridge and waited for me to turn from the stove. "Reese wants to put something out… about the pregnancy." He caught my eyes like he was trying to read my unspoken reaction before I gave my verbal one. "She says she's getting lots of queries."

"Because I'm fat."

He shook his head at my reply. But instead of denying it, went with sarcasm. "Yep, the size of a hippo."

"A hippo, Kelsea! Your uncle just called me a dirty, gray beast."

"Uncle Finn!"

As Finn rolled his eyes at having been played again, I said, "Okay." But, admittedly, it was slowly, and with a twinge of trepidation.

"Okay?" He stopped and leaned against the center island. "Okay with releasing it? Are you sure? Are you ready for that?"

"I don't know. Yes … no. Finn…" I looked down at my white top and black bottoms with definite baby bulge somewhere in between. "I mean, I hope they think I'm pregnant. Yeah. Okay. What does she have in mind? Press releases to some outlets?"

"Well…" He seemed to hesitate. "*Media Monthly* wants me to be one of their top ten sexiest husbands."

I dropped my stirring spoon. "Really?"

Finn rolled his eyes at my reaction. "I know it's ridiculous, but you could have at least humored my ego a little bit."

"Sorry." I pushed my lips onto his and backtracked. "Top ten? You're number one, baby."

"Uh-huh."

"Well, except maybe for that Ben Winthrop." I jokingly countered, citing the handsome, blonde television star.

"You better not say that if we go through with this interview." Finn joshed back poking me with his finger. "Besides, I don't think he qualifies. He's not married, is he?"

"I still have hope?" I teased and then turned more serious. "Is that what you want to do? The interview?"

"It's kind of embarrassing, but I know that stuff sells, and it will help. But just if you are okay with it. We would both be interviewed."

I took in a deep breath and truly thought about it. It would be the most I would have ever been "out there" as Finn's wife or, for that matter, ever. Finn protected my privacy fiercely because he believed in separating his career and his personal life. But I also had never liked being in the spotlight.

"For you?" I said. "I will do it. But only for my sexiest husband."

CHAPTER ELEVEN

"What did you think when you heard your husband was one of our top ten sexiest husbands?"

The question was posed from the *Media Monthly* reporter who, along with her photographer, was sitting across from Finn and I in the comfort of Finn's Manhattan penthouse.

The penthouse was a nice compromise as far as locales go. I didn't want a sterile location, but something that would relax me. And Finn didn't want anyone near our suburban New York home. That was too personal for him. Like Goldilocks, the penthouse's middle ground was just right.

I had asked, practically begged, Finn to tell me what he wanted me to say ... how to answer any questions. But he deferred, saying he wanted me to feel free to say whatever I felt. Finn should have known better. Since the first time we met, he had been witness to the side of me that used dry humor when I was nervous. And despite his hand being interlocked with mine and his calm demeanor, I was nervous.

When I started to say something but stopped to edit, Finn answered for me, giving a classic Lara answer, anyhow. "She asked how many guys turned it down in order for me to rank that high."

Grateful that he was putting me at ease, I smiled and wrinkled my nose at him while admitting, "I kind of did."

"You don't think your husband is sexy?" The reporter asked, obviously a little shocked.

"I do," I restated. "It's just, I don't think of him the way your magazine is referring to. I mean, God yeah, who can resist these abs," I said, releasing my hand momentarily to rub it over Finn's stomach, which was covered by a black V-neck T. "And that smile," I added when he did just that. "But that isn't what is truly sexy about Finn."

"Go on."

"Yeah, go on," Finn teasingly tagged in with the reporter.

He seemed much more at ease than he usually was when talking about his personal life to strangers. Maybe it was spending time with Kelsea, or maybe it was knowing the pregnancy was going well ... I wasn't sure. But I was definitely glad. If nothing else, it helped calm my nerves.

I lightly pushed on my husband's shoulder before turning serious. "It's the way he puts his whole heart into everything he does. How he cares about everyone around him— his fans and his bandmates." I briefly let my mind flutter to Carter, who I knew was really stepping up with helping his mom, brother, and sister. "But Finn's family is so special and important to him and, without a doubt, me. I know he loves me unconditionally. He is my best friend, first and foremost. That's what makes him sexy." When I turned from the reporter to Finn at the conclusion of my statement, he kissed me ever so softly and appreciatively.

"What was the first song that you ever sang for your wife?"

"The first song? Hmmm..." He looked at me. "I ... I don't know."

"The first time we met," I offered. "I was going to see

his band play on campus. What did you play? I guess that would be it."

"God, I don't know, classic stuff—rock, country. We did all kinds of covers. That was a long time ago now," Finn answered.

"'Lara's Song', though," the reporter interjected. "That, I'm guessing, would be your song."

Our song was "Roxanne." But that was something we kept private between the two of us. That was going to remain personal.

"Was 'Lara's Song' the song you used to woo her?" she continued her line of questioning.

Finn smiled with a soft laugh. "I didn't need to woo her."

"You didn't?" I tried an incredulous look on him.

"Did I?" he light-heartedly challenged.

"No," I admitted. When we reconnected years after college, I knew I was instantly falling for him. Well, if I was honest, it was even before that.

The reporter smiled, I'm sure recognizing the obvious, easy-going love between the two of us. "Since you met in college, do you ever go back for college reunions?"

"No," Finn immediately answered. "The only person I really would be interested in seeing I talk with every day."

I smiled at his sweetness and replied, "Ditto." Although it probably would be fun to go, I knew attending an alumni event would be a celebrity nightmare for Finn.

"But you weren't dating back in college, were you?" she continued having obviously done her Finn Murphy homework.

Feeling more relaxed and more myself, I answered with, "No. Sexy guy here didn't know a good thing when he saw it back then."

"Really? I think you may be rewriting history a little bit," he countered.

"Yeah," I conceded. "Our timing was just off." I took Finn's hand again.

"So you kept in touch?" was the next question for *Media Monthly* readers.

"No, unfortunately, we lost track of one another. Seven years," Finn answered with a legitimate touch of sadness for all those years lost.

"What brought you back together then?"

"Finn came to play a benefit concert where I work."

"It was your nephew's school, right?" The question was directed at Finn, but I am sure she knew the answer all along.

Finn looked from the reporter to me to Reese who was on her phone but still very much in sync with the interview. When she took a step toward us, Finn fielded the question himself. "That's right. But, listen, my sister has been through enough with …with Wyatt's …with Wyatt." It didn't matter that it was over two years since his death, Finn still stumbled on that devastating fact, especially when caught off guard and with strangers. "Can we please just leave that out?"

Reese stopped her stride as the reporter sympathetically complied. "Sure. I completely understand." She instead switched gears. "I need to ask another question, though." She looked pointedly at me. "I don't want to offend or anything, and I know what happened this past winter…"

There it was— the main reason we agreed to do the interview. I was nervous all over again. Because once I said the words and it was out in the public domain, it was going to be more real again. But, the fact was, it *was* real, and it was a good thing, and—

"Yes, I am pregnant." I interrupted both the reporter and my internal dialogue.

"Oh, well, congratulations," she offered genuinely.

"Thanks." Finn smiled warmly at me. "We feel very blessed."

"And it's okay that I print that?"

"Yeah. Sure," he agreed.

"How far along?" She turned her attention to me

146

because, after all, that was a girly question.

"I'm around my third trimester," I answered and then delivered the party line even though I hadn't been directly told to. "Everything is good. Just not up to making the social scene as much. So, unfortunately, no CMA Awards this year."

The last part of the statement made Finn and I particularly sad. It would be the first year since we became a couple that we wouldn't be together for the CMA awards— the place where we first became that said couple. But we both thought it was best that I not fly in the last stages of my pregnancy. We purposefully wanted to tell *Media Monthly* that ahead of time in order to squash any rumors as to why I wasn't there since the article was due out around the same time.

"Gotcha," the reporter said with a wink. "We'll make sure to let that be known." She then turned to Finn. "So we didn't ask you. What do *you* think is sexy?"

"Her. Just knowing that she is here and that she loves me." He stroked my hand with his thumb. "It doesn't get any better than that."

"In case you had any doubt, no one had to back out, Mrs. Murphy. Your husband was always and instantly on our top ten list."

I heard her. But I couldn't take my eyes off of him. And it had nothing to do with his physical beauty. It had everything to do with his heart.

"Yeah. Mine, too. Mine, too."

After the question/answer segment of the interview, the magazine photographer had to take some pictures. He already had a couple candids of us sitting on the sofa, so he just needed some solo shots of Finn. They had a professional backdrop and lighting equipment set up in the area where the foyer meets the living room.

When they suggested that Finn put in his green contacts, he refused. "The article is about being a husband. And my natural eyes are what my wife likes."

I met those eyes. I did like his natural gray eyes, but, more than that, I liked his thoughtful heart. I picked up the book I was reading and curled up on the sofa as the flash started snapping.

After a minute or two, I heard the reporter say to Finn and the photographer, "We want the sexy look. Give me that Finn Murphy sexy look."

Finn's reply was, "I don't have a sexy look. And, if I do, I'm not giving it until my wife looks at me."

I looked up from my book, silently laughing, and smiled. He didn't necessarily provide the photographer with a sexier look then, but his eyes did seem to brighten. And the clicking of the camera sped up as the lens was on Finn watching me.

Finn, Reese, the reporter, and the photographer then all moved into the nearby dining room. They sat at the table as the photos were downloaded to a laptop so they could make some selections for the article. Wanting my opinion, Finn called me over to join them.

After seeing the collection of photos, Finn returned to one. "What about this one?" he asked me. "I think I like this one. What do you think?"

"Yeah," I agreed.

"Yeah," he echoed in a tone that was an obvious mimic of my noncommittal response. "You don't like it?"

"What?" I asked again because at that exact moment the baby started somersaulting, or something close to it, in my stomach. I smiled, loving the feeling of an active, vital babe. "Yeah." I returned my attention to its daddy. "I like them all."

"I like them all." Finn repeated my words and started downright roaring laughing. He held his stomach as if he were the one with the baby inside. "I like them all," he said again actually needing to take a few steps away because he was laughing so hard. When I started laughing only because he was laughing, he said, "Lara, a lot of them are awful!"

They were. In one, his eyes were nearly closed, giving him a very drunk look. There were others taken from the wrong angle and still others that made him look pissed off.

"Well, it's a loaded question," I explained. "It's like me asking you if the jeans make me look fat."

"The jeans" —he looked at my maternity denim— "look good, and you are beautiful," he said, most honestly, without any of the laughter.

"Uh-huh. See there... 'I like them all.' That's the same thing as you saying I'm beautiful all the time." When Finn tried to interrupt with surely a protest to my statement, I forged on by clicking the mouse to find a particular picture. "I like this one, and the one you picked is nice, too."

Finn wrapped him arms around me and one more time started laughing with, "I like them all." Once again, it was like we were the only two in the room. "I like you," he said.

"Good thing," I replied as the photographer instinctively snapped a picture of the two of us in that moment—the photo that would end up running with the article.

***

About a week later, Finn flew out for just a couple days to do a country fest concert. It was one of those annual events that had nearly every country artist performing at some point over a three-day time span. He seemed to look forward to it, since he hadn't been touring and performing as much as he usually did. Of course, it was during this miniscule time span that I got life changing news.

At first, I wasn't even going to get up to answer the phone because it was our landline, and hardly anyone who truly knew us—aside from Finn's parents, occasionally— called that number. But I had to get up to pee anyway. So I walked past the phone to check out the caller ID. It had a name and non-local number that I did not recognize. But, for some reason, I felt this abnormal need to answer it.

I have always been overly guarded when it comes to strangers. Originally, it was because I was a single woman. But then, as a celebrity's wife, I needed to be on alert for individuals wanting something just because of Finn's fame.

I think the lawyer on the other end of the line was just as cautious with me. He confirmed who I was but only used my maiden name. And he made absolutely no reference to Finn. But then, the phone was only registered under my maiden name for that reason. When I asked what the call was regarding, he said he was representing a client whose name he could not divulge— a client who needed my assistance. I continued to listen, hearing the slight edge of desperation in his voice. Still, I was waiting for the con. He continued to ask me questions to confirm who I was, despite my giving extremely limited responses. Then, seemingly satisfied, he dropped the proverbial question bomb: had I given a baby boy up for adoption? He would be thirteen years old now.

My body froze, but my brain and insides were swirling faster than I could handle. I didn't answer him. First of all, I don't think I could have gotten a word out of my stunned, dry mouth. But, second, I didn't know what the end game of the conversation was. And, again, being overly leery, I certainly was not going to divulge anything that extremely personal to a stranger who I couldn't even see.

The lawyer filled the silent gap by telling me some devastating news. The boy, now a young teen who didn't know he was adopted, had cancer and was in need of a bone marrow transplant. I sank to the floor. The lawyer continued. The best solution was to find a close blood relative. They were able to track me down via the adoption documents and some research. I knew in my heart of hearts that it was not a scam. I think I subconsciously knew it before I even answered the phone. This was the little boy I had given up all those years ago, and he needed my help. But still I didn't speak.

"Miss Faulkner? I am assuming that we've got the right person. I know this may be a lot right now. Perhaps you would like to call me back?"

"Can I do that?" I managed. "I ...I need to talk with someone, and I will definitely get back to you."

"That's fine. You have my name and number, right?"

"Yeah—caller ID."

"Okay. Do what you need to do. Talk with who you need to talk with, and call me back. I am sure the family will be incredibly grateful."

The family. My son's family. My child who has cancer. I hadn't had morning sickness in a while, but the moment I hung up the phone, I ran to the bathroom and threw up.

After splashing water on my face, I sat down on the rocking recliner and stared blankly for a few moments. I hadn't known who adopted my son all those years ago. I hadn't wanted to know. Obviously, the adoptive family wanted to keep their privacy, too, as no names were given. But I had given a written consent of my information all those years ago for that sole reason ... in case there was any medical concerns. I had to help.

But I needed help myself. I needed help emotionally. This was so huge on so many levels. He was someone I could never forget but knew I would always live without. He was sick. Even if I hadn't given birth to that child, I would feel a tug— a need to do something– just as we had pulled together for a third-grader with heart problems at work a couple years before. That was the benefit concert that had brought Finn back into my life. I needed Finn now. I looked at my laptop sitting on the side table next to me. It was how I had left it when the phone rang—open to the website tracking Finn's plane back to New York. He was nearing the airport. I couldn't call him. I would have to wait until he got to the house. I needed to talk with him ... to have him listen ... to have him help me make sense of it all because, after all, he was going to be affected, too.

In the meantime, I pressed my fingers tightly to my face and paced the house. My mind was going too fast to even comprehend all the feelings I had—remorse, love, and fear topped them for sure. When I managed to slow down, a smidge of logic slid into the part of my brain that wasn't controlled by shock. I needed to legitimize what this man had told me on the phone. I went back to my computer and, after seeing that Finn's plane had landed, I searched online for the lawyer's name and phone number. There was a LinkedIn page, a Spokeo page, a law article written by him, and his company's main website. There were also sites that reviewed law partners, and all his ratings were either four or five stars. Everything I read seemed legitimate and top notch. And I knew the next thing I was going to have to do was dig up the papers from the adoption. I still had them, but they were buried and locked away, just as I had tried to do with all my memories of that time.

But Finn had texted just a few moments before telling me that he was on his way home. So I decided to finish reading the internet pages while I waited instead. I even looked up the law firm via the Better Business Bureau.

When the outside door announced Finn's entrance, I finally felt safe and secure. The anxiety that I hadn't realized settled into my core dissipated a little knowing that he was home. Somehow, Finn would be able to make everything better.

I stood up as he entered the great room and tried to put on a smile. "Hi, Cowboy."

"Hey, ba—" He verbally stopped himself looking at me more closely— the emotionally wrecked version of me. "Lara?" When I barreled into him, his voice became even more alert. "Shit! What's wrong?"

I hadn't cried the entire time. Now, I was letting go. The deluge of tears and shaking were so strong that Finn had a hard time even standing still with me in his arms. I know I was frightening him, but I couldn't get a word out. He tried to pull me away, but I clung, and I clung hard. He gave me a couple minutes like that before trying to settle us both down onto the sofa. Eventually, he got my face in his hands and looked me in the eyes.

"The baby is fine," I managed to get out first. "I'm fine."

His whole body seemed to relax, and he let his hands drop from my face down to my hands. "What is it then? You're scaring me."

And, in the comfort of my husband's arms, I poured out the story of the telephone call. Just like he had a few Septembers ago, when he first heard the story of my past, Finn listened with patience and understanding. Initially, he had some of the same concerns I did regarding legitimacy. But when I showed him the research online, in addition to some of the specific details the lawyer had mentioned, Finn agreed with my assessment. The child I gave birth to over thirteen years before was gravely sick, and his family needed my help.

"What do I do?" I asked Finn. My mind was still so muddled. I didn't know what direction to go in first. I would be lucky if I knew my shoe size at that point.

"Well, first, you need to take care of yourself." He touched my cheek. "Let's get something to eat and both take a moment to let this soak in. Then, I'll help you with whatever you need. You want to confirm everything and then see what the family needs from you. We can deal with that part tomorrow." God, he was so rational ... such a calming force.

"Okay." I breathed. "Okay. Thanks."

"Baby, you don't have to thank me." His voice softened even more. "It's a little boy and, even more so, it's you. I'll do anything I can." He touched my nose. "And I love you beyond words."

"The feeling is pretty damn mutual." I leaned my head into his taut, strong chest.

***

The whole situation was a legal and medical mess rolled into one. I called off work that next day, and Finn silenced his phone as we dealt with everything that we could. He was my rock, and he had to be over the next few days, as we learned new things about a deadly disease and the different steps in the process that would hopefully cure the child whose name I still did not know. Finn listened and advised, but I never mentioned his presence in my life to the outsiders on the phone. As far as they knew, I was still Miss Faulkner. The addition of country music's "Mr. Right Now" in the mix would only add unnecessary chaos to an already unbearable situation. Behind the scenes, he told me he would do whatever he could to help, and I knew he would. But we had to take things one step at a time. He had connections at St. Jude, but it didn't seem necessary. Between the adoption agency, their lawyer, their medical personnel, and my doctors, the kid was getting the best care possible. It was just a matter of waiting for results.

Then the guilt factor came into play. And I had a couple of reasons to feel guilty over the situation. First, there was a thirteen-year-old boy suffering—suffering from a disease that he very well might have gotten because of my genetics.

"You know there's no basis for that." Finn tried to reason with me.

"Right. I know. Environmental, blah, blah, blah."

"Lara, sometimes these things just happen. Each person's body is a different unique make-up. My dad had cancer but neither of his parents or siblings have had it. And, well, look at me ..." He paused with that sadness in his eyes. The fact that he suffered from a type of mental disorder was easily forgotten since his treatment was so effective.

It's funny that he was using the same rationalization

that I had used with him when we were first deciding whether to get pregnant or not. I had told him his parents didn't pass any mental illness onto him— a traumatic event triggered it. How was he going to pass it on to our child?

"Finn? Do you think they hate me?" Because I had grown up never being able to please my father, I felt like I was always seeking other people's approval.

"What? Who?"

"His parents. That little boy's parents," I said because he was always little to me.

"Beauty, why would they hate you? You gave them the most precious gift in the world. You gave them the love of a child."

I placed my hand protectively up to my blossoming stomach to feel my other child. "And he's sick. And I can't help."

That was where the second guilt factor came into play. After days of researching, talking with professionals, and visiting with my doctor, I knew I could not donate the bone marrow. Ironically, it was because I was pregnant. Even if I was a match, I would not be able to donate until several months after my pregnancy.

And then there was guilt factor number three. I insisted on being tested anyway. In less than a week, I knew I was a complete failure to that child. I hadn't been strong enough to keep him when he first started his life, and now I couldn't even help save his life. I wasn't a match.

It had been just one disappointment after another, and I was an emotional mess. People at work knew there was something wrong, but, of course, I couldn't tell them. No one knew of my previous life. I think they assumed Finn and I were having problems. So, I let them, even though nothing could have been further from the truth. That man held me every single time I walked in the door, got off the phone, or laid down at night. He made sure I was taking care of myself without being overbearing and listened when I needed to talk or just breathe.

Luckily, Baby Murphy was going with the proverbial flow. The child inside of me seemed to play off my senses. It settled down when I needed the calmness and, on occasion, showed some action to remind me how precious life could be.

Once we found out that I could not donate, another discussion from the medical camp emerged—Finn's and my baby might be a match. While Finn had been extremely supportive through everything, the fact that his unborn child would have a procedure done flew up immediate red flags. He went with me to see Dr. Weinstein, and we had a lengthy, in-depth conversation about what testing the baby would entail and, if he or she were a match, how the umbilical cord could be used. Siblings had a decent match rate, but our child would only be a half-sibling. While I was for at least finding out, Finn still wasn't convinced. It didn't matter, though, because we would have to wait until I was at least seven months along to test, and that, unfortunately, was still about another month away. At least the doctor had said, with a pleased look on his face, that the baby and I were in great physical condition. In fact, we were doing remarkably well, considering the amount of stress I was dealing with.

So, despite the trepidation, I had to concede to the final option. It was really the only route I had left to help that sick boy. I had to venture down those dark roads of my past and find someone I had never wanted to lay eyes on again—Macon.

CHAPTER TWELVE

Like the plague, I had successfully avoided any elements of that part of my life for as many years as that child had been alive. And now, with a few quick searches online and a seemingly innocent call to my mother, I had discovered where the man who fathered my firstborn child was living. Finn begged me to just track down a phone number and call. But I knew this was a conversation that, if it had any chance in succeeding, had to be done in person. So, I took a day off of work and gave our Halloween candy to neighbors to pass out. Then Finn and I set out to where it all began—my hometown—a suburb about an hour away from Pittsburgh.

We decided to drive instead of fly for a number of reasons. It was a lot harder for Finn to be spotted and identified if he wasn't turning in tickets and standing in lines for transportation. Even if we stopped along the road, it would only be momentary and no one would know our final destination. Plus, Finn rarely had a chance to drive any distances, and he loved it. It relaxed him. Which was another reason to drive— flying does the opposite for me. I certainly didn't need to add any more stress to the already taxing situation. And I really didn't want to fly that late in my pregnancy.

If it wasn't for the reason we were traveling across nearly the entire state of Pennsylvania, that trip would have been one of the most cherished times Finn and I spent together, just for the simple fact that it was the two of us, completely alone. We weren't in any of our residences, with distractions of our lives outside of our marriage. It was just us and the freedom of the road.

My stomach got more and more acidy as we neared our destination on, of all days, Devil's Night. Finn, surely sensing my anxiety, reached out his right hand for my left while he steered the car through the remaining roads to my childhood home. We arrived in plenty of time for dinner, but my mother was already in extreme cooking mode. Our plan was to stay with her for the night before starting on our real mission in the morning... which my mother knew nothing about. I think normally she would have been suspicious of our last-minute visit, since we had never done that before, but she was so over-the-moon about the idea of us being there that nothing else was registering.

Despite my mom's home cooking, dinner didn't make me feel much better. I was feeling a little guilty for not informing her of our true intentions. In fact, I hadn't told her anything about the phone call from the lawyer or the fact that "my son" needed bone marrow. Since she was the one who had helped me through the pregnancy so many years before, she would have been the most logical choice for a confidante. But my mother was a worrier. Plus, she didn't know the one secret I had kept from everybody except Finn— Macon was the father of that baby, not his fraternal twin brother Miller, who I had been dating at the time. I never wanted her to know about what happened that night at the waterfall— the alcohol consumption and the poor choices that I made for myself, as well as the ones others made for me. A pregnant teenage daughter had been embarrassing and disappointing enough, I am sure.

I would have, of course, been straightforward about the

bone marrow transplant had I thought my mom could have helped medically. She did cross my mind as a potential donor. But the medical personnel in charge already informed me that she was beyond the age of eligibility. So there was no sense in involving her just to have her worry, or be sad or, God forbid, take it upon herself to harass the Altman family.

When I went to excuse myself before dessert, my mother was instantly concerned. "Everything all right, sweetie?"

"Yeah, Mom. Just six months pregnant. Need to stretch. I'm gonna go up to my room for a bit," I said, as Finn pushed out his seat in a gentlemanly fashion. "Stay." I pleaded with my eyes for him to throw on his charm and talk my mom right into another conversation.

"Here, Elise, let me help clear." Finn took a couple of the plates before my mom could protest.

***

He found me a little while later in Lane's old room, which my mother had converted into a kind of craft room many years before. My room, however, remained a bedroom. Although, most of my stuff was gone. It was like she thought I would be the one, the vulnerable one, who would need to return. Whereas nothing could have been further from the truth.

"I thought yours was the second door on the right." I jumped at the sound of my husband's voice, having been a little lost in thought.

"Yeah." I turned my head to face him. "This was Lane's. He had the better window." When Finn pulled up a chair next to mine to look out that window, I suggested, "Prop your feet up. Lane and I used to do that all the time, just hoping there was a better life somewhere out there."

"I remember you telling me that." He spoke softly, taking my hand.

"I want you to know, there was. I found it. And if all of this" —I swirled my finger around the room— "led to you, then it was worth it. I can get past any regrets."

Before getting overly sentimental, I thanked Finn for intercepting my mother. He jokingly said that I owed him one and then told me, which I already knew, that she was upset that she wasn't going to be able to spend the following day with us. Before she knew of our last minute plans to visit, she had agreed to cover someone else's shift that next day. I didn't understand why she always felt a need to take on extra shifts. She lived comfortably, and Finn and I were more than willing to help out if that was not the case. But she always claimed that she did it because she was single and liked keeping busy and helping others. Regardless, the fact that she would be working actually made it easier for me to see Macon without adding extra suspicion.

I couldn't help but think that so much in life comes full circle. Such was the case with the Altman brothers. Miller, who wanted nothing to do with me or the rural, mediocre Pennsylvania life, had opted out of the college scene so he could move to coastal Virginia. Fast forward years later— he not only returned to a mediocre job but was living in his parents' house. Albeit, he bought the house from them when they decided to retire early and move south. And Macon, who went to college shortly after that infamous summer night years before, didn't appear to have fared much better. All I knew was that he had been living with Miller for long enough that it seemed relatively permanent.

It was bad enough that I had to be back in that town. But why, of all places, did I have to confront my past at the same exact location that had changed my existence forever? Why did it have to be that house with those woods behind it? It was karma, I suppose. It was my full circle. And it was going to happen, like it or not.

***

When Finn pulled up to the Altman house that next day, the memories not only came back, they crashed violently back. Just beyond that backyard were the woods that were home to the waterfall—where I had seen Miller with that girl ... where I had ran from ... where Macon and I and possibly others ... *STOP!* I shook the image from my head.

"You don't have to do this." Finn turned to me. "You have no obligations."

"I do," I said quietly, becoming that meek version of myself that I hadn't seen in such a long time.

We had agreed that Finn should stay in the car so he wasn't a distraction, either as a superstar or as my husband. So I kissed him quickly for luck and stepped out of the car. But the moment I did, my nerves returned full force, and I had to catch my breath.

Eagle-eye Finn didn't miss a beat. "Uh-huh. No way. Forget it," his voice called out via the open window, and I saw him starting for his car door.

I turned and leaned in the window. "I'm fine," I said and managed a partial, pretend smile.

Before he could rebut, I walked straight up the sidewalk to the small covered porch and rang the doorbell. It was a much more civilized approach than the pounding my father had done to the same door after finding out I was pregnant by whom he—and all interested parties—assumed was Miller. I didn't have long to flash back, though, because the door swiftly opened to expose the past right there in front of me in full color. There was no mistaking Macon. Although he and Miller were twins, they were fraternal and different in many ways.

"Yeah? What do you want?" he growled, and not because it was Halloween. As I hesitated trying just to take it all in, Macon continued, "Look it here, missy, you're too early and a little too old to be trick-or-treating. Unless it's just the tricks..." His smirk was the hardened type, just like his appearance—longer, ropey hair under an ill-fitting dark ball cap, an oversized army-green sweatshirt, and bloodshot eyes.

By the way he spoke to me, I figured he didn't recognize me. I ignored his rude remark and said, "No. I'm...It's Lara. Lara M ..." I started to announce my last name and then realized he wouldn't know me by that. "Faulkner."

"Lara Faul ..." He was squinting his eyes at me in an almost comical way, trying to place the name with the face. "Oh, Mill's old bitch."

Classy. How long until I can leave this God-forsaken world again? Please. Pretty please.

"Look, uh, Macon. There's something really important that I need to talk to you about."

"Yeah?"

When he propped his body against the doorframe, I wondered if he was doing it because he couldn't stand straight. I wasn't going to get close enough to smell his breath. "That baby ...our baby ...he's a young boy now, and he's sick."

"I thought you gave the kid up. And what's this about it being mine?" Both of the brothers had decided they didn't want to raise the kid or to know the paternity.

"He's yours." I tried not to cringe. "And I did."

"Then what?"

"The adoptive parents got a hold of me. He has cancer. He's going to die without a bone marrow transplant."

I didn't tear up. I probably would have had I not been semi-frightened of the scenario in front of me. I had never been scared of Macon before. As teens, we got along. He was rough around the edges but no one to be feared. Even that horrific night had just been bad decisions on both of our parts. It was just the fact that I was back, and he seemed so different ... and not in a positive way.

"Tough break," he said, confirming my personality assessment.

Trying not to be shocked by his callousness, I decided to keep going. "I'm not a bone marrow match, but you might be. You could save him."

"Oh, shit, no. I have nothing to do with it."

"Are you kidding me?" The shock was wearing off now, and I was returning to my more confident, post-Pennsylvania self.

"No, that kid, like I said, tough break. But, I ain't no baby daddy. There's no one drilling into me." He started with that evil-looking grin again. "Lara Faulkner, God, you're even prettier than before."

The second his hand even started to come up to touch my face, I heard the car door slam shut. I shrugged Macon's paw off my cheek and looked to Finn, who seemed to have flown up the sidewalk instead of walked. He couldn't have heard what Macon had said, but the action was not going to be acceptable in my husband's eyes.

Nodding his head toward Macon, Finn distinctly and firmly said, "Get your hands off of her."

Instead of complying, the human version of a devil allowed his hand to trail down my body to the side of my breast. It was repulsive enough to feel his hand on me through the fabric of my blue and white dress, but I didn't dare allow him to touch my blossoming stomach. I moved slightly away and hugged my light cardigan sweater closer to me.

"Off!" Finn reiterated a little stronger and put both of his hands up to protect me.

"Oh, yeah, right. You married the …you're the big shot rock star, huh?"

"Finn, it's okay," I said, secretly glad he was by my side, yet wanting to defuse any more friction.

"How'd you land that, Lar-Lar?" Macon sneered, making me feel like vomiting.

"Lara, let's go." Finn spoke to me but did not let his stare stray from Macon.

"No." I was becoming more bold, partly because Macon was pissing me off and partly because I knew Finn was by my side. "Macon, I need you to get tested."

"I already told you—" His statement was cut short by the presence of another person in the doorway—his double.

"Mill ..." I managed. Although we had not necessarily parted on the best of terms years before, seeing him brought back more innocent memories of a turbulent time.

"Hey, Lara," he said, casually looking me over as I was him.

His hair was longer and he had a whiskery kind of goatee that I couldn't immediately decide if I liked or not. He had bulked up. Or was it that Macon was so skinny? Miller was dressed monochromatically with a contrasting tie. From the information I got from my unsuspecting mother, I assumed it was his waiter job attire.

Coating his words with unattractive sarcasm, Macon turned to his brother and said, "Ah, the lovers reunite. Too late, for you, though. She's knocked up again." I couldn't help but cringe as his eyes diverted to my baby bulge.

"Christ, Macon, go sleep it off," Miller, a sober contrast to his brother, implored.

"Hell, no. I might have me another, though." He leaned a little closer toward me. "You know, maybe this bambino is mine, too."

That may as well have been an open invitation for my husband. Finn, who I noticed had been clenching his fists since the "knocked up" comment, first pushed Macon into the door and then threw a good blow across his face. "Stay the fuck away from her!"

I don't think I screamed out loud. Although, I did internally. I hadn't expected to enjoy the reunion, but I certainly didn't want a brawl.

"You'll regret that," Macon countered, rubbing his jaw.

"Try me." Finn egged him on, in pure macho mode.

"C'mon …" Miller took the role of referee, physically standing in the middle of the two men.

Ignoring his brother, Macon peered at Finn while answering his challenge. "I already tried" —he put his fingers up for air quotation marks— "the little teenage whore. Mmmm-hmmm." As he licked his lips and trolled his eyes up and down my body, Finn advanced toward him once again.

"Finn, stop! Don't!" I cried out, tugging at my protector's arm.

Miller wrangled up his brother and managed to awkwardly get him inside. Macon's Cheshire grin was the last thing I saw before they disappeared into the house. Finn could not stand still and I think wanted to go all Hulk on the door and tear it apart.

"Hey," I said in as calm of a voice as I could muster. "Let me look at you."

He turned to me with his eyes ablaze, but I knew that hatred wasn't directed toward me. "You shouldn't be here," he said, plainly and a little more rationally.

I pulled his gray ball cap from his head and put my hands up to his face to make sure that he hadn't been hurt. That was my priority right then. Luckily, Macon was too drunk to have even gotten a swing in.

"I can't believe—" I started to say as the door opened again.

Miller, now solo, seemed to restart our conversation. "Lara. Well, it's been a while."

"Yeah," I admitted while watching the two men eye each other and wondering if there was going to be even more drama.

"Miller," My ex formally introduced himself to Finn by extending his hand for a shake.

"Right." Finn, guard back up, refused Miller's hand and didn't return the courtesy of offering his own name.

"That's all right. Know who you are." Miller turned his eyes and conversation to me. "So, I heard. The kid was

Macon's, huh?"

"Yeah," I confirmed.

"For sure?" He seemed to be trying to get a better look at me now that there wasn't so much drama unfolding.

"Yeah." Everything was coming out monosyllabic. But, really, what else was there to say?

"How old now?" he continued.

"Thirteen." I took Finn's hand.

"Huh. Wow. Yeah. Damn." Miller summed up my thoughts—how it didn't seem possible that I could have a teenager.

"Listen," Finn interjected. "If you or your brother aren't going to help, then there's no point in us—"

"You want me to get tested? Yeah. I mean, it's a kid. I need to talk it over with my fiancée just in case, but she'll be fine with it. She has a kid."

Fiancée? I pondered that new information to myself but then quickly went back to the topic at hand. "Thanks."

"Yeah."

"But Macon would be better."

Macon was the real connection. He was the real chance for a match. The more removed the recipient was from the potential donor, the less chance there was of a match.

"Lara, he's either drunk or high. I don't think they'd accept him. And he's not getting clean for nobody or nothing. Believe me, we've tried. If he wasn't my brother, I wouldn't let him even stay here."

"But—" I started.

"You want me to do it, give me the info. But tag Macon out." Once I got the materials out of my purse and handed them to Miller, he said, "So, I'll let you know?"

"Not even a chance. Just the doctor." Even with reporters, Finn had never been this protective and possessive.

"Right." Miller seemed to respect Finn's stance ... perhaps because of the woman in his life?

"Thanks, Miller," I said and meant it genuinely.

"I'd invite you in or something, but I don't think—"

"No." I said.

And Finn echoed with, "We're going."

"Well, it was good seeing you," Miller offered politely.

"Yeah," I agreed.

We looked at each other for a moment, taking in the past and the present all at the same time. We knew back then, even before that night, that we weren't meant to be. But it shouldn't have ended the way that it had. I hate that word "closure." And I certainly didn't think I needed it. But, somehow, I had it—at least with Miller—that Saturday in October.

CHAPTER THIRTEEN

Finn was driving fast, but I knew he was in control. So I let the rush hit me, too. We both needed the combined sound of the roar of the engine and the wind blowing through the car to allow our minds to debrief.

When the throttle started to ease up, I took the opportunity to say what I knew I needed to. "I'm sorry. I—"

He glanced over at me, easing even a little more on the gas. "What are you sorry about?"

"I don't want you to have to deal with this. This is my crap. Macon ... he was—"

"He's an ass. What happened when you were younger should be in the past. He had no right saying that. You weren't the one who did something wrong."

"But I brought it all back by going to see him. I had to, though. I couldn't not try to help."

"No. You did the right thing." I knew he meant it by the softness of this voice, but I also knew he still hated every other part of what had transpired.

"I mean, he wasn't the classiest of guys, but, God, his life really went out of control. I can't believe it."

"It happens." A swift look of guilt swept his face.

Knowing very well that Finn's life could have went the direction of Macon's, I took his hand in mine. Caressing his palm, I ventured more into the topic. "What makes it happen?" When he looked at me a bit bewildered, I continued. "I want to know. I can't imagine becoming so addicted to something that's illegal or that bad for you. Why? Why can't you just say 'no?' Can you explain it? I'm ...I'm not judging you." I grasped tighter...more secure. "I just want to understand."

"It's to mask some type of pain—sometimes physical but a lot of times emotional. I didn't actually get pleasure out of drugs like so many people do. That's why when the docs figured out what was really going on with me..." He glanced over at me again, a wave of embarrassment washing over his face. He hated talking about what he considered a flaw.

"Thank God they did," I offered. "Thank God they looked beyond. What would have happened if they hadn't, and they totally disregarded everything else ... every other wonderful thing about you?"

"I wouldn't have you. I wouldn't be alive."

He said it so plainly and so matter-of-factly, it nearly broke my heart. And the way he responded so quickly made me certain that he had thought of that question probably more than once in his life. But what definitively tore my heart in pieces was that I realized his answer was most likely the honest truth. And I squeezed his hand hard to bring him comfort and reassurance.

He managed a mini-smile and continued. "Once I was regulated with the proper meds, I have never, ever even had the slightest of cravings. But for others, they don't think the good feeling they experience when high or drunk can be substituted with anything else. They need that euphoria ... constantly."

"I saw that with my dad. It didn't matter that he had a wife who loved him and two kids who needed him. He loved that damn bottle more." Finn brought my hand up to his mouth for a kiss, and I moved onto the next person who had found too much solace in a bottle. "But, Will, he's not like that."

"No," my husband agreed. "Will only slipped for a little bit because of…because of…."

Finn didn't need to finish the sentence with the proper noun. I already knew it. Wyatt.

"And Will is strong." Finn continued. "He's strong like you."

"I don't feel strong around here. This place is *my* pain. If I hadn't gotten out, I can't imagine what *my* life would have been like."

"Baby…"

"You know, can we just drive for a while? I just can't go back to the house right now … not right away. I … I need a break." The house I grew up in held so many painful memories. I needed a breather between that and the confrontation on the Altman's front porch.

"I'll drive for as long as you want me to, Beauty. We could even go straight back to New York if you wanted."

"No." I managed a semi-laugh. "I couldn't do that to my mom. Besides, our stuff is still at her house. And it will be fun to see the trick-or-treaters tonight, right? I just need to step away and breathe for a little bit."

"Have any place in mind?"

"Nope. Just drive. Getting lost right now kinda sounds good. You all right with that?"

"I'm with you," he replied.

We continued down a few country roads, soaking in the silence of the crisp autumn air and the beauty of the colorful leaves that were decorating more of the ground than the trees. We were becoming not only physically lost, but lost in our own thoughts. I know mine were of desperation for a child who needed my help so urgently. And, if I had to guess, Finn's were of helping and protecting me.

After a little while, I made a second request. "See that

171

convenience store place over there?"

"Yeah."

"You mind if we stop?"

"Sure. You need something?"

"I need to pee!"

"Don't you always." Finn laughed a cleansing laugh but obliged by pulling the car into the lot.

"Hey, you try having this pressure on your bladder all the time."

"I know." He punctuated his statement by squeezing my hand.

"You want me to get you something?" I asked, noting how he was scanning the parking lot, which appeared pretty full.

"Yeah. You mind? I don't feel like going in." He maneuvered the car into a spot and put it in park.

"I get it," I reassured him, knowing the possibility of running into fans. "Coffee?" I asked.

"Yeah. Maybe something small to munch on, too?"

"Okay, Munch," I teased, calling him by the childhood nickname his sister had given him over his love of snacks.

"Uh-huh…" He softly chuckled back.

"I can meet you at that white picnic table way over there as long as no one is around." I pointed to an obscure area down a path and near a tree.

"Sounds like a plan. Thanks, Beauty."

I scurried to the bathroom first. Sure, pregnancy had taken ahold, but my nerves were also wreaking havoc on my bladder. Next up was coffee and brownies. After paying, I turned from the register and noticed a woman, probably about my age, wearing a Finn Murphy concert T-shirt. Finn's black and white photo, complete with cowboy hat and guitar, was staring right at me. I always found myself in awe when a random reminder of my husband's fame appeared. Despite being on tour and attending awards ceremonies and other functions with him, I still didn't see Finn like that. He was my love … my friend …

my knight in shining armor.

"You a fan?" the woman asked after she caught me looking.

I smiled. "The biggest."

"Yeah." She sighed. "Really missed not seeing him this summer. Can't wait 'til next."

"Me either," I agreed, and snuck out to meet the magical music maker himself.

Luckily, either no one had discovered the picnic table or they thought it was too cold to sit outside. Because I found Finn sitting there alone, facing my approach. There was definitely a chill in the air, but nothing a warm beverage couldn't cure. That and the comfort of a man's arm wrapped around your shoulders.

Sliding onto the bench next to him, I handed Finn the coffee and brownie. "What's that?" I asked, peering down at the image on the electronic tablet in his hands.

"Statute of limitations," he said plainly and then took a sip of his dark, strong coffee.

"For wha..." I started but had read far enough to know the answer.

It was Pennsylvania's laws on felony rape in the first degree. I tried hard not to have the images of that night at the waterfall flash back into my mind. But words like "unconscious," "victim," and "intoxicants" pushed them right to the forefront.

"That's not what happened, baby." I separated slightly from him and looked into his sad eyes, knowing he only wanted to think of me as the purest of pure.

"Lara, you said you don't remember it. You woke up on the sofa the next morning. You didn't know what, or who..." His mouth couldn't finish the words, and his eyes couldn't stay on mine.

"No." I softly put my hand on his while I tried to erase the inevitable images of Macon and his friends that night.

"And I know you told me you thought there was something in that punch he gave you to drink."

"That's true." I sighed. "But, Finn, I don't want to bring all of this up again. I never did. Besides, look…" I pointed further down in the article. "It says the statute of limitations is twelve years. It would be too late, anyway."

"I get that. I do … everything you're saying. It's just …I want to take it all away for you."

I tossed my head, trying to shake away the tears. But they were starting to fall almost as rapidly as the colorful leaves swirling in the wind. The day, the trip, the past week or so were just too much.

"It'll be okay," he said, putting the tablet and his coffee down and drawing me into his chest. "Don't cry. God, this is what makes me so irate. It fires me up. I hate what this is doing to you." I could hear the irritation in his voice gain strength. Yet, it was such a contrast to the smooth rhythmic stroking of his hand on the back of my head.

I pulled away so that I could face him straight on. "I'm not crying because of that. I'm crying because of all you do for me, especially when you shouldn't have to."

"I just don't want you stressed."

"I'm—" I started with a senseless denial.

He looked me straight on. "You were grinding your teeth last night. You haven't done that in God, what, a couple years?"

Since right before we got engaged, I silently acknowledged. It took me all those years—from middle school on—to finally stop … to finally feel relaxed. "I was?" I was dismayed but not, when I thought of it, all that shocked. My location of horrors was the trigger for sure.

"Yeah." He softly caressed my jawline. "I'm telling you, Lara, if that mother fucker doesn't want to man up, that's one thing, but to put his hands on you …to say—"

"Finn, he's not worth you getting this upset—now or before. I hated—"

"I know." He cut me off, knowing the psychological impact that physical violence had on me. "I'm sorry you had to see that, and I'm sorry if I scared you." When I hesitated with a response, Finn, with eyes asking for forgiveness, said, "I know I did."

"A little," I admitted. "But I was anxious to start out with." When he placed his understanding hand gently on top of mine, I continued. "I can't believe he might be that little boy's only hope."

"You can't think that way. Maybe his brother…" His voice trailed off as he took a bite of his brownie.

I noticed how Finn never seemed to call Miller or Macon by their actual names. Was it too real for him that way? I knew what the mere thought of Audrey did to me.

"God, I hope Miller can somehow do something. I don't know that there's anyone else."

The child's only other biological aunt or uncle was my brother Lane. Lane knew nothing about me being pregnant or giving a child up for adoption, since he had already moved away when all of that had gone down. I would have certainly sacrificed my secret and humiliation if I thought it would have helped the kid. But, again, there was an issue with Lane being a donor. Because of a horrific hockey accident in high school, Lane had fractured his hipbone. Back then, what it meant was losing his athletic scholarship. Flash forward, what it meant was his ineligibility to be a bone marrow transplant donor.

"Lara, you've done everything you possibly could. It's in God's hands. It's time to take care of yourself. Besides, there are other important things to think about." When I didn't say anything, he nudged me.

"I know." I wrapped my cardigan tighter around me.

"You were supposed to ask 'like what?'"

"I know, Finn." I was sad. I was tired. But I would never forget our child. "I have to take care of the baby."

"Well, yeah, but also important things like eating bonbons and getting massages."

I swiped at a straggling tear. How damn lucky I was to have a man who knew when to push me and when I just needed a simple, funny jab. Grateful for him, I decided to play along. Although, it was the absolute truth.

"And my gorgeous, sweet husband who is going to give me both."

"Maybe at the same time." He smiled that smile that only Finn Murphy could. It was the one that charmed the heck out of concert T-shirt wearing women and, most importantly, his wife.

"Counting on it."

"I love you, Lara. I don't do things for you because I have to. I want to. I wouldn't know how not to."

"I thank God every day that you entered my life ... not just once but twice."

"I'm sure there's probably some exceptions to those days."

"Even on those, Finn."

***

Laying there in my childhood bedroom that night, I was wide awake listening to Finn's familiar soft slumber snore. It broke my heart knowing that I had dragged the love of my life into all of this mess with me ... that he had to meet the worst spider of them all—Macon Altman. Of course I knew Finn was aware of every sordid detail of that time and loved me in spite of it. But, yet, I was still embarrassed for him to be witness to the ugliness that had once been Lara Faulkner. And now that he had come face to face with the reality of it, how could he not be affected? How could he not look at me differently?

"Lara," his voice whispered to me as if he were dreaming. "Go to sleep, baby. I love you ... forever."

I couldn't turn around to face him without falling out of the diminutive bed. Besides, his arms were cocooning me securely in place. There was no way for him to have known what I had been thinking in that dark, silent room. But his insight into my internal thoughts was dead-on, and

I knew that was because of our unmistakable connection of love. And because of that, I was able to rest.

***

When we got back from Pittsburgh, Finn only had a couple days before he had to fly to Nashville for the CMA Awards. He normally would have been down there days before, but he postponed his arrival because of everything that was going on with me. Not that anyone was aware of his reason.

Hearing the last part of his phone conversation, which was surely dealing with just that topic, I said, "I bet your team liked you a lot more before you and I were a couple."

Finn placed the phone on the table and reclaimed his seat next to me on the sofa. "*I* didn't like me before you." He manipulated my body to turn slightly away so that he could massage my shoulders. "And, no, they're good. They love you. They're just finally earning the momentous amount of money I pay them." He was teasing, but I did know they were compensated well, as they duly deserved.

"I know it was a big deal for you to miss this time in Nashville and come with me instead."

"Wasn't even a decision to be made."

In reality, it was an easy year to legitimately skip some of the pre-hoopla days before the CMAs. He wasn't presenting any awards, and he had decided not to perform, either. The latter was mostly due to the fact that he didn't want to spotlight Carter's absence. And there wasn't a replacement drummer— temporary or otherwise. Finn and Carter were kind of at a standstill on what to do about the matter. Carter's mom appeared to be really making strides with her recovery. But my husband had confided in me on our journey back home that, while he couldn't imagine playing without Carter, he also didn't know how long he could wait. He had to think of his career, too.

I turned back to face him, forcing his hands to drop to

his sides. "I know you have a lot going on. I feel like I haven't been here for you. It's just … I've just been so overwhelmed by all of this."

"With due reason."

"I'm sorry we haven't been together."

"We were just in a car for over six hours. How much more togetherness do you want?" he teased, knowing very well I was talking about being intimate.

"You know what I mean," I lamented.

He kissed me sweetly. "I do."

"I just want you to know—"

It wasn't that I didn't love him. God, it was so much the opposite. I was just so …

He interrupted my verbal and non-verbal thoughts. "I know, Lara. I know." His hand caressed my face, putting me at ease.

"I'm sorry I can't make it to the CMAs."

"Love my mom, but she is not a good substitute at all." He joked about his mother being his date for the awards ceremony.

"At least it's not Audrey." I attempted to tease back, but it didn't really work.

"Lara…"

"What? I'm kidding. She doesn't threaten me."

"I'm not sure about that." He shook his head. "But there's no reason she should. Regardless, when I saw her at the morning show, she told me she kind of hoped her station wasn't nominated this year."

"Why?"

"Because it's wedding week, and she wouldn't be able to make it."

"Wedding week? What wedding?" Was that a radio promotion?

"Hers," he answered nonchalantly.

"You didn't tell me that!" I practically screeched at the shock of my nemesis being off the market.

"You didn't really give me a chance." I could tell he

wanted to laugh, but knew better.

"Hmmm…" I stalled for a mini-moment, jokingly thinking of our no-omission clause. "I think you withheld that a little on purpose, Finn Murphy."

"Maybe," he admitted. "But it's not like she's ever been something we can talk about casually."

"Married. Hmmm." I let that thought ponder in my brain. "Well, good for her," I said out loud, while internally wondering if she would even go through with it.

"Uh-huh." I think my husband was trying to keep it simple, knowing what a landmine Audrey was for both of us.

"I happen to like being married," I said in a semi-seductive tone.

"Me, too," he agreed. "And, just so you know, I looked. Her station wasn't nominated. I didn't even want you to think about the possibility of me running into her." He knew me so damn well.

Relieved, I light-heartedly brought up another ex. "What about Dorothy? She's not in the music industry too, is she?"

He nudged me with his hand. "Geez! No. I don't know. I have no idea. Besides, you really don't have anything to worry about there."

"Why not?"

"She came out of the closet a couple years after high school."

"What? Your date? The prom queen was gay?" I spouted out. "Did you know?"

"No. No one did. I'm not even sure she knew back then."

"I guess you didn't get any action on prom night then, huh?" I couldn't help but giggle.

He shook his head. "No."

"Well, you might get some now." I smiled.

I curled into my husband, laying my lips on the back of his neck. He tilted his head back for a moment, letting me taste him. When he turned to face me, I did the same. Feeling that magnetic force between us that had been there long before we ever connected as lovers, our mouths met one another's. The tenderness in our kissing was therapeutic, releasing, and full of pure love. Simultaneously, we started on the buttons and straps of each other's tops. I then coiled my finger around Finn's belt loop and dipped my fingers onto his hips.

"Those hands on my hips, Lara," he warned with a sexy smile before standing us up, pulling my dress down to the floor, and sweeping me into his arms in a romantic move.

"Finn," I cried out. "I'm getting too heavy."

"Hardly." He smiled as I grabbed onto his flexed arms.

"Okay, He-Man, can I take the bonbons with us, then?"

"Definitely," he answered with a nose scrunch and smile before squatting slightly to allow me to swipe the chocolaty treat off the coffee table. Finn had lived up to his promise, and had the bonbons and his magnificent hands ready that night after dinner. "Besides, Cincy won."

I laughed at the reference to our ongoing bet—one we had started even before we were married. Finn, the ultimate Bengals football fan, would get to lick chocolate off my body if Cincinnati won. And if they lost, I got a massage.

I let my tongue lap in his mouth as we entered the bedroom and cascaded onto our bed. When his lips found the back of my neck and his hand strummed my thigh, I called out his name. And then we were beautifully closer than close can be. And, for that moment, everything was good—our baby and us. If only everything else could be, too.

CHAPTER FOURTEEN

I held onto that feeling the next day while I was at work, and he was in Nashville getting ready for the biggest award show of the year. A full workload worked to my advantage that day. Not only did I not have the luxury of missing my strong, wonderful man, but I didn't have time to think about that poor boy who was struggling for life and a bone marrow match. When we returned from Pittsburgh, I let his family's representative know what had transpired, with apologies that I didn't have better news. I also had to respect Finn's wishes and wait at least a few weeks to make the decision about testing our unborn child—and with Finn, seven months meant at least eight.

Finn was texting me so much during the CMA ceremony, I almost felt like I was there. He ended up winning Entertainer of the Year for the second consecutive year. The shocked look on his face upon the announcement of his name was priceless. He had been surprised and overwhelmed the previous year with his first win. But he truly didn't expect a second, simply because he had cut out his summer tour and hadn't been as visible the past few months. The award, however, spoke of the power of his talent and the loved person that he was.

His acceptance speech was simple but heartfelt. After acknowledging his blushing mom in the audience, he spoke into the camera to me. "There is nothing generic about you or how I feel about you and, yet, it is so simple…I love you, Lara. I'll be home soon."

I smiled at his thoughtful remembrance of our speech talk on Grammy night and then tried to call him. But I knew all about the flurry of activity that happens at award ceremonies, especially when you win the coveted prize. So, getting his voice mail, I echoed his words and gave my congrats before going to sleep—my heart full of love and pride.

***

Finn kept true to his promise and came home right after the CMAs. While much of his time was occupied with press releases, phone calls, and scheduling, at least he was home. I was looking forward to us finally getting a true chance to relax and catch up with each other that weekend.

Mentally planning our dinner, I walked in the house on Friday with groceries in hand. I had texted Finn that I was going to be a little late because I was going to the grocery store after work. When I got no reply, I wondered if he was slightly upset due to our "leaving work on time" agreement.

Hence why I started my entrance with, "Remember, you love me, and I wasn't working—"

What I walked into wasn't a little reaction, though. It was more of a tirade, and one that I did not understand. I found Finn in the great room, uncharacteristically throwing his phone and picking up his tablet.

"Jesus Christ!" he shouted in the direction of the electronic device. "What the—?"

"What?" I beseeched, after setting the bags down and approaching him.

His eyes, more guarded than gorgeous gray, blazed my direction as he handed me his tablet. When his phone started to chime across the room, Finn groaned and went to retrieve it. In turn, I looked at the tablet display. My being late surely hadn't registered on the Finn Richter scale— not when I read the devastating details displayed on the screen. There was a clearly biased, one-sided article all about Finn ... and his altercation with Macon.

"Oh, my God," I managed to say, while reading the article.

It was obvious that Macon had gone to the press. There was a picture of him with bruises and cuts on his face. He blamed Finn for the wounds and called him crazy. On that word, I flinched and looked up at my husband. This article was the worst thing that could happen to a man who fought so hard to keep his personal life private, especially one who had been diagnosed with an undisclosed mental illness. I ached for Finn immediately. I wanted to go to him... to reach out to him, but I had to finish the article. Selfishly, I needed to know if any of our secrets had come to light.

To my relief, it was a short story. Its main focus was the photo and the accusation that country music's reigning king was guilty of assault and battery. I could feel his stress and anger from clear across the room as Finn talked on the phone. He was continuously looking over at me with the most curious, odd expression. Once he got off, I carefully placed his tablet on the coffee table and slowly walked toward him.

"How ...how did...?" While words were coming from my mouth, I was still too stunned to form a comprehensible sentence.

"Get away from me. Get away from me right now," he growled in a troubled, low voice that I barely recognized.

Shocked by what sounded like contempt, I did take a step away. I flashed back to Memorial Day. He had told me then if he ever asked me to get away from him that I should listen. He had been convinced that he had hurt me that weekend. And by the look on his face and the words coming from his mouth, I guessed he once again feared the same. But I knew back then that he wouldn't hurt me and that I couldn't leave him in pain. And nothing had changed.

"Finn—"

"Lara ..." he warned.

"Finn? What? I want to help you." I tried. I was scared for him ...not of him. I didn't want him going off the rails because of one illiterate son-of-a-bitch. "Let me."

"You've done enough," he said with a detached tone in his voice.

"I'm not sure what—" I was starting to get a feeling that I had not experienced since I left home after high school— that fear of the sudden explosion ... the feeling of not being safe ... the feeling of my father. Instinctively, I took a step back but remained calm, only to be interrupted by Finn answering his phone once more.

He started pacing almost uncontrollably. I was actually glad for the mini-break. It gave me a chance to breathe and absorb all that I had to take in from the moment I first entered the room. Finn finally hung up the phone and looked at me. I know I had that doe-eyed look on my face because, despite the respite, I was still in shock from what had been written and publicized in that article. But more than that, I was terribly distraught that my husband was so personally and traumatically affected by something that was a result of my choices.

"How can they just post that?" I asked once he was off the phone again. "They didn't contact you. That's like slander or something, right? You didn't do all that damage. You hit him once. You did not give him all of those injuries. We know that. What did he do? Did he purposefully hurt himself to hurt you?" I was thinking how hard Finn worked on his reputation and how this inaccurate representation threatened to bring it all down with one puff from the big bad wolf.

"Shit! I can't believe this," was his non-answer. "I can't believe we went there in the first place. Damn it!"

And there it was. It was because of me. It was all because of me.

"I'm sorry," I offered genuinely. "What's gonna happen?

"My legal team is already working on it." He appeared a tad calmer, but I think it was more because his mind was so internally distracted. Then the doorbell outwardly distracted him. Going to look at the front door camera, he said, "Well, there they are."

"Who?" I asked not understanding the intrusion.

No one ever rang our doorbell. We lived in a gated community. Obviously, it was someone Finn had expected.

"The cops."

"The cops?" What the hell?

"Yes, Lara. Not as quick as social media but…"

He didn't need to be condescending. I just didn't understand. It was all coming at me at once. The magnitude of the situation and its consequences just hadn't caught up to my swirling brain.

"They're not going to arrest you, are they?" I asked, thinking surely there was some other explanation.

"I don't know. Just let me deal with it. Go in the bedroom."

I looked at him with the slightest furling of my eyebrows. He knew I hated being dismissed. "But wh—"

"Just… Christ! God, just do it, okay?" he bellowed, causing me to twitch and jump.

Despite his outrage and controlling demeanor, I just wanted to hug him. I wanted to put my arms around him and somehow squeeze the pain away. But I knew that wasn't the solution. I bit my upper lip and nodded my head slowly up and down. When he dipped his eyes slightly in acknowledgement of his outburst and headed to the door, I honored his plea and escaped to the master bedroom.

I wanted to sob with a force worthy of Niagara Falls. But I knew I couldn't. The idea was for me to be invisible. So, I clutched my pillow up to my face and burst out a very muffled scream. It was an odd mixture of fear for my husband and hatred for Macon that brought the stifled reaction. It was also regret that I was the one who had brought the two of them together in the first place.

Wanting to know what was transpiring between Finn and the police, I managed to calm myself down, and I tried to listen. From what I could tell, Finn was not being charged with anything … yet. Macon's credibility was in question because he waited a while to make the accusation, and it was well documented when Finn was in Nashville versus the Pittsburgh area. I heard Finn admit to hitting Macon on Halloween but denied causing all the trauma that the photo portrayed. Something else must have happened after our visit, and Macon was totally taking advantage of his chance to screw with a celebrity for publicity. When Finn emphasized that he was defending me, I inched a little closer to the door.

"Was your wife injured, Mr. Murphy?"

"Physically? No," Finn answered.

"But you two were the ones who approached him?"

"We were in town visiting my wife's mother, and she was looking up old friends."

"So she is friends with the victim?" questioned the second of the two voices that were interrogating my husband.

"Well, I wouldn't say friends, and I most certainly wouldn't say victim." To give Finn credit, he kept his voice just at the right tone— not elevated and not too light. He was surely using his performer skills to pull that off because I knew how insanely outraged he was.

"Mr. Mur—" voice number one started.

But Finn answered the question more succinctly. "She

was friends with his brother."

"We understand high school sweethearts," voice number two chimed in like he was a member of the press core.

"They dated," Finn clarified because in his mind—and mine—there was a distinct difference from dating and being sweethearts. "See you know all this. I'm telling you exactly what went down. If he is saying anything different—"

"Is your wife available to speak with?" the first officer asked, and I froze like I had committed a crime.

"She's pregnant, and because of complications in the past, she is supposed to stay away from stress." Finn's honesty was intact until he added, "She's trying to nap."

"I might have heard something about her trouble before." Yep, Officer Number Two was definitely a *People* magazine reader. "Sorry."

"If we need something from her, we'll be in touch," said the other cop, but I could tell just by the tone in his voice that he wanted to be on Finn's side.

"Is that it then?" I heard Finn ask.

"For now," offered the second officer. "We'll be in touch one way or the other."

"Thanks. Let me walk you to … " Finn started but all three of the voices faded as they must have made their way to the front door.

I expected him to come to me then … to let me know what happened and to talk. But he didn't. So, I waited. But still no Finn. I wanted to cry. However, I put my own feelings aside and thought about him and all that he was experiencing. It would have been torture for anyone to be falsely accused of something. But to have that happen and be in the national spotlight? How can you deal with that without anger? And then to throw in Finn's diagnosis of PTSD … Even with his regular meds and meditation practices, I wasn't sure how he was going to hold up to the pressure of his world spinning apart.

I splashed some water on my face so I didn't look as awful as I felt and ventured out to see what I could do. I found him on the back deck overlooking our private yard and pool. His back was turned, so he didn't see me approach. Just as I was about to say something, I realized he was, once again, on the phone.

"Yeah. I'll be there." He spoke in a way that told me some of the fight had been drained from him. And who could blame him after such an upheaval? "My flight gets in around eleven tomorrow. So I guess I'll head straight there."

What? What flight? Tomorrow? That was news to me. God, where was he going now in the middle of all of this?

"Yeah," he continued to whomever was on the other end. "I know." His heavy exhale alluded to his exhaustion. "Look, I know. It's done. I had nothing to hide. I just told them the truth. We'll deal with it...I don't know... I know." The exhaustion was revving back up to agitation. "That's not for you to worry about... I know. All right. I got a lot ...I'll see you tomorrow." With that, he hung up the phone and placed it on the deck railing. He ran his fingers through his hair before dropping his head. Without turning around, somehow knowing that I was there, he spoke this time to me. "Say it."

"You're leaving?"

"Yeah. I've gotta go home."

"What?"

"I have to. I've got to go to Nashville and deal with this ...this mess."

Did he even realize what he had said? Home? Nashville was his home? He looked to his phone, which was threatening to vibrate off the ledge. Couldn't we have even a minute without being interrupted? And, during that minute, couldn't he at least turn around and look at me?

"I thought this was your home," I said meekly, feeling extremely hurt.

"God, Lara. C'mon. Really? Really?" At least that got

him to turn around, but only after he threw his fists angrily onto the deck rail. His dead-on stare told me not to further provoke what I hoped was just semantics regarding residences.

But I still didn't understand his leaving. "Can't you deal with it here?" I tried.

His answer was plain and abrupt. "No."

"Maybe I can go with you," I proposed but couldn't imagine a scenario where that would be ideal between flying and work.

"No." His response was just as firm.

"Wh—"

"It's best." He slightly turned away again to glance at his phone.

"No, it's not." How could us being apart be what was best?

"You shouldn't have anything to do with this."

What did that mean? Was that a dig? Because I had *everything* to do with the mess that he was in. Did he want or maybe need to be away from me? Why was it suddenly so hard to understand this man, who was my one and only love … my soulmate?

Assuming the worst, I said, regretfully, "But I did. That's the real reason you're going. Admit it."

"Lara…" The tone in his one word, my name, told me he didn't want to be pushed.

"Finn, we promised we wouldn't do that …we wouldn't leave."

Between Finn's fear of being left and my trust issues, especially when it involved someone who was angry, we were a complete combined mess. "Stop." There was much more force this time.

I started to plead. "I'm sorry."

"I know you are." His voice was a little softer and he, once again, turned fully around to look at me. "But, quite frankly, it doesn't matter. It happened."

Suddenly chilled, I crossed my arms over my chest and

tentatively asked, "Do you think the cops will question me?"

"I hope not."

"What? You don't trust me to back you up?"

"I trust you with my life." His words were slow and methodical and should have been reassuring. But he was still so distant. And he was still leaving.

"You just don't like me that much right now."

Struggling for the right words, I could tell he was exasperated but, yet, wanted to explain. "Listen, I'm upset. I think I have a right to be. And I need to take care of this. I can't let this escalate. I can't let this ... God!" His hands were visibly clenched as the realization seeped back into his brain. "I can't let this derail my career. I'm stressed. And I don't want you any more involved in it. Period." His voice started to rev back up. "I need you to just do what I'm asking. Please. Damn it, Lara, I told you before, you need to know to just let me be."

"I ..." I took a step toward him still having that undeniable desire to help. But the intensity radiating from his body told me to stop. "Okay," I surrendered.

"Okay," he echoed in a dismissive tone.

I couldn't debate with him anymore. He had asked me to back away now twice. It wasn't doing either of us any good. Never mind derailing his career, I couldn't let the stress derail him. Or, for that matter, us.

As I opened the patio door, I heard him yell out a general "Fuck!"

I paused squeezing my eyes tightly shut. But I knew there was nothing else at that point that I could say or do. So I continued to close the door poignantly behind me.

I decided to make the dinner that I had only a little while before imagined would be a relaxing meal. God, what had happened in such a short period of time? Cooking, I concluded, would at least keep my mind occupied. Besides, even if I didn't feel like it, I knew the baby inside me needed the nutrients. I heard the patio door open and close and then open once more a couple moments later. I could hear him start to play something on his guitar. But even in the strings, I could detect the frustration—the clipped and plangent sound … the missed notes.

When the landline rang, I paused my cooking and winced, hoping that it wasn't a reporter who had somehow retrieved that number. Thankfully, though, it was my in-laws digits on the caller ID. They would sometimes call the landline because Mrs. Murphy felt like it signified Finn and I together. She had a sentimental heart that way. I cringed at the irony and picked up the phone, anticipating that they wanted to speak with both of us because they had heard the news. It didn't take long, though, to realize it was truly just a social call and that they had no idea what hell their son was going through. But I knew it wasn't my place to tell them. And I also knew that Finn needed the calming force of his family. So, I gingerly approached the patio. My husband set his guitar aside and looked at me.

"Baby," I said with caution. "Your folks are on the phone. I think you need to talk to them."

"Did you call them?" he asked in an almost accusatory tone, like I had gone behind his back and called in reinforcements.

"No. They just happened to—"

"They don't know, then?"

"No. You need to tell them."

"Yeah." He picked up his guitar and followed me back into the house.

"I'll give you some privacy."

I'm not sure why I said that, besides just needing to say something. After all, the phone was mobile. And, in addition, the house was huge.

"That's all right, you don't have—"

"Gonna finish making dinner. Get some when you want."

"Hey," he said this time speaking into the phone.

"Yeah, she's fine, but there's something I need to tell you."

I watched as he walked up the stairs and the conversation with his folks started fading from earshot. Did he realize where he was going? His mind was surely so splintered at the moment. But somewhere deep down, he seemed to be craving innocence. It was innocence that talking with his childhood heroes could provide. And it was innocence that sitting in the future room of our soon-to-be newborn could offer. It was a sacred room, but one most worthy of its cause. It was the room, after all, where I had also found refuge when I first learned that I was pregnant again.

I prayed that talking with them would bring some kind of calmness into his soul, the way it usually did in times of crisis. I did not listen. I did not pry. And after a while, I ate dinner in the solitude of the kitchen, only knowing that his conversation had ended because I heard the guitar playing once again. This time the tunes were more melancholy, but at least controlled.

CHAPTER FIFTEEN

Hoping that Finn would find his way to me at some point, I took a shower and then decided to start reading our neighborhood's book club book. I cozied up under the covers of our bed and got lost in the make-believe world of a group of friends who decide to start life over by moving to Europe and reinventing themselves with fake names, families, and careers. In that moment, I personally thought it sounded like an excellent idea. When I actually began coming up with aliases for myself, though, I decided to put the book down, turn off the lights, close my eyes, and, instead, start mentally listing all the things that I, Lara Murphy, had to be thankful for.

Somewhere mid-list, Finn made his way into our bedroom. As he silently entered the adjoining bathroom, I added *not sleeping in different rooms* to my internal list. I reclosed my eyes and felt him crawl into his side of the bed. It was still a little early, but I think we both wanted the day to be done. Even though I was lying on my side, facing the opposite direction of my husband, I knew he was stretched out on his back.

He exhaled a strong, cleansing breath and remained silent for a few moments before saying, "I wish you were asleep."

Great, I thought sarcastically, he still didn't want to converse. "I could pretend to be if that's what you want." Admittedly, I said it in a bit of a snarky tone. Not only was I frustrated with not knowing how to help, but I was feeling a little emotionally rejected.

"No," he softly grumbled his own frustration. "That's not what I meant." He paused and then tried again. "Besides, you never could fool me with your pretend sleeping act."

I just couldn't read him, and with every word having been an emotional landmine since I entered our home, I kept it simple. "Oh, no?"

"Nope. That day after I first kissed you …right before my college graduation? I came into your room and you pretended to be asleep."

Geez! What? He was bringing up something that took place a decade ago … something so genuine in our hearts … one of our milestones that could have been so much more had it not been for my unwillingness to believe in love back then. All this time I had no idea that he knew I had been avoiding him that day.

"You knew that?" I finally turned and faced him.

His face was beaten by the day, but his voice was soft. "Yeah. I knew you didn't want to deal with what happened … how I felt. And I just let it be. Probably shouldn't have." He let that settle in my mind, knowing how we both had made a mistake by our actions that night long ago—silly denials that cost us seven years. "But, yes, I knew." After another slight pause, he brought us back to the current day and the harsh reality of our life. "I'll probably be gone for at least a couple days until we see what the press does."

"I understand."

I didn't completely. But everything seemed already determined. And there was no sense agitating the situation further.

He took a breath before speaking again. "Please don't fight me on this, but I talked with Nola. The three of them are coming over while I'm gone. They'll be here tomorrow morning." He continued his monologue in such a way that I knew he thought I would have an interjection. "I only told them the very basics— just what's been reported. The idea is that the press follows me to Tennessee. But if there is even an inkling that they are trying something with any of you, you let me know. If that happens, no work or school for you or Kelsea."

"Finn—" I started.

Instantly, he cut me off as if anticipating an antagonistic response. "I don't want to have to worry about you."

"I wasn't going to argue." I was actually kind of impressed that he thought things through as he much as he did. But I shouldn't have been; he was looking after his family. "It's just …it's not me I'm worried about."

While placing his hand on my stomach, Finn slowly blinked his naturally gray-hued eyes. But it wasn't the baby I was concerned about, either. It was him. I was worried about Finn, and I feared this was just the beginning of what he was going to have to endure.

I placed my hand on top of his, so that his was sandwiched between the baby bump and my palm. Did he understand that he was our glue? That he was what held us together? He needed to be strong and not give in to the negativity but instead feel our little trifecta of love. He took his other hand and spread it openly on the top of my head. He added slight pressure, which felt like an idyllic security blanket or a bulletproof vest for my brain. Then, right after catching my eyes with his, he gently moved that palm down to my face and held it there, essentially making me close my eyes. All he had wanted me to do since he first climbed in that bed was to relax and rest. I didn't know how I could. But for his sake, I tried and added one more thing to my gratitude list: *the sweet comfort of a secure hand.*

***

Neither of us got a decent night's sleep. I had felt the bed dip and expand as he had gotten up periodically throughout the night to pace. I noticed each time he checked the messages on his phone. He hadn't known I was watching. Or so I thought. Maybe he had. After the college story he had relayed, it was most likely that he did.

The combination of a lack of sleep and Finn being downright neurotically anxious put my emotions on overdrive as he was preparing to leave that next morning. I still didn't know where we stood. I knew he was upset, but I didn't know how big of a part of that was directed toward me. I knew he had every right to be. I had put him in the predicament, after all.

When Nola and her family were coming through the gates of our neighborhood, I finally realized everything was really happening. I looked down at Finn's packed bags right there in the foyer, and I totally lost it. I almost sagged to the floor I was crying so hard.

"God, Lara. Please. Don't. I can't leave when you're like this."

"Then don't."

Turning around in a circle, he partially put his arm out to me and then took it back. "I have to. We talked about this."

"I can't stand that I did this. I can't stand that you're leaving because of me…because of something I did."

"Look, when it comes down to it, it's me. I did it. I should have known he would try this shit."

"You wouldn't have done it, though, or even have been there if it wasn't for me."

"But I was, and I did. I just don't want you to be a part of it anymore."

I realized what a scene I was creating, and I understood

that I was only making a horrible situation worse. So, I tried. I mangled my fists up to my eyes and rubbed hard, willing the tears to stop flowing. And then I told him something that I hadn't even realized was subconsciously in my brain. "But you haven't kissed me."

Standing in front of me, he started shaking his head slowly back and forth. He was totally spent and deflated. "We're not back to that again."

I dipped my head in embarrassment. I supposed we were. Somewhere in the series of events of that previous night, I had reverted back to that insecure girl— the one who had reintroduced herself to Finn a couple years before and thought he didn't care because he hadn't kissed her when she was expecting him to. As it had turned out, nothing could have been further from the truth. Now, though, we were past that ... or we should have been.

He took his hands in mine and kindly, but tiredly, commanded, "Look at me."

But I was crying again, and I couldn't bring myself to meet his eyes. "I—"

"Uncle Finn!" Kelsea barreling though the door interrupted us instantly.

While Finn teetered from having Kelsea suddenly sucked onto his side, I took the opportunity to turn around and rapidly wipe my eyes. Via the open door, I could hear Will in the driveway telling Nola to hurry Finn along. I turned around then just as Nola was entering the foyer.

Oblivious to the drama that was unfolding around her, Kelsea ran to me. "Aunt Lara, this is so cool that we're having a sleepover at your house."

Nola officially entered and immediately hugged her brother. "Remember, you're strong. You are the best. You're more than this."

"Thanks," he said to her, while looking at me with concern over our unfinished conversation.

Breaking their embrace, Nola jokingly said, "Yeah, well,

don't let it go to that already big head of yours."

Not in the mood for their usual sibling banter, Finn instead turned to me. "Lar?"

Kneeling down at Kelsea's level, I was holding onto her more than she was holding onto me. "Have a safe trip," I managed to get out to my husband.

"I—" Finn started but was not allowed to continue.

"Listen, man, I'm not like one of your personal chauffeurs or assistants." Will entered, playfully hitting his brother-in-law. "I'll drive you to the airport, but I'm not carrying your bags." He looked my direction and tilted his head with a "Hey, Lara." He then started pushing Finn out the door. "C'mon, man. We're super crunched for time. I just heard there's some kind of construction closure."

"We got this," Nola reassured Finn as I nodded a confirmation.

With that, he sagged his shoulders and picked up his bag. I waited until he walked out the door and got into Will's car. And then I lost it—round II.

***

Nola forgave me being a terrible hostess and instead took it upon herself to reverse the roles, for which I was grateful. She let me escape to the master bedroom to recollect, regroup, and reenergize while making sure that Kelsea was sufficiently occupied. I eventually reemerged and accepted my sister-in-law's offer to make us some tea.

With Kelsea mesmerized by her electronic tablet, Nola tried to encourage me to tell her the details of what had led to the sudden family-bonding weekend. I didn't have the energy or desire to delve into it, and I wanted to respect whatever Finn had decided on regarding disclosure with his family. Although obviously curious, Nola seemed to understand that decision, at least for the time being. Instead, we sat and talked about mindless, suburban-type things like getting addicted to *Candy Crush Saga*, PTO, and whether to switch cell phone carriers.

That was, until Will eventually returned and walked back in the door. "God, they weren't kidding when they said that section was going to be a traffic nightmare."

"Did he get off okay?" Nola asked her husband.

"Yeah, dropped him off with just enough time. Though I'm sure Mr. Magic Music wouldn't have had a problem boarding last minute."

"Will!" Nola fake-admonished. We all knew Will was talking in jest; he and Finn may as well have been actual brothers instead of in-laws.

I was more serious, though, with my questioning. "How was he?"

Sensing my distress, Will answered me honestly. "You know, he was on the phone most of the time."

"Yeah."

"He just wanted me to make sure you guys were all okay." When I managed a half-hearted smile and Kelsea looked up from her game, Will continued, "So, what do you say? Want to get out of here? Do something?"

"I don't know," I said. "Maybe I should wait for Finn to call."

"Lara," Nola chided. "You need to get your mind off of this." God, it was like her brother's voice coming out of her body. "And your phone is mobile." She gave me a knowing smile.

"Okay," I relented, knowing my sister-in-law was right on all accounts. "Getting out would do me some good. And it's not like *we* are the recognizable ones."

"And, if so, that's why we have Will." Nola winked at her husband who flexed his muscles.

When Kelsea and I laughed, Will pretend pouted. "I'll forgive that," he joked. "So, where do we want to go?"

"Ballet!" Kelsea boisterously submitted her venue choice.

"No." Will's response was immediate. "I'm not sitting through that again. Besides, you have to get those tickets in advance." Before Kelsea could whine a protest, Will offered some other suggestions. "There's that local jazz fest thing going on. Or, bowling." He looked at me and my pregnant stomach. "Okay, maybe not bowling. But we should be able to agree on a movie."

"You know, I actually have four tickets to the community theater. Finn bought the series. We usually give them up, but with everything that's been going on …" I realized as I said it that they didn't realize *all* that was going on—just the recent punch-throwing. "A reminder came up yesterday on my phone. Kels, it's *The Secret Garden.*"

"What's that?" she asked.

"Same author as *A Little Princess*?" I offered.

When she scrunched up her nose in confusion, Nola lamented. "Guess we better bone up on the classics and do a little less of Disney's latest."

Sadly, I agreed. How could kids not know Frances Hodgson Burnett? She was my first form of escape at Kelsea's age.

And she turned out to be an escape that day, too. Seeing as it was a noon performance, we had to grab something quick to eat and be on our way. I was thrilled with the dark theater setting. No one would recognize me, and I wouldn't be obligated to talk—even if it was pleasant conversation with my in-laws. It would have been perfect had I not been checking my phone every couple of minutes, anticipating some kind of contact from Finn.

Finally, it came in the form of a text. *In TN. U O.K.?*

Following his lead and keeping it simple, I texted back. *Yep. U?*

O.K. Gotta run.

I stared at the phone until the backlight faded to black. I was glad to hear from him. After all, it was tradition that we let one another know once we had landed somewhere safely. But I expected more. What exactly, I wasn't quite sure. At least a heart symbol, or an "I love U"? How had life become this way? Numb, I decided instead to stare straight ahead and focus on the walled garden in front of me.

Sitting next to me and obviously noting my behavior, Nola whispered, "He's busy. Dealing with a lot of things."

"I know," I bravely acknowledged while allowing my sister-in-law to squeeze my hand in encouragement.

***

It wasn't until much later in the evening that I actually heard his voice. When "Roxanne" belted out from my phone, I nearly jumped. I had been hoping and waiting, but it still startled me. I excused myself from the backyard fire pit, where Nola, Will, and I had gathered.

"Good. I'm so glad you called," I admitted as my opening phone remark while entering the house.

"Sorry. It's been crazy. You should have called me if you needed me." His voice sounded more tired than usual but, at the same time, more at ease.

"I just…" I didn't need him to do anything for me. I just needed him. "You know, I was worried about you but didn't want to interrupt."

"That's it? No problems? Everything all right?"

"Yeah."

"You would tell me…"

"Yeah," I answered, while gingerly sitting on the recliner and propping up my feet. "I haven't seen much online. There's been a few calls from friends, but I haven't returned them." Then I added what he really wanted to know. "Everyone here is fine."

I didn't mention that there were some "camera campers" by the neighborhood gate when we had returned from the theater. But they didn't recognize Will and Nola, who were donning ball caps. And the back windows of the Jamison's car were tinted. So no outsiders could see me or Kelsea. So, I figured, moot point.

"That's partly because it broke on the weekend. But my people have been working on minimizing it."

"What about you, though? What's going on there? Is the press—"

"They know I'm in town. But that's okay. That was the whole idea. There've been a couple attempts to get me to speak, but it's being taken care of." There was a slight pause. "Lar?"

"Yeah?"

"I'm sorry, baby."

"What? Why? For what?" I sat up a little straighter.

"I love you so much. You know that, don't you?"

I may have been concerned about how he was dealing with everything, and I knew he had every reason to be upset. But I never, ever questioned his love. Still, hearing him voice those precious words brought grateful tears to my hormonal eyes.

"Finn, of course I know that."

"I'm sorry I got so mad. And I'm sorry that you felt this was your fault."

"Stop," I said, wiping the tears so that I could speak honestly. "You have every right to feel everything that you are feeling. God, your whole world was just turned upside down without any notice."

"No," he spoke plainly. "That happened in December."

December. God, when I fell ... when I lost our baby. How I ached for him. How much he sacrificed in his life because of me.

"Finn—"

"And everything else pales, Lara. Everything." His voice changed from clearly emotional to almost ominous. "Listen, there's something I need to tell you."

"Okay."

"I'm only telling you this because of our no omission clause. And I want to say, I really, really debated about it."

"What?"

My stomach, which had only just started to relax after hearing Finn's loving words for me, started to churn. Was it his meds again? Did he go off them with all this happening?

"He contacted me." He spoke very slowly and plainly as if bracing himself for my response.

"What? Who?" When I didn't get an immediate reply, my stomach lurched again. "Macon?"

His name had come out as a whisper. It was like Macon was a real life monster. And considering the trauma he was inflicting, he may as well have been.

"He sent a message on my website. It wasn't public," Finn added quickly. "It went straight to my team. They are the only ones who saw it and brought it to me."

"What? What did it say?"

"It's okay, Lara." Oh God, why did he preface it like that? "Lar?"

"Yeah?"

"It'll be fine."

"What? What will be?" The evasive responses were only making me that much more anxious.

"We've got it. Nothing will happen."

Quit protecting me! "Finn!"

"He said he could make all of this go away if I paid him off."

Blackmail? God, does that really happen? I thought that was just in primetime television shows.

"Oh, God." I sighed. "You're not going to give him any money, are you? I mean, you didn't do what he is accusing you of."

"That's not it, though."

Surely my stomach was on the floor by now. "Wha—"

"He said that if I didn't, he wasn't sure if he could keep 'Lar-Lar's' secret."

Vomit invaded my esophagus upon hearing not only the obnoxious name only Macon used for me but also the implied threat. "Oh, my God."

"Listen to me," my husband said firmly and confidently. "It's not going to happen. Everything is fine."

How was everything fine?! Finn was being accused of assault in the national press. The cops were questioning him. The son I gave up as an infant was fighting a terminal disease. And, now, his existence might be added to the tabloid fodder.

"Lara? My lawyers are working on it. I'm sorry, I had to tell them everything."

"No. That's okay. You should have."

"That boy" —with determination, he referenced the child I gave up— "will be protected. He's a minor. It won't come out. Besides, there's really not many legal ways they could trace his identity. You don't even know who he is."

"That's all that matters, then. I don't care about me," I spoke with the utmost honesty.

"Well, *you* didn't do anything wrong. It would only backfire on that motherfucker."

"You're not going to pay him then?"

"No. Not at all. It was a dumb move on his part. It actually gave my legal team more to go with. Not only blackmail in print but, statute of limitations or not, we could bring up what he did to you back then." He choked on his own words. "I'm telling you, Lara, he can accuse me of anything, but he crossed a line when he involved you in this."

"I'm sorry."

"That right there is why I didn't want to tell you. You don't need to be sorry, and you don't need to worry."

"I'm glad you told me," I said, softly. For, even though I was worried, truth in our relationship was so important to me.

"Let's talk about something else. I don't want you thinking of this anymore."

I knew that wasn't possible, but I agreed, knowing I had no other choice than to trust that the lawyers would keep everything sequestered. Plus, I wanted desperately to be back to a place with my husband that evoked a more innocent, carefree, blissful time. Everything had been so heavy between us, though, I couldn't just get away with some generic how-was-your-day comment.

"How about squash?" I tried instead.

Surely perplexed, Finn asked, "What?"

I explained. "I found a website that said the baby is now the size of an acorn or butternut squash." In the midst of everything, I knew I had to make our baby a priority. Researching weekly pregnancy charts online not only did that but helped my mind stay occupied on the positives in life.

"Hmmm. All right…"

"I gave Kelsea one to stick under her shirt."

That time I got a genuine, albeit soft and short, laugh from my husband. "I'm sure she loved that."

"She did." I smiled, hoping he could sense it across the line.

"Did you get a pic?"

"Nola took one of both of us together."

"I bet you both looked beautiful."

"Mmmm," was my non-descript, typical response.

I certainly didn't feel beautiful— especially not with the weight gain and the haggard effects of the recent emotional stress. But his statement calmed me. He made me feel, if not beautiful, safe and loved and secure. It was something "my Finn" would say.

"Beautiful," he reiterated, knowing me well. And then he asked, "They all right? Kels and Nol?"

"Yeah. Your niece decided that she wants to sleep in our bed. But she wouldn't go to sleep with me there. She kept talking up a storm."

"God, she's really just like him, huh?"

"Yeah," I said softly, knowing immediately that, without saying his name, my husband was referring to Wyatt—the little chatterbox that was silenced way too young.

"I'm sure you're pretty tired. Make sure you get some sleep."

"I will. I'm gonna head in there. She should be asleep by now, and now that I know you're okay…" Because even though my secret had been threatened, it was Finn's life that had been exposed and thrown into turmoil.

"I'll be okay." Before I could question his use of the future tense, he gave me a parent-like directive. "Lara, you call me if you need something."

"I will," I said with a touch of melancholy because I knew our conversation was drawing to its natural close.

"Promise me. Because I know you and—"

"I promise. But the only thing I need is to know—"

"I love you."

"Yeah. I know." My heart warmed. "I was going to say, I need you to understand that it goes both ways. You're not alone." I emphasized, fearing how this stress would affect him. I didn't want him to resort back to those feelings of abandonment and sadness and anger.

"Okay," he said plainly.

"Finn? You are so loved. There is a house full of people here to attest to that. And me and our little squash are first in line." I rubbed my active belly.

That seemed to warrant a more positive response. "Thanks, Beauty. I needed that, even though I know it, too. Sleep tight, Bed Bug."

CHAPTER SIXTEEN

Whether it was from pure exhaustion or knowing that—despite Macon's blackmail—Finn and I were in a better place than when he left, I did sleep very soundly that night. Neither Kelsea's open mouth gurgling, the awkwardness of a third-trimester pregnancy, nor fictitious bed bugs could keep me awake. I even slept through the three Jamisons getting up, having breakfast, and leaving for church.

Afterward, when Will came back to the house solo, I teased, "Where's your harem?"

"Wrong family member," he countered, making an obvious reference to Finn's female fan club.

"Yeah, don't I know it." I rolled my eyes, knowing I had to let that part of my husband's stardom roll off my shoulders.

"I think that boy would go gay before even looking at another woman besides you."

"He probably has that following, too." I chuckled, but was appreciative of Will's words.

"I don't want to know." He smiled. "To answer your question, though, I dropped Nol and the dancing diva off at her tap lessons. She has her recital coming up soon, and this is the final practice."

"Oh, you should have stayed."

"Hubby crooner was texting me—making sure you are really okay."

"So, you're here to babysit? I hope you told him to relax."

"Yes to the second. And, no, not here to babysit. I'm here to avoid the excessive amount of estrogen and drama that takes over at these dance things." When I laughed an agreement, he continued. "I just thought I would legitimately check on you and do some work before heading off to pick them up again."

"Thanks, Will."

"Yeah, well, I know Finn can be overprotective, but I think it's smart in this case. Nola and Kelsea are fine. They know everyone at dance, and it's a closed facility. I just wish we knew exactly what hap—" He stopped talking as my phone rang. "That's probably my pain-in-the-ass brother-in-law now. Would you please tell him, he put me in charge, and if I am in charge, everything is fine."

I laughed and looked at my phone, knowing it wasn't Finn. "It's my mom."

"Great. More girl talk!" he jested and left for his family's temporary guest quarters upstairs.

Sadly, I debated about whether or not to answer the phone. As far as I knew, my mother was unaware of the events taking place. Neither Finn nor I had told her what had transpired on the Altman front porch. She would have surely questioned my even going to their house. But had she caught wind of the incident via the press or through hometown gossip? I needed to know what, if anything, she knew, so she would know how to best handle it if need be.

The thought of explaining any of it filled me with angst, though, and it was duly noted in how I picked up the phone. "What mom?"

"Well, that's a greeting."

"Sorry. What do you need? I'm …I'm just dealing with

some things," I answered, pretty much convinced by the sound of her normal pitched and semi-slow voice that she was still unaware.

"What's going on?"

"Nothing. Just busy," I said and then turned the question once again to her. "What's up?"

"You'll never guess who I saw this morning." That was my mom— gossip central. It was actually quite surprising that she didn't know about the encounter.

"Who?" I asked just out of habit. I couldn't care less, especially under the circumstances. I was thinking it was probably somebody she knew in grade school who …

"Miller." She bombarded my thoughts like an explosion. Maybe she did know. "Miller Al—"

"Yes, I know who Miller is," I spoke quickly. "What did he want?"

"He was in the emergency room. I was working my shift. It's my long week. You know, I told you. I've hardly been home." She was starting to do the Elise Faulkner ramble.

I tried to refocus her. "Why? Is he hurt?"

I couldn't help but be concerned. What had happened? Despite our checkered past, Miller had never really done me terribly wrong. Plus, he seemed empathetic to the plight of the nephew he never knew.

My mother's answer came out in a loud whisper, and it couldn't have been more shocking. "His brother died … drunk driving."

Wait! What? Brother? Miller only had one brother. Stop! Slow down! What?!

Oblivious to my internal turmoil, my mother continued her tale. "Single vehicle, thank God. Glad he didn't take any innocent with him."

"What? Macon's dead? That can't be." This time, I was pretty sure my words were vocalized.

"Why? Why not? I heard he has been messed up with drugs for a while now."

"He just—" I actually stopped myself and took in a deep breath.

I had been making figure eights throughout our entire downstairs area. I was trying to process but just couldn't. What did it all mean? What did this mean for Finn? Oh, my God, and that boy. What if that selfish bastard really was that innocent boy's only chance? There would be no changing of minds or ...

"Just what?" My mother managed to reel me back in.

I was going to say that Macon had just been torturing my husband, but I lied, not wanting to have to explain the whole sordid tale. "I don't know. You know how it just seems like it can't happen to someone you know."

"It does, though. We know that." She obviously was recalling my father passing under similar circumstances. "Anyway ...Miller. So, he said he wants to talk with you. We're in the emergency room, his brother just died, and he's asking for your phone number! I wouldn't give it to him, of course. The nerve after all these years ... after what happened back then."

"Did he say anything?" I ignored her partial rant, knowing she thought, because of me, that Miller was the bad guy in the whole scenario years before. Now I needed to know if Miller told her any of the details that had been buried and omitted.

"Yeah! It gets worse!"

Oh, Jesus. Oh, my God. How could things get worse?

"When I wouldn't give him your number, he asked me to give you a message and gave me *his* phone number."

"What was the message?" My nerves were on epic tilt.

"He told me you didn't need to worry. What Macon was doing was wrong and there wouldn't be any more to come from it. What the heck does that mean? What does him drinking or doing drugs have to do with you?"

I needed a chance to think. There were more questions than answers bombarding my mind. First was my mom. How could she still be oblivious to everything? And how did Miller know not to tell her? Or, did he just assume that she knew? And what did his message mean —nothing more would come from Macon's reign of terror? Because he was dead? Or because Miller had some say in it?

"Oh, oh, oh, God, I ..." was all I managed to get out.

It wasn't a definite confirmation and, God, it came at the expense of a life. But, wow. What a waste. It was just another affirmation of how much addiction can alter your life. Regardless, after days of distress, I was finally feeling a little sense of relief— at least about the mess with Finn.

"Lara?" She still wanted some kind of answer.

I retraced back to my mother's question. "I ...his addictions have nothing to do with me." I responded honestly and then asked, "That was it then? That was all Miller had to say?"

"No. There's more!" she practically screeched. "I can't believe I am actually going to relay this message. But he told me to tell you that he's a match."

"What?"

"He's a match?" she said in the form of a question this time. "He's not talking about that online dating thing is he? He doesn't think you're going to do that? I just assumed he knew you were married. That's when I decided the guy is grieving and out of his mind. So, I just walked away."

It was one revelation after another. My mother's conversation with my ex was probably over in just a matter of minutes. But, it pulled a number of punches in rapid succession.

"He's a match? Miller's a match?" Of course I knew he wasn't speaking about dinner and movies and long walks on the beach but something much deeper— saving a life.

"Yeah."

"Oh, oh, wow. And you have his number?"

"His phone number?" she asked as if she had just heard the most appalling thing on Earth.

"Yeah. You said he gave you his phone number." I tried to remain calm, but anxious excitement was bubbling up in my core.

"Lara Ann!" she admonished.

Had my mind not been solely focused on the mission at hand, I would have been extremely disheartened that my mother would even think I would harbor the idea of entertaining another man. "Mom, it's all right. Could you just get me his number?"

"Uh…" She hesitated.

"Mom, please!" I urged and wondered if it was even worth the anguish. I'm sure I could easily click a few buttons online and figure a telephone number out.

"Well, it's in my purse," she answered back, sounding as if she was pacifying a crazy woman—which she may as well have been. "I'll have to go get it. It's in the other room."

"Thanks. Just text it. I'll look for it in the next couple of minutes. And I'll talk with you later." I hung up before she could ask any more questions, which surely were mounting with fluidity in her brain.

***

I had to call Miller. I had to talk with him … to know for sure. Although, I didn't doubt any of my mother's words. And I thought I knew Miller well enough to know that if he offered those two pieces of information to my mom, they were legit. But, I needed to talk with him. I would offer him my condolences and find out the details of, well, everything.

First, though, I needed to pee. And then I needed to get on my hometown's newspaper web page and confirm the accident. And then I needed to call Finn. He was my instinct. He was my go-to. He was my love.

When he picked up after a few rings, I could hear the flurry of voices in the background. "Finn?" I asked. "Where are you?"

"I'm meeting with some people. Everything all right?" I

noted that he always seemed to start with that question ever since my first fainting spell— it made me feel both sad and loved at the same time.

"I'm all right. Both me and the baby are fine," I reassured him and then came right out and said it. "Macon's dead. I'm not sure of the details, but it was drunk driving …last night, early this morning. He's dead."

"What?" He was obviously as shocked as I had been. "How do you know?"

"My mom."

"How does she know?" The noise from his end of the line seemed to diminish, and I imagined that he had left the room for a quieter setting.

"He was brought into the hospital. She was working that shift. And, I just looked at their local newspaper online."

"Oh, geez. Yeah, I'll pull it up." And then he added, "Well, can't say I'm going to be shedding a tear."

"It's a shame what happened with him, though."

"You have to stand up to your addictions. And I don't want to hear about how he was. Or that you were kids. What he did to you was criminal. Back then and now, really."

"And what he was doing to you."

"Don't worry about that. I'll deal with whatever happens."

"Finn, my mom saw Miller at the hospital, and he told her that we weren't going to have to worry about it anymore."

"Yeah? Well, I guess as long as he" —Miller's name still didn't dispense from my husband's mouth— "doesn't want to press charges."

"He won't."

There was a pause and then he said, "I should probably tell my team. Press will be interested in this, too. But since the whole assault thing was an exaggeration, and the police don't seem anxious to pursue it—"

"No?" I asked, feeling hopeful.

"Well, there hasn't been any follow-up, and I told you my lawyers got this."

"Good." I breathed in a little easier. "Finn? I have to call Miller."

"Why?" There was immediate agitation in his voice.

"I have to confirm things for all of our sakes. And I can see what he can do about the police."

"Lara, don't worry about it. The guy is dead."

"I have to call. I just need to confirm things."

"You want to wait until I come home?" I knew he wasn't really asking it as a question—it was more of a request.

But I only paid attention to the part I liked. "You're coming home?"

"Yeah, I should have never left you … not with this pregnancy … not with everything going on. You're not supposed to be stressed. I'm gonna see if someone can get me a flight out tomorrow. My team can take care of the press and whatever so I can take care of you. Okay?"

"Yeah. Yeah. More than. I miss you." Just then, Will came down the stairs with his keys jingling. I stopped him with a hand signal, asking him to give me one minute but not to leave.

"Ditto," Finn recited to my "miss you" comment.

"And I have good news."

"You just told me."

"No." I had a hard time, even if he was evil incarnate, thinking that someone dying was good news. "Finn, this is really good news."

"What?" I could hear relaxation start to seep into his bloodstream.

"Something else I have to confirm. But I want to tell you in person." Deep inside, somewhere, I didn't want to jinx the possibility that Miller was a bone marrow match. I needed to hear it from him directly …before telling Finn … before celebrating … before relaxing.

"You're not going to tell me you're pregnant are you?"

"No! Too late." I laughed, glad that we could joke about it.

"All right, baby. I'll call you when I know my flight details. Where's Will?"

"He's right here." I smiled.

"Can I talk with him?"

"Can you talk?" I asked Will.

"As long as it's not that pain-in-the-ass," Will jokingly bellowed, surely having heard who I was talking with.

"I'll give him pain-in-the-ass," Finn started yelling back from across the line.

"Okay, boys, save it for the ring." I laughed at both of them. "Here's Will," I said into the phone with the addendum of, "I love you."

"I love you, too. See you soon."

***

I waited until coming home from work the next day to call Miller. No matter how desperately I wanted to confirm that he would help rectify his brother's slanderous accusations and that he was a willing bone marrow match, I also understood that Macon had been Miller's brother … his only brother … his twin brother. And, even if things had deteriorated for Macon and possibly between the brothers, there was a bond, and Miller needed a day or so to digest and grieve before I entered the scenario.

Besides, with the Jamisons having gone back to their own abode—Finn had agreed the press threat could be managed without any more campouts at "Hotel Murphy"—I wanted to keep my mind off the fact that Finn was flying. He managed to charter a private plane to decrease the chances of anyone realizing he had left Tennessee. He could sneak back into the New York area around dinnertime.

I regretted my decision to make that phone call to

215

Miller while Finn was mid-flight. It was, as I should have anticipated, an extremely awkward conversation. My relationship with Miller was non-existent. We weren't boyfriend and girlfriend. We weren't friends. In all reality, we hadn't spoken in over thirteen years. And, with everything that the phone conversation had to entail, it was uncomfortable to say the least. Although, Miller was cordial and confirmed everything he had told my mother. He would be putting in a call to the necessary personnel so that he could be a bone marrow donor for the boy I had given up all those years ago. And, omitting the buried secrets part, he agreed to talk with the police to confirm what really happened the day that Finn and I had visited the Altman residence.

When I got off the phone, though, I couldn't stand still. My emotions were ravaging through my body. I was so grateful for everything Miller was doing in the midst of his grief, especially for someone he had no obligations toward. I wanted to talk with the only person who knew the whole story ... the only one who knew me. But he was miles away— high in the sky.

That turned out not to be the case, though. If I thought the phone conversation with Miller was troublesome, then the next one was absolutely terrifying. It was my worst nightmare come true.

When a person who talks and handles stressful situations for a living stumbles on her words and starts the conversation by making sure that you are sitting down, you know something is desperately wrong. When it is one of your husband's right-hand people, you start praying like you never have before. When you hear what she actually has to say, you crumble to the floor, realizing your world is falling completely apart.

I had been expecting a call from Finn saying that he had landed. But what I heard instead was Reese telling me that the plane had lost contact with air traffic control a while before. Nothing was known except that the pilot had radioed in that there was some kind of issue before the total loss of correspondence. Search parties were out and the owner of the plane was contacted. The owner, in turn, contacted Finn's staff, who had made the arrangements for the personal plane in the first place.

"Finn will have my hide for calling you," Reese said. "I know he wouldn't want you to worry."

Worry? Worry! I was so beyond worrying. I was in another realm of existence. I was so petrified, I couldn't speak. I couldn't even cry.

"Lara?" Reese's voice drew me back. "I thought you should know. I made the decision to call you. It's a small plane. So everything has been kept hush-hush so far. But if the story breaks, I didn't want you to hear about it on the news or from a reporter. Besides, I know if it was Roger, I … I would want to know."

"I … yeah … of course."

"He'll be all right. They're going to find him. Everyone's working hard on that."

"What about his parents?" I interrupted. My head was spinning, spinning, spinning.

"I only called you. If you think…that's up to you."

"You know nothing? Nothing?"

"I promise you, I will keep you posted as soon as I know anything and even if I don't."

"Oh my God, Reese. What do I do? Oh, my God!"

The baby started kicking like crazy, and I felt like I was going to throw up. I heard Reese say some supposedly soothing words, but I couldn't concentrate on them. I don't know if it was my head or my heart that was pounding louder. I needed to see him or, at least, hear him. Knowing that Reese had to concentrate on all that was going on there, I hung up the phone and, clinging it to my bosom, walked into the master bedroom. I curled into Finn's side of the bed and held his pillow securely against my body.

Closing my eyes, I willed him to be okay. "Please don't

leave me, Finn. Please. Please." I sobbed out loud.

Surely others had tried calling his cell phone, but I had to try, too. Maybe, just maybe, right? I hit the speed dial. There was no ring. It went straight to voice mail. God, even when just speaking, his melodic voice was smooth and special. But I wanted to hear it live. I didn't want the generic recording. I couldn't pull it together to leave a message. So, I hung up, momentarily collected myself, and dialed again. Once more, I focused on his jovial, calm, but brief voice box message. I tried to mimic his energy because if—when—he picked up his voice mail, I didn't want him to know how insanely scared I was.

"Call me. Call me, please. Let me know if…" I started to break. "I love you." I managed to squeak out before hanging up.

I stared. Oh, how I stared. I couldn't get out of my trance-like state. I couldn't move. I was in our bed holding onto our babe whose kicks were now soft flutters in my stomach. As I replayed over and over again all of our moments together, I tried to focus on the magical ones— the wedding, of course, … the engagement … coffee at Java Mug … my first visit to Nashville. But the regrets snuck in, too, especially the ones over the past couple of months. I could not believe how we had argued over the silliest of things. And mostly it was me being stubborn, and he wanting to make sure I was loved and safe. God, and that was essentially what led him onto that plane… that godforsaken plane. How could I live with myself knowing his love and need to protect me could have cost him his life?

And how had we left things? What was the last thing I had said to him? God, help me, I hoped that it was that I loved him. Was it? I couldn't remember. I couldn't remember.

"Finn!" Breaking the trance, I screamed his name so loud that I swear the house shook. But, yet, no one but my own ears could hear my pain.

I decided not to call Mr. and Mrs. Murphy. There was a big part of me that wanted to, but it was the selfish part. I just wanted someone to talk to. But I knew nothing. And even though I was appreciative of Reese calling me, I couldn't throw the agony of the unknown on my in-laws. I would wait until, God willing, I had a positive result to relay later.

When the phone rang again just a little while later, my blood pressure and hopes instantly rose at the same time. Having the fortitude to look at the caller ID first, I saw that it was Carter and answered immediately. "Carter? Carter? Is he with you?" My shaky voice matched my quivering hands.

"Lara?" Carter's voice came through the line. "Hey. No. But I heard what happened. I'm just calling because I thought you might need someone to talk to."

My heart dropped. Why wasn't it Finn? Or at least someone with news, positive news, about him? But I was very glad for Carter and his consideration. I did need someone. I needed someone who wasn't Finn's family and would only worry, yet someone I could trust to not say anything until, God helping, there was a happy ending.

"I don't know what's going on," I lamented, sinking back onto the headboard of the bed.

"We don't either. They called all of us. I'm on my way to meet up with the team. I'm ready, Lara-Li. I'm ready to drive and search or whatever."

"God, Carter. I can't lose him."

"You—"

I had someone to talk to, and I was talking. "He wouldn't have been on that plane. He wouldn't have even been in Nashville if it wasn't for me. I caused all of this. I caused all of this mess."

"You wouldn't have been able to stop him … with any of it. What happened or didn't happen in Pittsburgh—"

"It didn't." I emphasized. "Finn would not do that."

"I know, Lara." The way he spoke in a reassuring tone

told me he knew I was specifically making a point for him—a domestic abuse witness. "He protected you, though."

"That was all."

"What I was going to say was, having the press follow him here, that was on him. You know that. He would do anything for you."

I was downright bawling. "I don't want him to die for me."

I thought I heard a crack in Carter's voice, but it very well could have been one of my many. "He's ... are you kidding? Let me tell you something. Yesterday? We were all over at the ranch."

"Yeah?" I tried to follow Carter's voice.

"Yeah— an impromptu jam session. Your boy needed some support and to work out some of the crap. So the band was there."

That made me smile in between the sniffles. I could picture my handsome, sweet husband and his friends, getting lost in their love of music. I was glad he had them. It also made me smile and wonder if Carter was officially part of that group again.

"I'm sure that helped," I tried.

"It did. For all of us." He paused as if reflecting, and I was realizing that I was hearing a new Carter—a more mature version of an already great guy. "So when everyone left, I, y'know, stuck around a little bit. And Lara? He could not stop talking about you or that baby. He is so in love with you. He's not going to die. He has too much to live for." The momentary pause of tears ended, and I began to openly sob again until Carter broke in. "Hey, that was supposed to cheer you up. What happened to that tough broad that slapped me last summer?"

I semi-chuckled through my tears. I had, in fact, slapped him for dumping Vanessa so callously. "I'm missing my husband," I replied and then tried to will myself into a less depressive mood, if possible. "What happened to the insensitive guy who deserved that slap?"

"Touché, Mrs. Murphy." He laughed. "Hopefully that guy's gone. Listen, Finn would be pretty upset if he thought I made you cry."

Knowing what Carter said was true, I tried to please my absent husband by wiping my watering eyes and nose. "You're a really good friend, Carter. Finn is very lucky. Thanks for calling me."

"I'm the lucky one. You both have really been there for me. He's just lucky that he married so well." I could picture the signature charmer Carter smile as he finished those words.

"He did, didn't he?" I managed a little sarcasm.

Carter returned to being serious. "He's going to be fine. I'm pulling in now. I'll call if we know anything. And you, too, okay?"

"Yeah. Yeah."

Each agonizing minute after I hung up felt like an hour. Each drop of silence felt like closure —the kind I didn't want. Why would getting any kind of information take so long? I mentally worked backward to figure out how long it would take for all those phone calls to take place before Reese called me. Someone should have known something, especially in today's technological age.

And then, the worst thought crept in. If he and the pilot and whatever crew were all right, why hadn't they called? I didn't want to think what I was thinking. But, despite Carter's encouraging words, I was.

And I screamed again. "Finn!"

God, baby, hear me. Let me know you're okay. Once again, though, my external and internal pleas were followed by silence.

CHAPTER SEVENTEEN

Eventually, I managed to get myself up, knowing that the manic thoughts cycling through my overstimulated brain were causing me to be near hyperventilation. I needed to regulate my breathing. So, I started trailing through the house, noting and touching things of Finn's that I had taken for granted because they are always there. It wasn't his awards or any part of his music life that I noted, but the real him. It was the nearly identical teal and white polo shirts that swayed on the hook in the walk-in closet, perhaps forgotten as he had packed haphazardly …his unscented shaving cream near his sink …the kitchen corkboard filled with his handwritten reminders of events and important dates … the powder room's paint color, which he insisted on picking, and I reluctantly agreed looked great … the baby's room, where his guitar remained … the photos of us together scattered throughout … his tennis shoes near the mudroom, ready for a run … his shirt and shorts in the laundry basket next to them … the fire pit in our back yard that we built almost immediately after moving in—a fond replica of the one in Tennessee…

The phone, which may as well have been glued to my

hand, practically yelled at me, causing me to scream back and jump. Chilled by the November air, I was standing on the deck when the phone rang. It startled my deep thoughts so much that it didn't even register to me who was calling. The designer ring was "Roxanne." I breathed in deep. It was Finn. Or, as I quickly realized, no, it was Finn's phone. It didn't mean it was him. It could be anyone who had found his phone.

I pressed the button on my phone to answer. I listened. But I refused to speak. My silence represented the side of me that was afraid of happiness because I knew it could so easily be taken away.

"Lara?" his voice questioned.

I'm not sure what you would consider my response to be. A sigh? A wail? A cry? Ultimately, though, it was relief. I had never felt such immediate gratitude and relief.

"Lar? Lara? I'm okay."

And then I started bawling. I let loose for all the angst and terror I had felt since Reese called with the terrifying news. I was holding my face, and then I was holding our baby. And I was bawling.

"Lara, God, baby." I heard his voice call out through the phone. "It's okay. Please. It's all right."

"Finn?" I managed to squeak out because I still needed that last ounce of confirmation.

"Lara, it's me. I need you to calm down and talk to me, okay?" I could tell he was worried about me but trying his best to use a soothing voice for my benefit.

I let out an enormous puff of air to help erase the tension in my shoulders and stop the tears. Then I managed a sassy, yet true response. "I hate planes."

His voice immediately got lighter with a semi-laugh. "I know, Beauty. I'm not too much of a fan, either, right now."

"But I love you more than I hate them," I answered even more honestly, while still wiping the silent tears from my cheeks.

"Yeah?" I could hear the appreciation of my words in his voice.

"You're okay?" I asked the question that was truly my only concern.

"Yeah. We're all fine."

"Where are you? What happened?" I asked while swaying side to side, still trying to get the jitters to subside.

"We're ...I don't know ...somewhere in eastern PA. The plane lost pressure and then contact. But it's not as bad as it seems. It happened pretty quick, and I didn't even really realize what was going on. We were able to land safely. It was just in the middle of a cornfield. So, there was no reception, and we had to walk a while to get to someone's house."

"Is that where you're at now? Some farmhouse?" I asked, thinking how the owners must have thought it was some sort of reality TV prank— a country music superstar showing up at their door looking for a lift.

"Sorta. Firemen came. We're in town now."

"Why didn't you call me right away? I've been worried sick, Finn." At least, though, with the sound of his voice, that nauseous, doomed feeling was dissipating, and I was finally able to sit down.

"Sorry. I called as soon as I could. We were concerned about getting someone out here. We called 9-1-1, of course, and then we were calling anyone associated with the plane. And I didn't even know you knew something went wrong."

"Reese called me."

"Yeah, she told me. I hadn't even checked voice mail. She shouldn't have called you. There was no reason for you to—"

"Yes, she should have." I defended her. "I'm your wife. I nee—" I stopped myself. "Oh, God. You're okay, right? Really?"

It was hitting me then—really and truly. He could have died. In most cases, when you hear of something like that, the plane disintegrated ... no survivors.

"Yes. I promise. Everyone got checked out by medical personnel just as a precaution. I'm more worried about you right now."

"I'm ... I'm okay."

"Where are you? What are you doing?"

"I'm out back. Just breathing. Sitting now and breathing. I'm ... I'm good."

"That's good. Relax." As I did just that, he continued. "How's the baby doing?"

"Fine."

"Good. You get something to eat and drink, Lara."

"Yeah. I will."

"Make sure—"

"I will."

"All right." It was his turn to take a deeper breath. And then, "Beauty, they mentioned that you might have called my folks. It's okay if you did. I just need to know. Should I call them?"

"I didn't. I'm sorry. Should I have? I debated...with Nola and Will, too. I just wanted some word before I did."

"No. They didn't need to know. But if something ever happens, and it makes you feel better to talk with them, you should do that. They have each other, and they will be there for you."

"God Finn, don't even say that." I semi-cried out an answer, knowing I never wanted to go through that heart-wrenching fear again. "You're not getting on a plane again, are you?"

"No, baby, it's fine. I think for this leg of the trip, I'm driving. They're gonna take me to get a rental car. I'll be able to drive straight home." After the slightest of pauses, he tacked on, "To you."

"You're sure?" A second wave of relief was washing over me.

"Yep. From where we're at, it's only a few hours away—maybe not even three."

"I want to see you. I love you so much."

"Remember, more than you hate planes," he repeated my statement with what I determined was a smile.

"I do. I love you more than anything." Another fresh round of tears started.

"God, Lar, please, don't cry."

"Can't ask me that right now," I said honestly. "But at least they're tears of relief."

"I love you, baby."

Once again, I tried to harbor the tears. "I don't want to hang up."

"I know. I don't either, believe me. But there's so much going on here. The sooner I can get all of this cleared, the sooner I can get that car," he said. "Get something to eat, and then do me a favor."

"You want me to do you a favor?" I teased, finally feeling a little more relaxed, despite a wet face. "You need to come home for me to do that."

Finn's laughter was a most welcome sound. He obviously knew what I was referring to—how I had asked Finn to make love to me the very first time. Luckily, we were able to joke seductively about it. "All the more reason for me to get that car." He laughed. "But, no. Will you call my folks? It would make me feel better that you have them to talk to and that they know everything is all right before any of this breaks in the press."

"Yeah. Yeah. That's fine."

"I love you, Lara. Everything's okay," he added, knowing the second part of his statement was just as important to me as the first at that moment.

"I love you, too," I echoed. But, knowing our conversation was coming to a close, I choked on the last words. "Be safe."

"I will." He must have known I couldn't hang up first. So, he let silence fill the line for a moment or two before he ended our connection.

I finally leaned back on the chaise and closed my eyes.

He was safe. He had called. He was alive. He was coming home. And I remembered—I had told him I loved him … a couple of times.

I put the phone up against my heart and crossed my hands over it. I could, indeed, breathe. And it felt so good. I sat in that serenity pose for a little while and was just about ready to call Finn's parents when a text came in.

There was a photograph of Finn gnawing on a corn stalk with a big grin. My husband's accompanying written words said, *What I'm bringing home for dinner this week.*

The term LOL, in my opinion, is vastly overused. But it was so entirely accurate in this case.

I laughed hard, still finding new waves of utter relief. Then I texted back: *Ha! Ha! Just bring your SEXY self home. XOXO*

Did U C the article?

The *Media Monthly* edition with the top ten sexiest husbands had come out that day. One was sent directly to the house and, yes, I saw it. I had even read it before getting that phone call from Reese. And now that everything was all right again, I hoped that the article would really do what we had intended for it to do. It was beautifully written and truly showcased the heart of Finn's sexiness and our love. Hopefully, that and, ironically, the airplane survival tale would positively overshadow all of the darkness that had overtaken us.

I texted back. *Yeah. Have it here. Not as good as the real thing, tho. I love U, Cowboy.*

Ditto, Rox. C U soon.

***

"Hi, Honey," Finn's mother answered the phone. "We were just talking about you. Zak just walked in the door, and he said we should call and see how you are with Finn away. We know it's hard on him, of course, with these accusations, but you—"

Still trying to calm the last of my accelerated nerves, I interrupted her banter. "So, he's home?" I asked about my father-in-law. "You're both there?" That was the reason I had called their landline. I wanted both of them to hear the news at the same time. I really didn't want to repeat the horrific tale.

"Yeah." From the way she slowly spoke that one simple word, I could tell she recognized the cautious tone in my voice.

"Good."

"Lara, what's wrong, sweetie?"

At least I could supply my in-laws with a revised tale of the day—happy ending intact. They were going to get a cushioned version. It was much better than the scary slap of reality that Reese unfortunately had to deliver to me earlier in the day.

"All right. So, everything is okay," I started. "I just talked with him."

"With? With who? Finn?"

"There was an accident. His plane went down."

Before I could get another word out, and despite me providing the prerequisite of telling her that he was okay, Mrs. Murphy was Finn's mother, and she let out an animalistic screech that only a loving parent could. This followed by, "Zak! Zak!"

I heard Mr. Murphy's breathy voice across the line. "Good Heavens! What?"

"Pick up the other line. Lara's on the phone. Something happened. The plane...Lara?"

"Listen—" I tried.

But I was interrupted by my father-in-law. "Lara, darlin', what's going on?" His voice sounded as sturdy as ever, but I suspect part of that was just the patriarchal role he took on. He loved his son as much as we did.

"He's fine. He's fine," I tried again.

"Okay. He's fine." Mr. Murphy was speaking into the phone, but the comment was directed to his wife. "Thalia, let her talk."

As I detailed all that I knew, I could hear the relief expel from both of their voices. Finn had been right. I did need to talk with his parents, as much as for their benefit as mine. Telling them out loud was cathartic. It was confirmation that he was, indeed, all right. And it felt good to talk to someone, especially to someone who loved Finn as much as I did. Finn had been right. I could almost see him smirking in his car miles and miles away.

Our conversation concluded with my in-laws wondering if I needed anything, and me answering with the honest truth. "Me? No. I just need him to be home safely."

"He will be." Mrs. Murphy, who had regained her composure midway through our conversation, was back to being her confident self.

"I'll have him call you when he's back," I offered.

Mr. Murphy dissented. "He's going to want to be with you and our future grandbaby. Just have him send us a text, and then we'll talk tomorrow."

After agreeing and hanging up, I tried to find some other ways to occupy my time during the waiting-for-Finn vigil. I decided to call Reese and thank her for all that she did for Finn, as well as for me. She seemed extremely hurried, as I imagined she would be in the midst of trying to make sure everything was copacetic on their end. But she did tell me how grateful she was that everything had worked out—even though Finn, as she had predicted, was beyond furious with her for calling me. I reassured her that it would all be fine. I would make sure of it. And then, as I was more relaxed, my previous conversation with her floated into my brain. I asked who Roger was. Although not possible, I swore I could see her blush over the phone. She explained that she had finally fallen in love with a New York sports agent. Which, in hindsight, made sense. That was why she was already in the city when we did the *Media Monthly* interview, and why she never seemed to mind being in the area for business with Finn. Knowing how much I loved *my* man, I couldn't have been happier for her.

At the tail end of my conversation with Reese, Carter got on the line. "I told you so. Your boy has no kryptonite. There's nothing that will bring him down."

I knew that wasn't true, though. Being left … having others go…that was his kryptonite. And it would have been mine, too, if he had not survived that plane crash. But, feeling particularly grateful for life and love, I chuckled at Carter's comment and thanked him also before hanging up.

Next, I tried to clean, read, and even nap, but nothing seemed to work. I couldn't get my mind off of everything that had happened—Macon's accusation, his death, Miller's match, and Finn. God, I had almost lost him. I could not have lived through that. The thought was just simply unbearable.

When he finally pulled into the driveway in his black SUV rental, I leaped up from my perch at the foyer window and burst out the front door. I must have looked rather ridiculous, considering my pregnancy and the non-seasonal, floral dress I was wearing. But as I ran to his driver's side, illuminated just by the trigger light of the driveway, I didn't care. Nothing would have stopped my reunion with my husband.

A wide, closed-mouth smile spread across his face as he stepped from the vehicle. "Hi, baby," he managed to say before I plowed right into his torso. Holding me securely, I felt his hand gently, lovingly stroking the back of my hair. Although his words were muffled due to my face being implanted in his chest, I heard them after a few minutes. "What? You would think my plane went down or something." He tried to lighten the situation.

I pulled my face slightly away. And with a tsk and a tear, I said, "I need to see you." I bracketed my palms on his rugged face. "I have to really make sure you are good."

His whisper in my ear was both calming and, admittedly, sexy. "I'm good."

"I'm not letting you go."

"I hope not," he said. "C'mon, maybe we should go inside, though." He interloped one hand with mine and shut the car door with the other.

I leaned my head onto his shoulder and, snug to his side, let him guide us through the open front door. "You're home," I said with relief, as if the threshold held magical powers.

"I think I owe you something." He stopped in front of the foyer's built-in bench.

"What?" I asked completely perplexed. What on Earth could he owe me after all I had put him through?

"Right here, in fact." And before I could once again question, he leaned in and kissed me softly and sweetly.

I closed my eyes for a second and nodded my head in acknowledgement. I had questioned him, in the midst of all that stress when he was initially leaving New York, about not kissing me. I had been so wrong to do so. It was my deep-rooted insecurities taking hold. I knew better. I knew our love. And so did he. But, from his action, I knew that troubled departure had taken a painful place in his soul, too. And he was pushing the rewind button.

I smiled at him and his generous, thoughtful heart. "What about you? What can I do for you? You've been through so much."

"Take care of yourself and this little one" —he placed his hand on my blossoming belly— "and you are taking care of me."

"Finn?" I spoke his name with obvious concern.

Taking care of the baby was a given. Finn's well-being was what was immediately concerning me. He looked worn but physically okay. But with the accusations, our argument, Macon, the plane ... how was he handling it all? There was so much.

"Lara, I'm fine," he said, in a reassuring, yet tired,

voice. Grabbing my hand once more, he started to lead me into the great room. "And I haven't forgotten. I want to hear that news of yours. But if it's okay, I just want to hold you first."

"Yeah. That sounds perfect." Everything could wait, I thought as we both simultaneously sank onto the great room's sofa. Instantly finding our natural fit in each other's arms, I closed my eyes and just concentrated on his touch and smell, so relieved to still have the opportunity to do so. Then I said, "I completely get it now, and I think we're even."

"What? What do you mean?" He released his lips from the top of my head.

"Today—these horrible hours—this was my December."

I didn't need to explain my statement. He knew. He knew all too well.

He gently turned my face toward him. "I'm sorry you had to go through that. No one should ever feel that God-awful fear ... the prospect of complete devastation."

"I guess it's the trade you make for loving someone as much as I love you."

His eyes grew misty then as he gave me a committed kiss. "The whole 'it's better to love and lost' thing? Let's just stick with the love part. Because I am, and always will be, in love with you one hundred percent. Losing you is not an option."

"Same goes for me, Cowboy." We sat there for a few silent, serene moments before I remembered to tell him to text his parents.

"Yeah." He grabbed his phone and began to type. "Thanks for calling them." After finishing his finger movements on the phone, he coasted me back into his arms.

"Sure. It helped. Your dad is a rock. He—"

The returning text interrupted us. Finn looked down at his phone and started to laugh. "I can still catch the end of the Cincy game, right?"

I smacked his arm. "I can't believe you just said that!" But I smiled, glad that he was thinking of something besides all the heaviness that was surrounding us.

He rubbed his arm overly dramatically. "Yep. Still got the full swing intact." His grin was wide. "And blame Pop. I forgot until he just texted me the score. And, yes, Beauty, I can pass on Monday Night Football tonight."

I turned and let my tongue slip into his mouth a few times before resting my head onto his chest and slyly turning the television on via the nearby remote. "Let's watch the game."

"Really?" he asked with genuine shock.

"Why? Are you going to forfeit?"

"No! I will never forfeit, especially with a winning season." He smiled. "We're going all the way this year."

"Well, aren't you confident?" I teased, but I knew with Cincinnati's record that he had every reason to be. I eased back into his strong body. "I'd love to just do something completely normal like watch football with you. If I fall asleep, though, it's okay. We can talk tomorrow. I already called off." And then I added, "And my massage can wait until tomorrow, too."

He kissed me on the nose while wrapping the throw blanket around me. "You wish."

CHAPTER EIGHTEEN

I had decided to play hooky from work the next day. I was tired from all the emotional drama unfolding. But more so, I wasn't willing to let Finn out of my sight. Just like he had hovered over me after my near-death experience, I did the same with him. I clung to his presence, needing to make sure he was safe. Of course, he didn't object. I'm sure he would have been quite happy if I didn't return to work until after the baby was born. But he knew better than to step on that minefield again.

If I was taking the day off to be with him, he vowed to take the day off and be with me. Finn ignored most of the calls coming into his phone, except for those bringing him word that the press was aware of and running with the story of the fallen plane. Between the farmhouse owners and the firefighters, we both knew it was pretty much a given that the news would come out. Finn, however, let Reese and company take care of putting a positive spin on the whole incident which actually helped deflect from the Macon debacle.

When Finn hung up from his curt phone conversation with Reese, I took the opportunity to try to pacify that particular situation. "Ease up on her, Finn."

Due to Cincinnati's loss, my husband's hands were massaging my feet, which were lazily propped on his lap. "I—"

But I wasn't going to let him even try to rationalize his behavior toward a woman that only was doing what was best. "She didn't do anything wrong."

"She—"

"She didn't. I needed to know." I pushed my feet together so, although they were still in his masterful hands, Finn had to halt his actions and give me his full attention. "She was doing everything she possibly could between me, the plane, the press, you name it, and she was worried about you. You are lucky you have her ... and Carter, too." I tacked on at the end.

"Carter?" He looked up with slightly more interest. After I told Finn about Carter calling, he blew it off with sarcasm, but I knew he was touched. "Eh, he was just worried about his meal ticket being gone."

"Finn…" I tsked.

He began kneading my feet again while filling me in on the details of his visit with the drummer. Carter was, indeed, back in the band. His siblings were pitching in. Genevieve had turned sixteen during those months. So, Carter had helped her get her driver's license. Plus, he hired someone to help with laundry, dishes, dusting, and whatever else their mom might need.

"I'm sure that is a big relief for both of you."

"It is." Finn paused and then continued. "I didn't realize how much he liked Vanessa."

I slowly nodded. I wondered if Vanessa even knew. I wondered if what happened with his family made him realize it even more so himself. And I wondered if it mattered— if he would ever try again with her. But I knew it wasn't my place to interfere.

My place was right there on that sofa with the one who I had no doubts, whatsoever, about how he felt. "I understand you had a lot to say about me, too," I teased with a shy, yet semi-seductive smile.

For as much as Finn could blush, he did. But, at the same account, he answered with confidence. "That's nothing new, though, Beauty." When I kissed him my appreciation, he backtracked our conversation. "I'll play nice with Reese. Now tell me about this good news of yours."

A soft smile blossomed on my face. I couldn't help but smile every time I thought of the miracle. "It's about Miller," I started.

"You told me it was good news."

His fingers seemed a little firmer on my feet. It was kind of endearing to see Finn slightly jealous. Although there certainly was no reason to be … ever.

"I called him."

"Yeah. I really wish you would have waited."

"Just listen." I sighed and then continued. "I had to call. There was something I needed to make sure was true."

"You told me. Your mom said he would help. Great, but it doesn't really matter. I can take care of it. I—" Finn started putting on his macho, protective, invincible routine.

But I interrupted. "He's telling the police the true story. He was a witness. That's fine. But that's not all." I paused and, looking definitively into his eyes, said, "He's a match, Finn."

"What?"

"Miller. He's a match for my..." I stumbled over the correct terminology. What was that boy to me? Would I ever find the right word? Realizing that wasn't what was important, I forged on with the point I was trying to make. "He's going to be the bone marrow donor for that boy."

My husband's hands instantly stopped their motion on my feet, but he still held them in a comforting grip. "Yeah?"

"Yeah," I repeated, with an at-ease feeling warming my

entire body.

Finn adjusted my feet so that he could scooch closer to me. Taking my hands in his now, he spoke most genuinely. "God, Lara, that's great. That's … well, that's … I'm so happy for you and for that kid."

"Yeah."

"Man … wow." When he shook his head ever so slightly, I noticed he was trying hard to hold back his emotions. The past few days—heck, our past few months—had taken a toll on my husband. But I knew knowing that a child's life was going to be saved countered so much of that for him.

"Finn …" Equally emotional, my voice choked on his name with an appreciation for all he was.

He pulled me into his chest and rested his lips on top of my head. After a moment, that same compassionate man turned the tables in a half-joking way. "Well, I guess the guy's good for something at least."

I shook more than laughed. In my husband's eyes, the Altman brothers would eternally be "the bad guys." And his wife would never be more than the most innocent creature on Earth, no matter how many times I insisted that I had made wrong choices all those years ago, too. Thankfully, I had managed to change just as Finn had. But our pasts, no matter how many years or miles away, would always be a part of us.

***

While we were pretty convinced that all the sordid details of my past and Finn's role in the present part of it would never come out in the press, he and I collectively came to the decision to sit our families down and tell them the whole tale. They all knew different bits and parts. But after recent events, they all had questions. And after all the support and love they gave us, they deserved to know the truth. I just needed to get over my fear that they would be embarrassed or repulsed by me when that truth came out.

The opportune time came in the form of an appropriate, fast-approaching holiday— Thanksgiving. Wanting to tell everyone the truth all at that the same time and not have to keep repeating it, Finn and I offered to host the holiday at our abode. So, this time our gathering would include not only the Murphy side of the family, but my mother and brother as well. Lane usually had his holiday dinner with McEllie's family, and my mom did volunteer work. But they both agreed to come— unfortunately, sans McEllie—once I insisted how important it was.

Of course, initially, there were all the hugs, belly touchings, and "glad you're alive, Finn's" from everyone. But when Will and Kelsea headed out to pick up Will's parents from the airport, Finn and I knew it was the ideal time. With the exception of Will, we had everyone who had an emotional investment in the story in one room. But we also wanted to guard Kelsea from hearing anything. She was too young and innocent. Let her have that while she still could.

Once I started talking, I couldn't stop. My words were coming out a mile a minute, but I didn't dare make eye contact with anyone. The only contact I had was my husband's hand stroking mine in a reassuring way as he sat next to me on the loveseat. Even though many words were tumbling from my mouth, I really hadn't said a lot. I omitted a lot of the details but managed to get out the crux of what had lead us back to the country roads of Pennsylvania. I had given birth to a baby boy when I was fresh out of high school. And I had given him up for adoption.

"You what?" It was Lane who blurted out the question.

My mom was quick on his heels, though. "Oh, Lara. We don't have to bring all of this up. It's Thanksgiving."

I couldn't understand how a Wednesday or Thursday in August would be any more appropriate to tell your entire family that you were a teenage slut. But, I kept those thoughts to myself and said, "I have to explain."

"She really is a good girl." My mom immediately began apologizing on my behalf. "She—"

"Mom!" I semi-forcefully cut her off.

It was my tale to tell. I needed to get through it. And she needed to let me do it.

"Mom, you knew about this?" My brother was now on his feet, kind of swaying back and forth in front of Finn and I.

"Well, yeah, I—" she started, and then, as if she time-warped rapidly into the past, she cut herself off and began to hum.

I looked at my brother. He knew what I was thinking. One of our mother's nervous traits was humming. It had been one of her coping mechanisms when our dad would bellow in his drunken rage. And now she wasn't dealing well with the past finding its way to her present.

Lane noticed, but he didn't care. He was obsessed with what I had said and the fact that he had not known anything about it. "What? I don't understand. Where was I? Why didn't I know?"

My answer came out a little more forcefully than I intended. "You left! You high-tailed it out of there as soon as you could. You left me to still deal with—" I could actually feel my blood pressure starting to elevate.

Finn, noticing and empathizing with the fear of being left, calmly said to me, "Hey ..." and put his lips to my head so that I would slow down.

I gave my husband a half smile of appreciation and then, with more composure, said to Lane, "You left."

"I didn't know." Still agitated, he didn't sit.

"I didn't want you to know. I didn't want anyone to know." I managed to look around the room to the rest of my audience, whose expressions appeared slightly shocked, but very attentive.

"Keep going," Finn encouraged.

"But obviously you've known, huh?" Lane spoke first to Finn and then turned to me. "When did you tell Muhammad Ali?"

"Lane, stop." I started to get up, but Finn's hands on my thighs urged me to stay seated.

"What does that mean ... Muhammad Ali?" my mom questioned, still remarkably out of the loop regarding Finn punching Macon.

I ignored her and answered what Lane really wanted to know. "Finn has known since right before we started dating. He had every right to know and that comment—"

"Lara, you don't have to ..." Finn interrupted and clasped my hand confidently in his. "Listen, that's why we got all of you together to explain what happened...what all of that 'Muhammad Ali' business" —he glared at my brother, surely more to defend me than himself—"was about. I didn't want Lara to have to go through it a couple times. We wanted you all here at once."

"The thing in the press and with the police? That was somehow because of Lara giving up a baby years ago?" Nola was maybe starting to put things together.

"The police?" Mrs. Murphy was shocked.

As only a brother could, Finn rolled his eyes at his sister. He hadn't told his parents that the police had questioned him. He just let them know that it was in the press, it was an exaggeration, and he was dealing with it. So now he had to douse that flame, too. "Nothing to worry about." He looked to his mother. "They just asked a few questions about what I told you—the guy accused me of assaulting him. It was dropped."

Dropped ...officially ...thankfully. A good part of that was because the accuser was unreliable and dead. But it was also because Miller did his part and talked with the police.

My mother didn't let go of her questioning. "What assault and what does this have to do with that little boy all those years ago?"

Finn let me get up this time and walk around, while he stood to the side. I took a deep breath and related the details about getting the call regarding the boy I gave up for adoption and his fight for life. I hated that all the attention was on me. I was fine giving computer instructions to a large group of people. But my closest family members finding out well-buried truths? I couldn't stand it. I forged on, though, telling the collective tribe how we wanted to help find a bone marrow match, and since I couldn't be one, the next best possible solution was his biological father. Then I mentioned the trip to my hometown and Macon.

"Lara, honey, you mean Miller." My mother thought she had corrected me.

"No, Mom," I admitted but looked down and made my way over to Finn. "Macon."

"But—" she started again.

"Mom, Macon was the baby's father." I briefly caught her eyes with mine.

"Macon?" Nola tagged in. "That's the guy who accused Finn, right? But who is he?"

I reclaimed Finn's hand and slightly leaned into him. "Miller was my boyfriend in high school. Macon was his brother."

I knew my mom had to be swirling. She thought she was the one who knew everything about what happened back then. She had known most of it. After all, it was she who helped me through the pregnancy and giving the baby up. She just didn't know the exact circumstances of how that baby was created and who the father was.

"It was just one time," I said mostly for her benefit. "I was upset with Miller ... and with Dad. And I was drinking. It was—"

"And he didn't give you a choice," Finn interjected, never letting that part of the story go— the part that made it seem like I was completely innocent.

"Finn..." I flashed a warning but knew it was too late.

I hadn't wanted to tell that part. There was no reason to. It had no real bearing on the story other than to add more distress and discomfort to an already immensely awkward topic.

"Lara, they need to know." He looked at me determined, our bodies now slightly separated. But he did, thankfully, stop with that comment.

"What?!" Lane yelled in reaction to the fact that Finn basically said that Macon had raped me.

At the same time, my mother, who looked like she might pass out, cried out, "Oh, my God."

"Let it go," I tried. "It's over. My priority is that sick little boy."

My mother-in-law, whether to help me out, or because she didn't want to hear any more about her daughter-in-law's sexual encounters, asked, "So this Macon person ... is he a match?"

"He refused to admit to anything or to be tested," I answered.

Finn followed up. "He was drunk or high or something when we were there, and he had his hands on her." The tension mounted in his jaw as he relived our encounter at the Altman house. "He—"

"So you socked him one. Good for you!" I would have laughed at my father-in-law's demeanor had the conversation not been so serious.

"Zak!" Mrs. Murphy reprimanded her husband.

But he just reiterated confidently with, "Good for you."

My mom was finally piecing it together. "Miller ...Miller's a match, though. That's what he meant. That's what he was telling me when Macon died."

"Wait. What? That guy you punched died?" It was Nola's turn.

"Yeah," Finn seemed to be growing tired of this game of twenty questions. We easily forgot how cocooned we had been with the information. "But he didn't die because of that. He—"

"Drunk driving," my mother interjected. "Ah, these men and their alcohol! At least he didn't hurt anyone else."

Having no desire to revisit my dad's alcoholic past, I clung to the positive part of my mother's previous statement. "And, yes. Miller is a match, and he's going to do it."

"Oh, well, that's great. Thank goodness," came the voice of my mother-in-law.

"Yeah. I'm just sorry that any of you had to be involved in it, especially with what happened with Macon and what he accused Finn of." I found myself drawn back into Finn's comforting side nervously awaiting my jury's verdict.

"Lara, darlin', we're so sorry that you had to go through all of that." Mr. Murphy stood his towering, broad body up. "You know you have our support."

My shoulders eased slightly. I so wanted my in-laws' acceptance. And, probably due to the messed-up relationship I had had with my father, I particularly craved it from Finn's dad. "Thank you. That means the world to me. You have no idea." And then I hid my eyes in Finn's beige shirt, not wanting my extended family to see me tear up at their compassion.

"And, Son, we couldn't be prouder. You are the true meaning of the word man. We love you both." I could feel Finn reach out and shake his father's hand.

I looked at Mr. Murphy then. He and the entire Murphy clan were the epitome of what a family was supposed to be. I momentarily left the security of my husband's arms and gave a thankful hug to my father-in-law.

"And here I thought you were going to tell us you found out what you are having!" Mrs. Murphy chimed in, eliminating a lot of the solemn atmosphere that had—with due cause—set in.

"I was beginning to wonder if you were separating." That comment was my mother's.

"Mom!" I exclaimed and then attached, "Really?"

"Well, that match thing had me a little concerned." She referenced our previous telephone conversation.

"Geez! That wasn't match dot com!" I exclaimed.

"Well, I know that now," she said as both of us watched Lane take a few steps away and look out the French doors to the patio.

"We're not getting a divorce." I simultaneously shook my head and rolled my eyes.

"Ever." Finn pointedly reclaimed me back into his arms.

"Ever," I echoed, knowing the comfort and truth of his words.

Just then, Kelsea came tearing in through the front door. Her actions were pure kindergarten, but her words mimicked those of an adult. "What did I miss?"

Mr. Murphy grabbed at her belly causing her to giggle. "You missed your Pop-Pop gobbling you up like the turkey."

I was glad for the innocent interruption, and it appeared Finn was, too. "You okay?" he discreetly asked me.

"I love you," was my affirmative answer.

"Forever, Beauty."

As Finn rested his head alongside mine, Lane took the opportunity to approach us. "Thanks for taking care of her, man." He did one of those macho nods toward my husband to make sure that everything was copacetic.

"It's a privilege," Finn swooned. "But she does a pretty good job herself."

"Unfortunately, she had to learn to." It sounded like a regretful confession coming from my brother.

"Lane ..." What to say and how to say it? I pondered. "I'm sorry I came down on you. You had every right to leave back then. I just wasn't the survivor you thought I was." I recalled the words my brother had said to me when he had left home after graduating from high school.

"I may have been wrong about leaving—" he started.

"No—" I tried to protest.

But he continued. "But I definitely wasn't wrong about you being a survivor."

My brother and I weren't huggers. We didn't grow up in a household where affection was a given, regular occurrence. So when Lane put his arms around me briefly then, I truly understood the impact my tale had on him. And I knew it was because of the two men flanking me that it was true. I was a survivor. And I would continue to be one as long as I knew I had their love and support.

Next to Finn calling and telling me he was alive and safe after the plane incident, it was hard to think of another time where I felt so much relief. Unburdening myself of the secret that I had been holding from my closest family members was almost like being reborn. I didn't realize how much guilt I had been holding onto … not only for my actions all those years ago but for the recent ones when I had purposefully omitted telling my loved ones the truth about my past. Just as Finn had neglected telling me about his PTSD diagnosis in fear that I would think differently of him, I had done the same to our family. But I should have known and trusted their love for me.

***

"Beauty," he mumbled in his partially-awake state. "What are you doing?"

It was a legitimate question. It had been hours since all our guests had either left or gone to sleep. It was hours after *we* had gone to sleep. But despite it being the middle of the night, I was wide awake and sitting smack in the middle of the empty, upstairs room.

"Couldn't sleep," I answered the obvious.

"Heartburn again?" He fully entered the room and came to a seated position next to me on the floor.

"A little," I admitted to one of the non-joys of pregnancy.

"Me, too," he jested. "Too much pumpkin pie." He took the object from my hands— the first picture of that little boy all those years ago. "That's him, huh?" His voice this time was softer and more serene.

"Yeah. Only picture. Haven't looked at it in years." But, of course, he had been on my mind more than ever. "You upset?"

"No, baby. I wish you would have shown me sooner." He kissed the top of my head and handed the image back to me.

"That was it. Right after that picture, I gave him up. It was such the right thing to do. That day? That day I went into labor?" Flashbacks invaded my mind. "My father was in one of his alcohol induced moods—swearing, degrading my mom." On Finn's frustrated half breath, half grunt, I continued. "I told that little boy, as I handed him over, that he deserved the best life. And he got it. I know that. And I know this little one" —I rubbed my belly in recognition of our own child-to-be— "is going to have the best life, too. We're gonna make sure of that."

"We are." Finn's mouth curled up with pure joy.

After a beat, I tried to bring some levity back by looking around the vacant nursery. "I think maybe the best life might include some furniture, though."

"You ready for that?"

This time I spoke a little more quietly, as though if I said it too loud the castle would crumble. "Yeah. I think we should start."

He punctuated my nose with the tip of his finger before dragging it slowly down to my lips. His lips replaced his finger with a kiss as sweet and as pure as a newborn. "I love you. Everything is going to be okay." He then tilted his head down to my ballooning stomach. "Hey there, kiddo. You have the best mom. She is so brave. I can't wait for you to meet her."

It was the first time he really, truly spoke to our child like that. It gave me hope. It made me want to believe because he was allowing himself to believe. And if I trusted anyone to not steer me wrong, it was that beautiful man beside me. But, then again, I had believed before, and it had left me devastated and empty and lost.

CHAPTER NINETEEN

The busy rush of the holiday season kept both my mind and Finn's on other things than obsessing over what could go wrong. We remained focused on being happy, especially since the entire Macon debacle had been quickly replaced in the press with the heroics of the plane crash. Then his team decided to release his newest single a little early. They wanted to push feelings of good will and joy. And, of course, encourage people to open their wallets and pocketbooks. He was busy promoting the single but would only commit to either doing a quick couple hours in the city or phone interviews. He refused to go anywhere any long distance until the baby was born. And I loved him even more.

One evening in the middle of December, while he was holed up in his studio, I went to pick up some take-out for our late dinner and *It's a Wonderful Life* viewing. Headphones suctioned to his ears, he was behind the partition, singing and bobbing his head to the music when I returned. Acknowledging my entrance with a smile, he continued while holding up a finger, signaling for me to give him a minute. I obliged, knowing better than to interrupt the artist at work, and motioned for him to meet me upstairs.

A few moments later, once I had my feet stretched out on the coffee table, Finn made his way into the great room. He stopped mid-way to the sofa and smiled the softest, most serene smile I think I had ever seen on my handsome man. "Hi," he said.

"Hi," I mimicked, questioning his demeanor. "What's up?"

"You look so beautiful."

Sheez. He captured me with those words every time he said them. It was because I knew he truly believed them, and I—especially in my end-of-day, late pregnancy state—never did.

When I shook my head in denial, he added corroborating evidence to his statement. "How your hands are just resting on your stomach."

I looked down. "Didn't even notice."

"That's what's beautiful. It's so natural." Sitting next to me on the sofa, he greeted me again …this time with a kiss. "Hi. I have good news for you."

"Yeah?" I managed to expel while resting my head on his chest.

"Lar?" He used the shortened version of my name and then waited for me to look at him. When I did, he said, "While you were gone, there was a call on the landline. The transplant procedure started."

I know my mouth dropped open a bit. Then I raised my eyebrows slightly as my head ever so slowly bobbed up and down. "And?"

"There's not much to tell, I guess. It's just the first step. But, you know, it's happening … which means everything should be fine."

I exhaled. "Who called?"

"Somebody representing the boy. They wanted you to know and to thank you again."

"Oh. Oh, God. Oh, good. That's so, so good."

"Yeah. Yeah, it is." He wiped a tear from my cheek

that I hadn't even known had taken residency. "It's because of you, Beauty," he said, making that one tear turn into a mini-onslaught of others. "Hey..." He instinctively held me tighter. "This is good news. No tears allowed."

I sat up and rubbed my eyes dry. "It's very good news."

"It is. It makes everything seem worth it."

I looked at my caring husband. There had been so much drama over those couple of months. But we were strong. We had love on our side. We had survived. And now, so would that innocent, young boy.

I hit the unmute button on the television. The movie was just about to begin. Of course we could watch it at any other given day of the year, but it felt so serene to know that others in his family were doing the same exact thing as us at the same time— even if they were miles and miles away. It was peaceful knowing that the baby growing rapidly inside of me would know such wholesome traditions, too.

***

We honored our little girl—our daughter, Chloe—on the anniversary of the day that we lost her. We decided to make what could have been a gut-wrenching day for us, happy for others. Not to say that it wasn't hard. It was damn hard. When the day came, I wanted to back out, and I knew Finn would have in a heartbeat. He was sturdy and tough in so many ways, but dealing with grief was never going to be a strength of his. It was the fresh kicks of a very active little one in my womb that encouraged me to take my husband's hand, though, and do what we had set out to do.

The staff and the patients in the hospital where I had laid silent exactly a year prior were surprised, for sure— surprised and elated. The smiles on their faces made it worthwhile as they gathered in the small lobby just a short hallway down from where my room had been. They listened—and sometimes joined in—as Finn sang a few songs, while never letting go of my hand or allowing me to drift from his side. I know it was a huge comfort to me, but I suspect it was just as much to him. Afterward, he signed a few autographs, and we personally found the staff that had been so dedicated to me a year before to let them know that we were having a lunch catered for them.

And before we left, we spoke with an administrator confirming that we would make an annual gift to the pediatric wing in honor of our little one lost. Because of our financial security, it was something we were able to easily do, and it made the most sense for Finn. He had an extremely difficult time going to Wyatt's grave. So, any type of physical memorial for Chloe wouldn't have brought him any type of serenity. But, this would. And I had her mementos from her nursery and the feeling in my heart that she was always with me.

***

And then we were immediately thrown into the flurry of Christmas. Breaking the tradition of traveling to Louisville, we had the whole Murphy/Jamison/Faulkner crew at our place, since I was too late in my pregnancy to fly. Although the entire clan could be overwhelming, I cherished every moment, knowing that I didn't have that opportunity the year before.

Once everyone returned home, Finn and I celebrated our second wedding anniversary, a day late, but on our own. We went to the penthouse for a peaceful, quiet evening. As Finn got started on the fireplace and nostalgic s'mores, I went to the bedroom to change into pajamas.

When I was coming back down, I couldn't help but notice how my husband was watching me descend the staircase. I wished it was because I was in sexy, irresistible lingerie and he was thinking of all the ways to take them off me. But I knew better. I was in oversized cottony pajamas, and I was coming down a flight of steps. I knew he was nervous. But I gave him a look to let me be. And he stayed still, although clearly perched ready to spring into action.

There was not much occasion for me to go up the steps at our house in the suburbs, but, if I did, I was careful and used to it. The penthouse staircase was new territory…at least to my pregnant self. Had Finn thought of it, I am sure he would have brought the bed and everything else down to the first floor before our arrival. But I took my time, and I did not wear anything on my feet. And, of course, I wasn't feeling faint. So, I made it down safely.

Trying to ignore the exhale from my husband's mouth, I brought out the bag I had previously stashed in the closet and turned to him. "Are you ready for your gift?" I asked, slowly sinking my body onto the sofa.

"Aren't I always?" His relaxed smile emerged.

"Yes!" I tsked, thinking of how he turned into a little kid when presents were involved.

Finn gave me a quick kiss, reached into the bag, and started pulling out his gifts, which I always made sure were more sentimental than monetary. When puzzlement stretched across his face, I explained my theme of Number Two and Second. There was a watch to time the seconds between contractions, a box of diapers for all the "number twos" he would be changing, and finally, two photographs framed of the two of us—one from when we were just friends in college and one from our wedding.

"It took us two times to get it right, but we did it," I explained.

"We did, didn't we?" But there was something about the way he said it and the way he looked down that made me a bit concerned. Before I could question, though, he gave me an answer. "Lar? I'm sorry. I didn't write you a journal this year."

"What? No. I didn't expect you to," I said honestly but

still concerned that he seemed pretty upset about it. "I don't know how you did that last year." I cherished the journal he wrote in every day during our first year of marriage, but I most certainly didn't expect another.

"No. You don't understand. I wanted to. I just—"

I knew. My accident. The world stopped. And so, obviously, did the journal entries.

"I'm sorry. I couldn't. I just couldn't anymore."

"Fi—"

He wouldn't let me console him or even get his name out. He was adamant on telling me his reason. "It has nothing to do with how much I love you. I want you to know—"

"Finn!" I couldn't take it. I put my hands up to parenthesize his face. "God, baby, I know that. I know. If there is anything I know, it's how much you love me."

"Do you even know what day that was ... the first time you woke up just for a little bit from the coma?"

"What?" I was so focused on his feelings of pain and regret that I barely heard his question. But I quickly regathered my thoughts and searched back to that day in the hospital. It was all still a little foggy ... not because of any type of brain injury, but I am sure because I wanted to mentally block out that horrible time. "Uh...yeah. It was the end of December."

"The twenty-seventh." He pinpointed the exact date. "I knew it was a sign. It was our anniversary." When I smiled at his constant compassion and consideration, he continued. "I went with Nola, and I broke down. I bawled like a baby, Lara. I had never been so happy in my life than when you woke up. So, I asked Nola to find me some paper and give me some space. I thought I was going to write some lyrics, but I wrote you a letter instead."

I was getting emotional just thinking of that day and picturing my husband going through everything he had to endure. "But I didn't get a—"

"I didn't give it to you. You had a lot going on those

next few months."

"We both did," I quietly corrected, knowing he had lost just as much, too.

"Instead, I decided to keep it and then write you a letter on every anniversary month."

A smile emerged on my face before I even knew it was happening. Without even reading them, just the presence of those letters made my heart swell. I knew the power and thoughtfulness of Finn Murphy's words.

"I know it was probably the worst time of your life and you might not want to—"

I couldn't let him finish that statement. I brought my hands back up to his cheeks and kissed him strongly and for an extended moment. "Listen to me," I said with emphasis and determination. "Any year I have you by my side, loving me, being my man, could never, ever be a bad year. The twenty-nine years before were the bad years. So this year isn't even on the radar. I love you, Finn. I love you for everything you are and for all the love you have brought into my life."

"I love you, too, baby."

"Can I see my letters now?" I smiled softly.

"Yeah," was his quiet response, as he handed me the individual envelopes tied in a white ribbon.

December 27th

I have never seen a sight as beautiful as when you opened your eyes today. And I have never heard a voice more angelic than when you whispered that first word— my name – even if that was all I got for today. I know you are going to come back. I pray that you can feel my love while you sleep and try to recover. Can you sense my lips on yours, willing you to come back? Even when the medical staff urges me not to, can you feel me snuggled up against you? I pray that you do and that you know there is so much to come back for. Thank you for fighting, Beauty. Keep getting better. Wake up again. Even though I know when you do you are going to be upset and confused when you realize all that happened. And I will take that. I will take that on for you. I will take it just so that you aren't taken away from me. I love you more than words on paper or in a song or in a vow can ever, ever express. You are more than my wife—you are my best friend, my life, my reason for living. I hope I am yours.

Reliving that day through the eyes and heart of my husband brought nearly every emotion imaginable to the surface. But pain and regret were no longer on that list. Most of all, I felt loved, safe, treasured, and important. Not that I didn't feel that way every day with Finn, but it was rejuvenating to step back months later and put the events of December and January in perspective. I could have never done that clearly back then. We had lost something so precious in a split second that day. But it wasn't our enduring love, and it never would be.

"Finn," I managed to whisper out. "You are." I placed my lips on his and curled into the cottony fabric of his long-sleeved, green shirt taking in the smell that was uniquely him. "Can I read the others?"

"If you want to."

"Of course I do."

"Read. I'm gonna go call my folks and make sure they got in okay." Finn's parents were only flying back that day, whereas the rest of our family took off the day before.

"Yeah. Okay." I tugged at his hand to invite him into a quick kiss before he got up. "Tell them I said hi."

"I will," he agreed before grabbing his phone and exiting the room.

I inhaled a deep, calming breath and poured myself into the most heartfelt prose I could ever read. The next letter, written in January, talked about how he felt knowing I was finally at home and that I was his greatest, most cherished reward in life. The letters in March and April spoke about the times we had made love again after the accident, how much he loved and needed me, and how he knew how hard I was trying, but all he needed was for us to be us, so we could make it through. Some of the other letters detailed the excitement and worries about the new pregnancy, as well as our summertime adventures. But there was always a reoccurring theme of how much he loved me, underscored by how much he wanted to protect me.

That was never as prevalent as in the October letter, when there was so much up in the air regarding the bone marrow transplant and our decision to go to Pittsburgh to confront my past. Little did he know our life was going to continue to spiral downward for a while after that. But he also snuck in an extra letter, with a more positive spin, a few days later. It was dated "CMA night—a different anniversary."

The November letter fell on the day after Thanksgiving. We still had a house full of guests. But, somehow, Finn managed to write me a letter.

November 27th

I'm sitting here only illuminated by the light of our lava lamp. It just turned midnight, I'm just coming to bed, and it is now officially one of our month anniversaries. You are sound asleep. You look more peaceful and at rest than I can remember in quite a while. It makes me want to smile and cry at the same time. Smile because it is such a beautiful sight, but cry because you haven't had the tranquility to be able to do so. And you deserve that. I know there have been many stressors in your life, especially the past few months, and that sometimes I have contributed to those, for which I am truly sorry. I cannot fully express, or even comprehend myself, how much it meant seeing you unburden yourself yesterday of something that you have been holding onto and in for so long. I know you were scared to let that part of your defense down. And if anyone knows how that feels, it is me, Beauty. But you had nothing, I mean nothing, to be ashamed or fearful of. You are one of the bravest people I know. And you are so loved, as I hope you know and witnessed yesterday. We all love you. I know we gave our thanks and clanked glasses around the dinner table, but there is so much more I wanted to say. I am so thankful for you, Lara. I am thankful that fate, more than once, brought us together. And I am thankful that despite all the obstacles that we have had to overcome, you are with me. I am thankful for your compassion, your honesty, your sassiness, your commitment, your touch, your eyes and lips (and other body parts ;)). But, most of all, I am thankful for your love. I am thankful that you are my forever. I love you, baby.

I carefully placed that letter back into its envelope and brought all of them up to my chest. I always thought I couldn't love him more, but, right then, my heart was going to explode with adoration. I closed my eyes, thinking of how lucky and thankful I was to have Finn. He may not be open to the world when it came to personal stuff, but he never shied away, whether it was the written or verbal word, with me.

I opened my eyes upon hearing his voice. He was still talking on the phone with his parents but was descending the staircase. Their conversation seemed to be coming to an end.

"Yeah, I guess that probably will be the next time." Finn spoke into the phone with a smile in his voice. "I know," he said after a beat. "I'm looking at her right now." He threw in a wink in my direction as I cumbersomely started to get my pregnant body off the sofa. "I will," he spoke again into the phone, followed by a pause, and then, "You, too. See ya."

Finn hit the call end button at the same time I met him in the middle of the living room. Silently, I wrapped my arms around his fit torso and laid my head on his chest. His lips rested on the top of my head.

After a couple moments of the sweet, silent stillness of our bodies entwined, I spoke in typical Lara fashion. "Don't think writing down a few mushy words is going to get you out of diaper duty."

I felt Finn's head shake back and forth above mine before he pulled me slightly away to look in my eyes. "Did I say I was thankful for your sassiness?"

"I think you did." My smile was chased by a tear. I put my hands up to his cheeks. "I'm too emotional to tell you how much those letters mean to me. I'm not the lyricist you are. I would say thank you, but that's not enough. I would say I love you, but I know you know that. Finn, I—"

"Keep being my girl and that's more than enough."

I moved my hands to the back of his head and brought it down to me. I kissed him then as sweetly as I possibly could. Being his girl was the easiest thing in the world.

***

"I can't believe you won't let me open this before you leave," I whined.

"First of all, I am not leaving," he countered with a smile, but I knew how much he detested that "L" word.

"Finn, you're leaving …" I paused for emphasis. "me…" Again with the dramatic pause. "on New Year's Eve."

"Lara, stop that. I know you are just trying to open the last envelope before you're supposed to." He smiled again while making sure his outfit—his performing outfit— was just right as he stood in front of the floor length mirror in the penthouse's master suite. "You know I am not leaving you, and you know I will be back before midnight."

I pushed out my bottom lip to exaggerate a pout. But he just touched it with his fingertip and gave me a kiss. I knew I had lost.

"I expect a decent New Year's Eve kiss, Roxanne."

"Well, it's guaranteed to be better than last year's." A coma kiss has to be on the bottom of the list of best kisses.

Finn closed his eyes momentarily at the memory and opened them just as the doorman called to say that the car service had arrived. He laced his hand in mine and I walked with him to the front door. "I love you."

"I love you, too," I said as he swung his bag onto his shoulder. "Break a leg."

He quickly pecked me on the lips and stuck his pointer finger out at me. "Wait to open it."

"I will," I lamented.

There had been one more letter that Finn hadn't given me initially for our anniversary. He presented it to me the following day, but it was sealed and marked, *Do not open until New Year's Eve.* It had been lying on the penthouse living room mantle, teasing me ever since.

"See you tonight," he said.

"Not before I see you."

"You promise to watch, right?"

"Of course."

Finn was performing in the televised New Year's Eve celebration at Times Square. He would play two songs early in the evening so that he could still make it back, somehow, despite the chaos of Manhattan that night, to ring in the New Year with me. After all, there was no way I was going to be able to attend with just a couple weeks until my due date.

It was an important gig for him for a number of reasons. But one of the biggest was because he was going to finally announce his upcoming summer tour. And what a tour it was going to be. For the first time ever, my husband was going to be playing a number of football stadiums, and the Entertainer of the Year was expected to sell them out. It was another whole new level of stardom for Finn— one which he was excited about, especially knowing that, barring any complications, the baby and I could join him.

*****

After Finn left, I was so tempted to open that envelope. If it was at all like the others, I knew it would be sentimental, and I privately cursed Finn for not letting me open it yet. But he had his reasons, and I trusted and respected that, even if it was minor torture.

Finn first performed his current hit near the top of the show. Despite there being a snow and rain mix earlier in the day, luckily there was no precipitation that evening. But the temperature was still a chilly twenty-seven degrees. Even though he was moving and singing, he had to be cold. I mentally made a note to have some cocoa, along with champagne, ready for his return.

After the song, he briefly talked about his upcoming tour, which drew outrageously loud cheers from the crowd. Then the show went to a commercial saying that Finn would be back for another song later in the program. I took the opportunity to text him.

Cold? Was the single word I used.

I expected it would take him a little bit of time to respond. He would be mixing it up with the fans and hosts, as well as getting his band prepped for the next song. But it was less than ten minutes later when he texted back. Sadly, I knew that was the part of Finn that always felt like he needed to be on alert when it came to me, especially since Memphis.

U can warm me up later.

I smiled and returned the text. *For sure. No smooches w/ anyone but me.*

Never. No opening the letter til it's time.

When??? The suspense was starting to drive me a little loco.

Soon. You'll know. I love U.

Me too, Cowboy.

Finn's next appearance was in the middle of the next hour. There wasn't much opening banter—just an introduction stating that he would be performing a new song. That's usually how those things played out—get the crowd started with your number one hit and then get them hooked for the next one. The band started to play some light instrumentals, and Finn reached for his microphone.

Instead of singing, he looked straight into the camera and said, "Now, Beauty."

Completely focused on his face and wondering which song on the album it would be, it barely registered to me what he was saying ... to me. Oh! I quickly grabbed the envelope and opened it.

Happy Anniversary ... and New Year
This past year has been a journey of winding, hilly, detoured roads, both figuratively and literally. But there is no one I would rather travel them with than you. You are my home. You are my love. You are in every lyric. You are the only salutation for every love letter I will ever write.

That was the first page. On the second were lyrics to a song I had never heard before. A song titled "Love Letters (to my wife)." It was the song that Finn had just started singing on screen. I tried to follow along with the written words, but I was too mesmerized by the live performance on TV. It was another ballad like "Lara's Song." So, he stood still at the mic and either had his eyes shut or seemingly peering right at me. There wasn't a specific mention of me in the lyrics this time, but every scenario that was painted in the poetry of the words were extremely specific to us and our year.

As rowdy as Finn had the crowd going during his first performance, the gathering this time was the complete opposite. They were still and quiet ...their eyes wide and appreciative. On the final note, they erupted into applause, and Finn winked at the camera. Like a silly schoolgirl, I winked back. He had done it again. My heart really was going to go off the charts.

CHAPTER TWENTY

"Are you going to answer it?" Finn asked from behind the steering wheel. "Who is it?" He casually glanced my direction.

Coming home from the hardware store, after getting some little necessities for the nursery, I was in the passenger seat of Finn's car. It was my phone that was ringing, and it was someone I wasn't expecting. "Miller," I replied plainly.

Even though I had contemplated a number of times whether to call him, I was nervous and anxious seeing his number on my caller ID. I wanted so desperately to know what was going on with the transplant and, more importantly, whether it was a success. But I didn't know if it was my right. I hadn't heard anything more from the family's representative, and Miller had made no contact after our initial talk just after Macon had died. I had to accept that I did my part and now that part was over.

Finn turned a little more definitively in my direction and then swung right back around to face the windshield. I don't think it was my imagination that his hands grasped the steering wheel a little stronger. He didn't say anything, but I needed to.

Pressing the green call button, I held the phone up to my ear. "Hello?" I asked generically, wanting to sound casual.

"Lara?" Miller's voice asked across the line.

"Yeah." I rested my free left hand on my husband's thigh.

"It's Miller," came the voice from the past.

"Hi, Miller." When my voice cracked, Finn placed his right hand on top of mine. Glad to feel his touch, I closed my eyes and turned my hand so that it could be interlocked with his. I needed my husband's reassurance as much as he needed mine.

"How are you?" Miller asked just as generically.

"Good. You know, just very pregnant ... waiting for the baby."

Finn shook his head in a disapproving way. I'm not sure if it was the casual way I spoke with Miller or if it was because he thought our baby was too personal. I had no idea what to say, though. This was an awkward conversation all the way around.

"Oh, right," Miller acknowledged. "When?"

"About a week." Finn turned my direction this time when I spoke.

"Oh...good, I guess. Do you know what you're having?"

"No. We're ... it's a surprise."

Finn removed his hand from mine that time. But, in his defense, we were entering the driveway, and he needed to reach over and press the garage remote. I couldn't help but note his tension, though. Miller was saying something as Finn moved the gearshift into park and turned the car off. He got out of his side of the car as I did mine.

"Do you want me to grab anything?" I asked my husband.

"What?" Miller was unaware that I was involved in two conversations.

"No," Finn answered while shutting the garage door. "I

got it."

"Sorry," I said into the phone. "I was talking with Finn."

"Oh. How is he?"

We were walking into the house when I answered. "He's good."

Finn actually grumbled and set a couple of the items down on the kitchen counter. As he did, I rubbed my hand on his. He squeezed back quickly, released, and then grabbed a beer from the fridge. "I'm gonna get started upstairs. Come up when you're done." And he gave me a quick but possessive kiss as his closing statement.

After the initial awkwardness, Miller and I had a nice conversation. Being a participant in the transplant, he knew a lot of details and shared with me what he could, even though a lot of his part of the procedure was just him. Everything at that point was completed and seemed to be successful. There would be some follow-up, and Miller had asked to be updated every so often about the boy's well-being if possible. Thankfully, the family had agreed.

I thanked Miller profusely, not only for the selfless act of donating his bone marrow, but for contacting me. "I really, really do appreciate it," I said. "It ... it means so much when you are under no obligation. I mean, especially after..." I paused because our conversation had been going well. Dare I risk blowing it? "Well, with what went down this fall." There, I said it.

"I told you then—it's a kid. It's a kid's life. As far as that goes, there was no choice."

"I'm sorry about Macon."

"Let's not go there." He barely breathed before barreling on. "The other choices that were made? Y'know, back then ... back when we were teenagers? God, I'm sorry if I handled that wrong. I'm sorry that ... well, you had to deal with it all by yourself."

Shit! I wasn't prepared for that. This whole

conversation was emotional enough without regrets from so long ago that really had no relevance in the present.

I answered him the same way I had when I talked about it with Finn. It was something I believed, or had to, in order to move on. "We were all so young. We all made mistakes. And regarding the consequence of that... that night? Getting pregnant? There really was only one way it was going to end. And it was for the best."

"You're happy now, though, right?" It was a slight change of subject.

"I am." I moved my free hand down to my balloon of a belly and rubbed. "I am. But the more important thing is, that kid is happy and healthy. I really believe it."

"Yeah, Lara. I know that's true."

"Thanks, Miller. I can't say it enough. And, if you don't mind, please, please let me know if you hear anything else?"

"Sure thing," was his immediate response, but I wondered if he truly would.

"Be happy, too."

"I will," he said, before finding the end button.

When I hung up the phone, a fresh new wave of relief washed over my body. After Thanksgiving, I thought I felt contentment. But after that conversation with Miller, I not only felt content, but inner peace as well. Everything was finally going to be all right. Everyone was safe, happy, and healthy. I could breathe. And, I guess, cry. Because suddenly the hormones raged, and I broke into tears.

Finn bounded down the stairs finding me on the sofa mid-deluge. "What's wrong?" He knelt in front of me. "Lara? What's wrong? What did he say? If he even said something ... something that hurt you ..." He let the sentence fade as his grip on my knees tightened.

"Finn..." I wiped my tears. "Come closer. Kiss me."

"What?"

"Kiss me," I reiterated.

He sat on the sofa and gently obliged. "Talk to me."

"I love you. Everything is fine. Everything is back to being the way it's supposed to be."

***

I loved that, despite his wealth and connections, Finn was still a grounded boy from Louisville. He didn't hire out jobs that we could do ourselves. I know part of that was his deep-seated issue with privacy, but a lot of it was also the joy that we got in doing things together.

Just as we had personally decorated the house when we moved in, we were doing the same for the baby's room. Since Thanksgiving, the nursery had finally begun to take shape. We had assembled and moved into place—admittedly Finn more than I—the essentials, like the crib, changing table, armoire, and rocker. In addition, the bassinet was in our room and the car seat in Finn's car.

Everything was in place … everything but the baby. The due date came and went, and then it just became a waiting game. And I wasn't good with waiting. I wanted that baby, and I wanted him or her now.

And then, for as slow as things seemed to be happening, when the time came, about a week late, it seemed to have happened in the proverbial blink of an eye. It was late in the evening… of course. And Finn wasn't there… of course.

Giving in once more to that late third trimester exhaustion, I had gone to sleep. I wasn't alarmed or surprised when I found myself awake just a short time later, though. It hadn't been uncommon between the irregular sleeping hours, Braxton Hicks, and the need to pee … which was what I thought was happening.

But that wasn't the case. Once I was a little more awake, I knew better. I had done this part once before in my life. And this time, I was a lot more calm.

I took in the moment for a fraction of a second, picked up my phone, and texted Finn. *My water just broke.*

His text response came a couple minutes later, after I had managed to call the doctor's service. *Am I being punked?*

With a new sense of was-I-really-ready-to-do-this reality setting in, I texted back. *I wish. I think it's time. It's gonna B a long night.*

***

Finn was in the doorway of our first floor master suite in just over five minutes, which was pretty remarkable considering he was at our neighbor's house a couple streets down watching the NFL playoffs. "You're serious, right?" He was panting more than speaking from running several blocks back home.

Having just finished putting on my clothes, I was tying my hair back when I looked at my harried husband. "It's a good thing you are a runner. And I thought I was the one that needed to be doing the breathing exercises," I teased.

"Lara…" He didn't appreciate my humor. "Are you really? Are we doing this? Tonight?"

"Yeah. I just need to put on a little lipstick."

"What?" he practically roared. His hands went to his hips. Whether it was to portray his irritation or to steady his still slightly staggered breathing, I wasn't sure. "Let's go. You don't need makeup."

"I don't want to scare Junior," I teased and took his hands in mine just to calm him down. "We've got time. I called the doctor. Just get the bags." Because, God knows, we had to have two because of all the items we needed …not just for me, but for the baby, and for Finn.

What was wrong with me? Was I really this calm? I found myself actually enjoying the rare role reversal of Finn being the one who didn't want to be late. It wasn't exactly fair, though. I knew he was worried. The last time Finn was in the hospital with a pregnant me … well…Was that why I was calm? Was it a mask? Was I procrastinating? After months and months of waiting and wanting this child, was I still scared of what could potentially go wrong? Or was I scared that I could actually, finally find the happiness that a child could bring?

Grabbing the labor bags, which had been waiting next to the tall dresser for weeks, Finn said, "I'll start the car."

"Baby?" I called out, forcing him to turn and look at me. My calmness was still intact, but, suddenly, I was thinking things through. I was planning ... nesting in a way. I was being a mom. "Are you okay to drive? Were you drinking? Should I drive?" But before he could answer, the baby weighed in with a bona fide real contraction. "Ahhh, that was tight," I acknowledged bringing my hand to my abdomen.

"No. You can't drive. Good grief." He shook his head and brought his concerned gaze up from my enlarged stomach to my eyes. "I'm good."

"Sure?"

"Lara, I wouldn't do anything to risk either of you. If I thought that, I would have gotten any of our friends, our sober friends, to drive instead of just running out of there like a madman." He slowly spoke the next words with reassurance. "I hardly drank."

All of that I knew was one hundred percent true. I could see it in his demeanor. And I knew he wouldn't lie about something that could affect the life of his wife and unborn child. And the fact was, Finn didn't ever drink that much, especially when he was around a group. Yes, we had become close to our neighbors. But he was still conscientious about his reputation and how he could be portrayed in the public eye, especially when it concerned any type of drug or alcohol.

"C'mon. I don't want to be that story about the baby being delivered on the side of the road." He reached out for my hand.

I was about to agree when I noticed my watch and realized I needed to start monitoring the timing of the contractions. "You'll probably need a good drink, though, once we get into full labor."

"That may be true," he admitted and smiled as he finally got my hand in his.

We managed to cross the threshold of our bedroom before I stopped. "Finn?"

"Yeah?"

I noted the slight impatience in his voice. He wanted to be in that car. He wanted to be at that hospital where he knew there were medical personnel waiting to take care of me. But I needed to breathe. I needed to soak the moment in … the moment of us—Lara and Finn—in our home before it all changed. It would be a beautiful, wonderful, amazing change, but it would be the last time we were going to just a be a couple. And it made me excited and nervous at the same time. I'm pretty sure the smile I attempted in his direction depicted all of those emotions in one.

By the squeeze of his hand in mine, I knew he understood, as he always miraculously seemed to when it came to me. "Everything is going to be all right … even better." For the first time since he entered our home that night, I felt him truly relax. It was evident in the way he slowly and reassuringly kissed me. And it was evident in the way he was able to follow it up with a tease. "C'mon, let's go meet little Cinci." Finn had been jokingly threatening to name our child Cinci for a girl and Bengy for a boy if the Bengals made it to the Super Bowl.

"I did not agree to that bet!" I immediately bellowed while playfully smacking his toned arm. "Besides, they didn't win!" I had seen the fourth quarter score on my phone screen before trying to go to sleep earlier, and Cincinnati had been down eighteen to twenty-three. "They didn't, did they?"

"No. You'll get that massage," he lamented.

"I think I'm going to need one," I agreed. "And take that jersey off right now," I directed, speaking of the

Halloween-colored Cincinnati Bengals jersey he was wearing. "That will not be the first thing our baby sees its daddy wearing."

"I love you." He showcased that smile that made me swoon every time.

"Strip!" I half laughed.

Copying my laughter and raising his eyebrows suggestively, he teasingly, in his best *Magic Mike* impression, removed his football jersey to reveal a black, long sleeved, V-neck shirt which hugged his fit frame just perfectly. "Can we go now, please?"

I wrapped my ballooning body into his and said the words that made everything always all right. "I love you, too."

Despite frigid January temperatures, we were fortunate not to have to deal with any form of precipitation on our commute to the hospital. And because it was the middle of the night, there was also limited traffic on the road and little activity at the hospital. In fact, Finn and I were able to enter without even one "Finn Murphy" spotting. Of course, the doctor meeting us at a side door and escorting us via a private elevator into our luxurious, private birthing suite helped, too.

And we certainly didn't have to worry about that road side delivery. Baby Murphy ended up not being in a huge hurry to arrive once it started it's opening act. As it turned out, we would have hours to go.

Once the medical personnel had us settled in and all necessary forms were filled out, we were told to relax. It was just another version of the waiting game. Finn pulled out his phone and crawled into the bed next to me.

"Whatcha say? Labor selfie?" He held the phone up in front of us.

Glad that he seemed so much more relaxed since our arrival at the hospital and talk with the doctor, I agreed. "Might need a wide angle lens." I chuckled at my large self. "A little different than our skinny summer tour pics."

"Still beautiful," he claimed and clicked a few before showing them to me.

"You gonna send them to your family?" I asked.

"Nope." He ceremoniously powered the phone off and placed it on the nightstand. Resituating himself so that I could lean comfortably in his arms, he clarified. "You and me. I just want you and me. Everyone will know soon enough—our families, the press, our neighbors." He chuckled and added, "Well, they might already know. But I want us … just us. This is our moment. You good with that?"

"Finn, you know I am."

"I love you, Beauty. And I am so proud to be your husband." When the tears automatically started rolling down my face, Finn wiped them with the backside of his thumbs and said, "Hey, Juniorette doesn't need to see her mom all puffy eyed." He gently leaned over and grabbed his earbuds. Putting one in my ear and the other in his, he said, "I made you a labor mix."

I leaned forward and looked at him. "You did?"

"Of course. There's some classical, but it's really eclectic."

"I just want you."

"You have me." He played with a piece of my hair that had fallen loose from my ponytail. "But let's just listen."

I leaned back into the strength of his arms and waited for the music to fill my ear. First up was Finn's voice, but it wasn't one of his singles. It was our song. It was "Roxanne." I tilted my head slightly to catch his face, which lit up in a smile. I loved this version. It was softer and emphasized the words differently. It was what he heard when he listened to the song and when he called me that name. I squeezed his hand in love and appreciation. And then I squeezed it much harder as another contraction ripped through my body. Finn hit pause, helped me through, and timed the contraction.

Once it was over, I took a deep breath and said, "I

think it's a hit."

"You good?"

"Yeah. I want to listen to more."

"You got it." Finn snuggled me back into him, and we listened to his mix of songs that in one way or another had special meaning to us and our relationship.

Included, of course, was a rough track of "Love Letters (to my wife)," which I thought was even more beautiful than the New Year's Eve version. Finn claimed that he wasn't releasing it, despite a number of people posting and inquiring about how to purchase it. The bootlegged version from television was the only format besides the one floating in our joint earbuds.

After a little while, Finn stopped the music, stating that he was hungry. With the baby seemingly not arriving in the immediate future, the nursing staff provided him with a take-out menu from a nearby all-night diner, because God knows he wasn't going to leave my side to go down to the cafeteria. So, in the early hours of the morning, while Finn munched on plain, thin-crusted pizza sans the beer, which I am sure he wanted, I sucked on hard candy and water. There was no resting for me, or even meditating for Finn, because the contractions were strategically cumbersome enough to prevent such relaxation. Instead, as luck would have it—if you are Finn Murphy, that is—the Louisville basketball game was being replayed on a sports channel. So, as a distraction from the contractions growing stronger and closer, we watched the Cardinals race back and forth across the hardwood, scoring two and three pointers effortlessly. Well, Finn watched a little more intently than I did. I started rereading one of the pregnancy books I brought along in my bag while savoring my husband's back rub.

"Louie!" Finn exclaimed as if the most brilliant idea popped into his head. "Louie," he repeated, with obvious reference to his hometown and the team on the screen. "That can be the baby's name! Or ..." He paused but quickly came up with a girl version. "Louise."

I laughed. "Over my dead body."

He stopped suddenly mid-rub and looked at me straight on. "Don't. Don't say that."

Oh. Oh, God. "I'm sorry." I touched his kind, heartfelt face. "I wasn't think—"

"That's all I am thinking about."

"I know. I'm sure it's hard not to. But that part is over, Finn. I'm okay. The ba— Ahhh!" I screeched as another, seemingly stronger contraction hit, and I dug my hand into his. "The baby is doing just fine." I finished after a couple huge exhales.

"Jesus! Can't we do something?"

"Lara," A nurse entered the room as if answering my husband's plea. "How you doing?"

As she started checking monitors and parts of my contorted body, I responded. "I think better than him." I smirked in Finn's direction.

"Isn't that always the case." The nurse shook her head jokingly at Finn. Turning back to me, she said, "You're ready, huh?"

"Yeah." I knew it was time. Even though it had been over a decade since I had been in active labor, it seemed like yesterday. I knew we had reached the next phase. And, God, yeah, I was ready.

"What about you?" She glanced in my husband's direction.

"My girl's ready. Then, so am I." He kissed me on the forehead for an extended moment, only releasing as the next contraction rocked my body.

***

"Lara, Finn, you have a beautiful baby boy."

I heard the doctor say the words, and then the world became a blur. A baby. A boy. Lara and Finn. Beautiful. Everything was all right. Everything truly was the way it was supposed to be. I was with the man of my dreams, and we had a child of our own— a little boy. How did that happen?

I know I heard something about the cord being cut and everything checking out, but I was in my own world. I think the doctor was asking me something. Did I want to hold him?

It was Finn's voice that actually broke me free. "Lar?"

"He's okay?" I asked, realizing my first words as a mom truly sounded like a mom.

"All looks good," Dr. Weinstein confirmed. "And a handsome little one at that, too."

"Finn?"

"Yeah, Beauty?"

"He's ours?" I asked, not even trying to hold the emotions in.

"He's ours," he confirmed.

Knowing the underlying fear that came from losing two babies one way or another, my husband gently brushed my hair away from my face and softly kissed me. He then took the baby from Dr. Weinstein and held him like a pro. It was then that I realized Finn had much more experience with infants than I did. After all, he was Uncle Finn first … before he was a husband or even a rock star.

"Oh, God, Lara. Look at him. You did so good. He is amazing." Slightly teary eyed, he repositioned himself in the chair next to me and tilted so I could see our son.

"Just like his dad," I said.

"He's like a little miracle— our second chance." Finn looked absolutely in awe of his son.

I put my hand up to the baby's head and gently brushed the slightest trickle of hair. Although maybe a shade darker, it definitely seemed to mimic Finn's. And although I knew they could change, his eyes seemed to be all his daddy's, too.

"Chance," I echoed.

Finn met my eyes with his and then looked down again

to our son. We both felt it at the same time. "Chance," Finn repeated and nodded his head in my direction.

We had everything set and ready to accept a child into our home. But we still hadn't seriously discussed a name. Except, that if it was a boy, we knew without a doubt what the middle name would be. But there in the delivery room, as clear as day, we now knew the first name, too.

"Yep," I agreed.

"Chance," Finn said again. "Chance Wyatt Murphy, welcome home, little man. It's a wonderful life."

SNEAK PEEK AT *TEARDROP IN MY EYE*

CHAPTER ONE

Two strong hands grabbed me from behind, startling me so much that I jumped and let out a partial scream. I hated sudden, loud noises and things that seemingly came out of nowhere. The emotional scars of my childhood still lingered, no matter how far I traveled or how much I wished them away.

Thankfully, though, I relaxed just as quickly. It was because I knew those familiar hands wrapped around me now. And I loved those hands holding me close. I had missed feeling them so much while he was away.

"Hi, baby," he cooed in my ear, before having his soft lips survey my upper neck.

Loving the feeling, I let him explore for a moment before turning around and meeting his lips for a legitimate "welcome home" kiss. I knew Finn had just arrived home from the airport. Sure, he had texted me, but it was also in his eyes. Those natural gray eyes were watery and he was blinking—a sure tell sign that he had just removed his performer green contact lenses.

"Hi." I smiled, pleased to see the real Finn Murphy. I took off my silver winter coat and laid it on top of Finn's carryon luggage, which was resting on the tall kitchen counter chair.

"God, I'm glad to be home. Everything good?"

"Mmmm-hmmm," I murmured, and leaned into his fit

chest covered by a partially unbuttoned gray and white plaid shirt. I had missed him. A week had seemed so long, especially since I had been used to having him around full time for the past few months.

"How's my girl?"

I loved when Finn called me that. It made me feel like I belonged. It made me feel loved…and young.

But it wasn't me he was talking about this time. And I was okay with it. She was the only one I would share my title with.

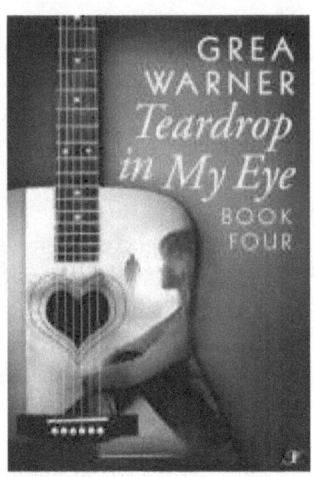

See how Lara and Finn's romance began...

A young woman content with her solitary life.

A rising country music star.

They were friends once …until their lives took them down separate roads.

Now, years later, when a child volunteers his uncle to sing for a fundraiser, LARA FAULKNER realizes it is none other than her college pal, FINN MURPHY. As the two get a chance to reconnect, Lara reveals to a compassionate Finn details of her shocking past and the traumatic decision she had to make.

Through trust and love, the bond between Finn and Lara deepens as the country singer manages to get an emotionally scarred Lara to let down her self-proclaimed walls. But will secrets, lies, and tragedy cause a bumpy detour on their road to complete happiness?

Emotional, dramatic, heartwarming… fall in love with COUNTRY ROADS – the first in a continuing series by author Grea Warner.

Available at all major retailers.

Check out this Amazing new series by Grea Warner...

How did a sheltered girl from Carolina end up in a national scandal involving one of Hollywood's most powerful music couples?

When want-a-be singer Bethany Opala tries out for a TV talent show, she is rejected. But then comes an amazing offer ... a songwriter's dream. Bethany has the opportunity to learn and develop her skills with top music manager, Ryan Thompson.

With a mutual passion for music and words, Bethany and Ryan's writing partnership develops into something more ... something love songs are written about. And while it isn't wrong, it isn't right, at least in the public eye.

Surrounded by secrecy and half-truths, Bethany doesn't know how much she should put up with. Especially, when one more rejection could scar her for good. Will her decision to leave not only Ryan, but the music business and California, come down to the toss of a coin?

ABOUT THE AUTHOR

There really wasn't any other path. Grea Warner knew from a young age that she wanted to write. She was born to write. First it was in diaries with little metal keys and in written tales that she slipped to friends in study hall. School newspapers, a college television drama, and internships in the soap opera world were next. After producing and writing a local show, she decided to delve into the world of the novelist. When her fingers aren't tapping out her latest book filled with angst and romance, Grea can be found hiking the trails or jamming to her favorite country artists on the radio.

Website: http://www.greawarner.com
Facebook: https://www.facebook.com/grea.warner.7
Twitter:@grea_warner